"Hyllos?" Elleni ventured ; very wrong with her hus rigid, not moving or even appe lowed hard and reached out to touch the nearest paıı ʋı ᴵᵌᵉ husband's body, his covered right elbow. It was cold, hard, and rough like it had been baked in mud for a week under the blazing sun. Elleni reached up and grabbed his hand, but he did not flinch or grab her back. His skin felt cold, like his clothes, and solid – unlike any flesh she had felt before. Rakhel let go of her hand and cowered by the open doorway. Elleni did not blame the girl for being scared.

"Hyllos, talk to me." Once again, her words fell on deaf ears. Elleni moved her hands to touch his face. It too felt cool and unyielding. She recoiled, taking a step back towards the red door. What ailment had befallen her husband, to hold him rigid as he stood like, like...?

She could not see properly in the gloom, so she left the andron to fetch some light. She returned with Rakhel close to her back. Elleni held the lit torch before her and edged closer towards the kyrios of the house.

Both girls screamed as one. Elleni dropped the torch as they fled the andron and the house—mistress and slave, hand in hand, running away from the horrors of their home. Their screams echoed down the streets of Athens.

Hyllos, general and citizen of mighty Athens, had been turned to stone.

THE MEDOUSA MURDERS

BY ALEXANDER ARROWSMITH

For Mark West

To Mary

Enjoy

Alexander Horcenits

PROLOGUE

ATHENS 432 BC – SPRING

The nature of his return to Athens was much different to his departure.

It was in the dead hours of the night that he stepped off the Corinthian merchant ship. Hardly anyone paid him or his tall companion any mind, not even the crew of the ship on which he had been a passenger for two long weeks. But his absence from the great city-state of Athens had been much longer. Twelve cruel, dark years, eleven of them imprisoned at the oars of the very Persian ships he had left to destroy one summer's day. He had been a youth then, ready to battle the enemy at all costs: death or glory.

What he found at sea was not glory, but the death of his shipmates and the indignity of being plucked from the waters by his enemy without killing a single Persian. Then the irony of being chained like a slave to power their ships, used to kill his fellow Athenians and Greeks. His pride did not last long. He bore the healed scars on his back from the Persian whips, but the scars deep in his mind would never heal. He wondered if his callused fingers could still manage to do the things he once excelled at, before joining the Nautical Astoi.

The wooden dock ran above the waves that lapped up against the ships at port. The ships' crews, navy mob, water rats, and painted whores passed him as he stood rooted to the dock's planks.

He wondered if anyone remembered him. Wondered if his parents were still alive, and if the woman he loved waited for his return. Taking a deep breath of Athenian air for the first time in over a decade, he pressed forwards through the port of Pireás, heading up to the city he had never thought to see again. The long walls on either side dominated the skyline. His silent companion followed him, like a huge shadow moving through the night.

His weary feet and damaged soul were close to the Piraean Gate when he first heard the news. Catching snippets of conversation, he picked up enough information by the time he reached the city's gates to gather what had happened this very morning. The great General Polydektos had been charged with the murder of his wife and daughter. The name rang a bell, like an echo from a past life. It was good to hear Greek voices once again. He pressed on through the city gates, unnoticed. There were no parades for him as a returning war hero, no garlands of laurels; only the dark streets of the lower Polis.

Yet stepping inside the city once more seemed to bring renewed hope to his heart and strength to his weary feet. He was divided: where to go first? His parents' house or the woman he loved? Or perhaps the other place that had kept him going during his long imprisonment. He decided on the latter and made his way through the streets of Athens, once more a free man and citizen of the greatest city-state in the world.

CHAPTER ONE

ATHENS 432 BC – SIX MONTHS LATER

Polydektos had not been prouder since his own son, Sokos, had joined the army of mighty Athens. Sokos was dead, and no one would ever replace him, but Talaemenes came close.

Polydektos could just about make out the youth two lines from the rear of the ten phalanxes of men. Five phalanxes were stationed on each side of the Sacred Way, the road leading up to the Dipylon Gate. Rows upon rows of men clad in their finest, polished armoured breastplates, greaves, and bronze helms. Many had shields showing a sacred blue owl of Athena on a white or gold background, while others' shields had warships or family crests, but all had their spear tips pointing to the sky, glinting in the sunlight.

Talaemenes was barely five months into his ephebos military service, yet today he was dressed as a proper soldier of Athens. All of his fellow youths, including Polydektos's nephew Euneas, were there to make up the numbers for this display of Athenian military might. Neither Talaemenes nor Euneas was training as a hoplite. Because of Polydektos's wealth and backing, Talaemenes had the finest armour and could afford a horse, so he served with the hippeus cavalry. Euneas, much to his father Eretmenos's displeasure, had joined the Athenian navy. He was one of the Nautai Astoi, and he hoped that after his training had ended, he would be posted on board one of the two sacred ships of Athens. Yet today, they were needed to bolster the ranks.

Polydektos could recall the vow he gave at eighteen when

he joined the epheboi. *I will not disgrace these sacred arms. I will not desert my companions in battle. I will defend our sacred and public institutions. I will leave my native land better and greater, as far as I am able. I will obey the magistrates and the laws and defend them against those who seek to destroy them. My Witnesses are the gods Agraulos, Hestia, Enyo, Enyalio, Ares, Athene the Warrior, Zeus, Thallo, Auxo, Hegemone, Herakles, and the boundaries of my native land, wheat, barley, vines, olive trees, fig trees.* A ghost of a smile crossed his face as he recalled the uncomplicated days of his youth.

The day was a perfect present from the gods, sunny with wisps of clouds and a cool breeze to keep the temperature down. Polydektos stood on a raised wooden stand erected by the roadside in front of the gates that led into the great polis. He was dressed in his general's attire, glad that he could fit into his armour once again. The heat shimmered around the waiting soldiers and it felt like they were all standing in front of an open oven. Polydektos felt an itch form on the top of his head under his helm. He could not remove his bronze helmet to scratch it. He could only tilt his head to the left, hoping the movement would tip his helm that way and relieve the itch. All it did was to send sweat rolling down his cheek and neck, making him feel even more uncomfortable. He did not want to be here, but Perikles himself had asked him to attend, as one of Athens's most famous strategoi. Normally he would have politely declined the request to draw him back into the limelight, but it was an important day, and Perikles was a close friend.

Six months had passed since his beloved wife and daughter had been murdered, and he felt the guilt of their loss every waking hour of the day. In half a year, Polydektos's life had changed immeasurably. His family were all dead, along with all his household metics and slaves. The only other woman that he loved had betrayed him. His young lover, Talaemenes, had left to start his two years in the military, and his former villa had been knocked down—the villa where, six months ago, his hetaira slave Gala—secret leader of a group of Dionysos worshippers calling themselves Maenads—had butchered his family.

All to gain his love.

He had personally overseen the demolition of his villa. He had sold half of the lands, and the other half he gave to the priests at the temple of Athene, to build a small temple over the ruins of his home. He felt like a homeless beggar, with no roof over his head to call his own. He let go the rooms he rented at the House of Javelins, where he used to visit Gala. He then had spent two weeks with his sister and brother-in-law, but it was far too close to his old villa, and Eretmenos's daily apologising for his servant Borilos's part in the murders of Polydektos's wife and daughter got on his nerves. So he had stayed with Alkmaion, an old war comrade, but Alkmaion's wife's constant nagging of the man had nearly turned Polydektos to drink, and he had sworn that off. He stayed with Sokrates for a month, but there too, the temptations of rich food and wine were too much. After the philosopher had gone off to fight in Potidaea, Polydektos had spent the last two months with Darios, another ex-soldier who lived alone. This had been more to his liking. He liked the seclusion, but he knew he needed someplace on his own sooner rather than later. A small place not too far from the Gymnasium would be ideal. He promised himself, when his formal show of strength and the subsequent reception was over, he would find himself a new place to live.

Polydektos looked up to the higher parts of the stage where the great and the good were assembled waiting for their honoured guests to arrive. Perikles caught his eye and wiped at his forehead. Polydektos nodded back and swept his eyes over the seven hundred hoplites, dignitaries, citizens, councillors of the Boule and Prytaneis. All their eyes glanced down the Sacred Way to the west, awaiting the visitors.

It took another sweltering thirty minutes for the ambassadorial cortege to finally grace them with their presence. When they did, even Polydektos had to admit they did it with confidence and style. One chariot took the lead, with the other two in a V-shape behind it, matching the design of the shields adorning both sides. The first chariot was drawn by two beautiful tall stallions, one white and one black. They both had bronze faceplates with red feathered plumes, matching the driver of the chariot. They had not sent some wizened old man to the talks, but a man in his prime. The ambassador was at the reins of the leading chariot, wearing no armour, but a simple short kilt and a red cape around his shoulder. His bare chest highlighted his bravery in coming to Athens without an army at his back.

Behind him in the left-hand chariot was a younger replica of the ambassador, clearly his son. The right-hand chariot was driven by a woman so striking that even Polydektos noticed. She was tall and strong, and her long raven hair flowed out behind her, held in place with only a simple gold band around her forehead. She wore a red dress to match the appearance of her husband and their son, slashed from her right shoulder to her left hip, exposing her left breast. Polydektos admired her show of defiance to expose her heart, unprotected by armour.

The Spartans had arrived in Athens.

To his regret, Polydektos did not get to see Talaemenes again that day. The youth had returned to his military training, while Perikles had requested that Polydektos come to the reception for the Spartan ambassador held at the proxenos's large villa. Palamon was the proxenos chosen by the city of Athens to host the Spartan delegation. He was from a wealthy family and had the trust of Perikles. He had a large estate in Skambonidai in the northern part of the city—large enough to house the ambassador, his family, and their entourage. He was chosen to show off the prosperity and greatness of Athens to the visiting Spartan delegation.

Polydektos hung at the corners of the large indoor court and refused the wine the slaves offered him. They had no fruit juice, so he filled his cup with the water intended for the wine. He nodded to a few people he knew and returned to his position by a supporting roof column. It was less well-lit than the rest of the court, and he hoped that people would get the message and leave him alone. For the most part, they did. He was a man tainted by the murders of his family. Not through any guilt laid upon him, but through the implication that associating with him might end one's life sooner than the gods willed it to be so. Polydektos preferred the solitary life, but he did miss his companion Talaemenes now he was training to be in a new cavalry unit. What he would give to be eighteen and starting out his military career again. The friendships and camaraderie he found in his formative years to become a hoplite citizen of Athens were some of the greatest bonds he had ever forged.

He took a sip from his cup, sucking the slightly warm water through his teeth. After too much bland water, he certainly missed the taste of wine, but not the aftereffects. It had been a long six-month struggle to get back into his old fighting gear, and he would never go back to being that fat, drunk, whoring oaf again. There were a lot of things he could never go back to. He thought of his dead wife and children, but his wave of grief was interrupted by the entrance of the main players of this show of a reception.

From one side of the room swept Perikles, dressed in a simple white robe with blue owls in a pattern around the borders. Behind him were his two legitimate sons from his first marriage, Paralos and Xanthippos. Following them were a few of Perikles's close advisors and friends, including the outspoken sculptor, Pheidias.

From the left, the Spartans entered. First came Lydos, tall and strong, oiled and washed from his journey, but still wearing his loose red chiton, baring his left breast. Behind him was his son Isandros, taller but leaner than his father, dressed the same. Only the ambassador's wife had changed. She still wore a blood-red dress, but it slipped off her shoulders, held up by two heavy gold chains that crisscrossed around her neck. It was unlike any dress that an Athenian wife would be seen in. The swell of her breasts was temptingly seen and her waist was shown off by another gold ringlet-forged belt.

She certainly stole the attention from Perikles, her host, and her husband. Maybe that was part of the Spartans' ploy? Polydektos sipped at his tepid water and finally managed to take his eyes off the Spartan woman when Palamon, the proxenos and host, began to speak.

"Welcome all, to my humble home. It is a great honour to have such noble and great men under my roof this night. I welcome Perikles, our greatest leader, and his sons. I also welcome the Spartan ambassador sent by King Archidamos the Second:

Lydos, with his son and wife. I hope this reception can help forge a greater understanding between Athens and Sparta; we are all Greeks, after all. Eat, drink, and enjoy all the comforts Dionysos provides tonight, my friends."

Polydektos stiffened at the mere mention of that particular god. He had had enough of the reception already. As the groups mixed around the courtyard to chat, Polydektos decided to go. He had done his duty as a citizen of the polis today by showing his face at the reception; now it was time to leave. He found a table to place his cup and made for the exit.

"Leaving the party so early, General Polydektos?" a woman's voice boldly asked as he had nearly made his escape through an archway leading to a long corridor and the way out.

Cursing the luck of the gods, he stopped and turned his frown into at least a more neutral expression before spinning around to discover the identity of the person behind him. He was surprised to see that the Spartan Ambassador's wife was addressing him. Her long, pale neck cocked questioningly to one side, and she was holding two cups of red wine in her hands.

"Yes," was his tart reply. He did not need to give false excuses to the wife of a Spartan in his own city.

"That is a shame, because of all the people here, you were the one person I was looking forward to meeting." She raised a cup to her painted lips and took a sip of wine.

"Even above Perikles and the other great and the good?" Polydektos replied, holding back any flattery or politeness from the stunningly attractive woman before him.

"You are famed as a warrior and military leader, yet have no political aspirations. These are almost Spartan traits." She smiled at him and took a sip of wine from the other cup.

Polydektos eyed her suspiciously. He had learnt by his great loss never to underestimate the cunning and resolve of a woman. He had no time for women now; only the ghosts of his wife and daughter touched his thoughts. He just wanted to leave this gathering, full of hot air and men who loved the sound of their own voices, and disappear into the night. If he insulted her, maybe she would hurry back to her husband's side and let him depart. "I thought Spartan women were plain of stature and dress and wore no adornments of gold?"

The Ambassador's wife grinned. "So, you find me not plain and wish me to remove my gold chains?" She handed a wine cup to Polydektos and reached for the pin holding one of the crossed chains over her left breast.

"What are you doing, woman?" Polydektos looked round to see if anyone was looking at them.

"I dress as a woman to please my hosts. Perhaps you prefer your women naked and supplicant?"

"I prefer no woman in my life at all and wish to leave," he said, thrusting the cup of wine back at her, spilling a few drops onto the back of his hand.

She left the pin but did not retake the cup. "I do not wish to make the great General Polydektos so uncomfortable he would miss out on the unveiling of the statue by the sculptor Skaios. He has the finest hands, gentle but strong, and has exported his works to Sparta, I've become a great patron of his over the years. It would be sad if you were to miss the unveiling. I promise to keep my clothes on and act as the plain Spartan lady you think we all are."

Polydektos opened his mouth but said nothing.

a strong voice broke Polydektos out of his spell. "I see you have met my beautiful wife, Eione."

Lydos, the Spartan ambassador, sidled up and kissed the painted cheek of his wife—and put a protective arm around her, Polydektos noted.

"I am—"

"I know who you are, Polydektos, son of Praxilios. It is good to meet a fellow soldier and not these prattlers of politics and lies." Lydos reached out an arm. Polydektos swapped his wine from one hand to the other and grasped the offered arm at the elbow as the tall strong Spartan grasped his.

"This is no place for old soldiers, I fear. I was about to take my leave." Polydektos tried to move his arm, but the Spartan held it tightly.

"I hoped you would stay so we could talk of battles and wars we have won. You are a friend to Perikles, are you not? Does he not wish you to stay in his exalted company longer, General?"

Polydektos managed to pull his arm from the strong grip of the Spartan Ambassador at last. "I count Perikles as a friend yes, but I am no general anymore. Just a citizen of the great city-state of Athens, nothing more."

"Then maybe you could counsel me on the ways of Athens, from one soldier to the other, both now having less exciting lives to lead."

"I would have thought being an ambassador and walking into a rival's city exciting, or at least enough to make you feel nervous."

"But the Athenians built two long, high walls after the Persian wars—surely signs of a city that is nervous about invasion by land, by...*superior* forces." Lydos kept his eyes fixed on Polydektos as he sipped his wine.

"Athens has strong men and strong foundations, Ambassador. We have a great empire to protect and many allies too. We are ready for war, but seek only peace with the other Greek nations. And my friend Perikles does love to build things," Polydektos countered. The wine on his skin and the aroma from the cup were tempting him to drink.

"Sparta and its king also want peace, so the fates are with you, Athenian. It is your leader that pushed the Megarian Decree and broke the peace treaty held by Sparta for over thirty years. Maybe Athens should drive out the *Curse of the Goddess*. Then peace between our two great city-states would run an easier course, like a river without a dam," Lydos said the last words in a low hissed voice. Though the ambassador did not name him, Polydektos knew what the *Curse of the Goddess* meant; that Perikles should be exiled for inheriting his mother's family's connection to some sacrilegious murders some two hundred years ago.

"You would like that, perhaps. An old tactic of war: cut off the middle head of Kerberos and the others will be more supplicant. If you wish to remove Perikles, you'd better bring a big army, Lydos of Sparta. Maybe you should consider driving out the *Curse of Taenarus*. before you make demands of Athens." Polydektos insulted the ambassador back, for he had no fear of the man, or of death anymore. He had little left to lose but his own life. The Athenians had not forgotten when the Spartans had murdered some Helot suppliants from the temple of Poseidon at Taenarus. It was a tit-for-tat reply, for the King Archidamus of Sparta to be exiled because of it.

Eione stepped in between the two warriors and pointed as nonchalantly as she could back to the centre of the courtyard, where men were gathering around a sheet-covered sculpture. "They are about to unveil the sculpture. Perikles, Skaios, and even Pheidias are in attendance. Shall we join them, husband?" Eione put a gentle hand on her angry husband's bicep. He glowered at Polydektos, but let himself be led away.

Polydektos smiled to himself and moved over to a corner to get a view of the proceedings, far away from the circus and the Spartans. He would see this latest work unveiled and then be on his merry way. Slaves refilled the wine cups of everyone present, except Polydektos. He had put down the cup the exotic Spartan woman had given him.

Perikles and Palamon stood to one side of the covered statue and Skaios, its sculptor, stood to the other. Pheidias, Athens's other famed artist, stood drinking wine and looking on intently. The Spartan delegation was to the fore of the crowd that had formed a semi-circle in front of the piece.

"My honoured guests and friends from home and abroad, I welcome you all into my humble home this night to foster the hand of friendship between the greatest city-states the world has ever known. I commissioned Skaios to depict this friendship of two strong states, working together for the good of all Greece. His works are well-known from Corinth to Kos, from the Akropolis to the Temple of Apollon in Sparta. I can think of no better man to have hewn this marble edifice to two beloved gods. It brings joy to my heart to finally reveal the product of his months of toil, love, and labour. I give you: 'Hands Across The Evrotas River.'

With a beaming smile of joy and hubris, Palamon, the proxenos, pulled the sheet to reveal the joined twin statues in all their glory. There was the expected sound of awe from the crowd and then the giggles started, quickly followed by unreserved raucous laughter.

The statues were supposed to be depictions of Athene and Ares clasping hands like friends over the River Evrotas, which the Spartans had to cross to invade Attica. Even Polydektos, who was no lover of art, saw what was wrong with the statue right away. Most of the large sculpture of the two Gods was fine; Ares stood naked and proud with a golden helm thrown back off his forehead. Athene, clasping hands over the river, was modestly dressed for a female goddess and held a colourful shield with the Gorgon Sister painted on it. Their heads were the problem. Ares was always shown smooth of face, almost feminine in features, and yet he had been given a full black beard and his penis had been painted bright red at the tip like he had the pox.

Athene had the body of a woman, but a face everyone in the room, indeed the whole of Athens, recognised: Perikles himself.

Polydektos wished he had the cup of wine to toast this piece of comic artistry, but others did not share his amusement.

"What is this?" Palamon pleaded with both had towards the shaken sculptor.

Lydos and Perikles, whose heads were depicted on the Gods' necks, had faces like thunder. Pheidias, the rival sculptor, was crying with laughter, along with the amused crowd.

"This is not mine," Skaios pleaded, his fingers intertwined. He collapsed before the gods he had hewn out of marble and began to weep. "I did not do this; someone has altered the heads. Perikles, Lydos, you have to believe me—I would not have shown this atrocity if I had known."

Lydos pointed an accusing finger at the Athenian leader. "So, this is Athenian hospitality. Insulting your guests and mocking the gods. They say you think yourself above the Olympus in Sparta, Perikles, but this takes the honey cake."

"Are Spartans so dull of wit to think I would sanction this abomination? Palamon, cover this up again. This insult will find you in the law courts in the morning, Skaios, mark my words." Perikles was red with anger and stormed off, with his angry-looking sons and the laughing Pheidias trailing behind.

"You will pay for this, sculptor," Lydos said. "It is lucky you are on Athenian soil. In Sparta, your whiny head would be rolling in the dust by now. Come, wife, son, let us return to our quarters." Lydos pushed his strapping son before him and dragged his wife painfully by the arm out of the courtyard.

"It wasn't me," Skaios wailed to anyone who would listen. "I didn't sculpt those heads. Someone changed them at the last moment." His reputation was now in tatters, and the mockery of the peace sculpture could see him exiled or even executed.

The crowd dispersed silently. Polydektos had seen enough. If he had known receptions could be so amusing, he would have come to many more. He was near the rear of the crowd so left without any fuss. It was a long walk back to Darios's home in the dark. This convinced him that he must find a place to live, even a small home near the centre of the city and maybe a farm outside the walls.

He was at the end of the lane, near Palamon's property, lit by many surrounding torches, when Skaios ran past and promptly tripped over a rock and went sprawling in the dust. Polydektos, in spite of not wanting to get involved, helped the blubbering artist to his feet.

"I didn't do this. Why would someone change the heads of the statues I've long worked upon?"

Polydektos held the sculptor at arm's length. "I know not, citizen. And I care even less." He walked off into the night. He was done with the politics of Athens for one night. He hoped never to be drawn into its malicious machinations ever again. He left Skaios crying for his art beside the lane. His bed was half an hour's walk away and calling to him like a siren.

CHAPTER TWO

Euneas wasn't really in the mood for drinking and carousing, but he and most of the epheboi had been given the night off after the evening meal for attending the welcoming ceremony for the Spartan ambassadorial delegation. He attended a banquet at the home of one of his fellow college friends, and then, after groping the fluke-girl playing there, he headed for the seedier parts of the polis.

His friend Ibykos already looked like he hadn't put much water into his wine tonight. He was also an ephebos, but training to be a hoplite rather than joining the mighty Athenian Navy as Euneas planned. Euneas also spotted Talaemenes, Polydektos's companion and ex-lover, at the far end of the large, loud tavern. They exchanged pleasant waves from across the tavern, but that was all. Euneas was still embarrassed about accusing him and his uncle of murder six months ago. Luckily, because Talaemenes was a hippeus, they had different social and military circles. Navy, cavalry, and infantry may work in unison at sea and on the battlefield, but in Athens, they mostly kept to their segregated training groups. Talaemenes had only just begun his training, so Euneas was five months ahead of him. After a year, his training would continue on board a trireme. Then after another year, he hoped to serve on one of the two sacred vessels of Athens. When Ibykos and Talaemenes were sent to the far-flung edges of the Athenian empire after a year, Euneas might even be serving onboard the ship that took them there.

A gap opened at the bar, and he and three of his fellow nautai astoi pressed against it and tried to get the attention of the metic serving. The barman was a burly, bald man from the island of Rhodes, with a very hairy chest and shoulders. Euneas tried to grab one of the serving girls, but his friends, overeager for their drinks, stumbled into a thin man staring into his wine cup. They knocked the remains of the man's wine over the bar and his bare knees.

"Will you critics ever leave me alone?" the drunk-looking man shouted into Euneas's face as he pushed him back against his friends.

"I am sorry, my friend, a thousand apologies. Let me fill up your cup once more," Euneas offered with a smile.

"So you can drop poison into it, no doubt?" the man roared, then punched the startled Euneas on the nose. The shock of the sudden attack, more than the power behind the punch, sent Euneas sprawling backwards into his friends. The group ended up in a tangled heap of arms and legs on the sticky tavern floor.

The half-drunk man ran away before they could get up, and Euneas rose just in time to see him pushing Talaemenes into the doorframe.

"Hey you, go to the crows!" Talaemenes called after the fleeing man as he rubbed the side of his head.

"Where did the bastard go?" Euneas appeared at the doorway next to Talaemenes, cupping his bloody nose. "We won't let him offend our honour."

"That way." Talaemenes pointed in the direction the man had taken flight.

"I give you thanks, Talaemenes, you are a good man," Euneas said, patting the other man's shoulder before hurtling into the night after the drunk.

Talaemenes rubbed his head and left the tavern, only to be accosted by another man in the doorway. This man, in his early thirties, left a fine white powder on his arms when he grabbed them. "Have you seen Skaios, the sculptor? I only went out to piss and saw him hit someone and run out the tavern. He is not in his right mind and as drunk as a Spartan's wife on her wedding night."

"That way." Talaemenes pointed after the fleeing heels of Euneas and his two companions.

The man raced after the three nautai astoi, leaving Talaemenes bemused and alone. After a moment's hesitation, fearing the hotheaded Euneas might beat his attacker to death, Talaemenes raced after the other parties in the interest of keeping the peace, or at least saving Euneas from another visit to the law courts this year.

This part of the city was dimly lit at the best of times, but at this hour the torches and braziers dotted around the streets were half-burnt out. Talaemenes could hear the whoops and cries of Euneas and his companions in the close, winding streets as they pursued the sculptor. Skaios's drinking companion darted through the shadows at a fair pace and Talaemenes had to put on a burst of speed to keep up. As he headed deep into the tightly packed, poorer streets, he realised he was slightly lost.

A low, thick fog was rolling in from the sea, and it covered the ankles of the young Athenian ephebos. He had evil dreams of such low fogs, yet in his dreams, they were tainted blue and green and brought death to whomever they touched. Talaemenes tried to retreat, but he suddenly heard a cry of shock from the eerie streets somewhere behind him. Apart from the damp smell of the sea and the low graveyard mist, this part of the city was silent again. Another cry of fright echoed close by, followed by the sound of running feet. Talaemenes pulled out the small knife he always kept hidden under his clothes and headed towards the sounds as directly as the streets would allow.

The torches dotted intermittently around the area were soft and appeared smudged because of the rolling fog.

"Skaios?" someone called out into the night.

Talaemenes assumed it was the sculptor's companion, as the voice had a note of concern in it. The sound came from a different direction to the cry of fright.

"Euneas, over here," called a different voice from another and more distant direction.

Talaemenes wasn't sure which way to turn. The fog muffled the voices he heard and he was disoriented in his own city for the first time since he was a child. Something hissed like a serpent, no more than a corner away, and Talaemenes felt he was caught in a vivid nightmare and would wake up in his cot back at the military college.

He had decided to investigate the hissing sound when he saw someone wearing a cloak pass along the bottom of the lane which he had just traversed. He only caught a glimpse of the person's face because of the poor light and the fog, but it was hideous to behold. A flash of boar-like tusks protruded from beside a wide open mouth from which a long, pointed tongue flicked. They had a hood cast down over their eyes and nose. As soon as he saw them, they were lost to the dark behind the next row of houses and shops.

Talaemenes walked backwards slowly and then with great pace, fearful of what he had seen. Someone ran out of the fog towards him from a connecting criss-cross lane. They both crashed to the floor hard. Without taking the time to stand, Talaemenes scrambled back on his behind, though the mist that hid most of his assailant's body from view. He grabbed at the man and pulled him out of the low fog, his knife at the man's nose.

"Please don't hurt me. It is I, Olos. We bumped into each other at the tavern. I'm looking for my mentor, Skaios," the man almost shrieked in fear. "I was scared by the fog. It seems Morpheus himself has been sent to swallow us."

Talaemenes lowered his knife from the man's throat and together they helped each other to their feet.

"This fog does seem unnatural. Come, we will stick together and search for your mentor."

Talaemenes had only got these words out when he heard there came an ear-piercing scream of fear and pain from around the next corner. Olos and Talaemenes exchanged worried looks and then hurried around the corner to find it empty. The cry had been so close that they surely would have expected to see someone close by, but there was nothing but the swirling ankle-high mist.

"I'm certain, as Zeus is my witness, that that was Skaios, screaming in fright or agony," Olos said, keeping close to Talaemenes.

There was one lit torch in this narrow lane, and Talaemenes

grabbed it from its sconce on the side of a weaver's shop. He held it low and moved down the lane with Olos in tow. "Someone might be hurt and hidden under this accursed fog."

Olos was terrified and could only nod in reply.

Talaemenes swished the torch back and forth across the ground, causing the fog to retreat for a few seconds to reveal the paving stones of the street underfoot. He did this along half the length of the narrow lane until one sweep of the torch near the left-hand side against a wall revealed an object.

"By the Gods, no!" Olos put his trembling hands over his open mouth.

Talaemenes swept the torch low again and reached down to pick up two of the four items of clothing left on the side of the street. One was a faded off-white chiton tunic. The other a brighter, newer blue outer himation that he recalled the sculptor Skaios was wearing when he bumped Talaemenes into the doorframe.

"Do these belong to Skaios?" Talaemenes asked, handing the garments over to Olos's shaking hands. He reached down with his free hand again to collect a pair of sandals.

"Yes, these are his clothes." Olos gulped air audibly, looking at the blood stains on both garments.

"Then wherever he is, he is as naked as the day he was birthed, and wounded," Talaemenes said as he swept the lower torch to the ground, finding the odd drop of blood, but no other clues to the whereabouts of the sculptor.

Many loud approaching footfalls from the other end of the lane caused both men to stand. Talaemenes readied his knife to protect them. Three shadowy figures approached in a hurry, and Talaemenes thrust the torch forwards to see their faces.

It was Euneas and his two naval college companions.

"Talaemenes, it is good to see you safe" Euneas clasped the other Epheboi's arm in an out-of-breath welcome. "Many strange things we have seen in our pursuit of the man who punched me, but no sign of him have we found."

"What do you have there?" One of Euneas's companions called Metron asked, pointing at the bloody clothes Olos was holding. The other man in their group was looking around them like he expected them to be attacked at any second.

"My mentor's clothes. Skaios, the man who drunkenly attacked you at the tavern," Olos mournfully replied.

"Then where is this Skaios? I wish to have a word or two with him about his manners," Euneas said, brandishing his fists.

"We know not." Olos shook his head.

"We heard a fearful scream and rushed here to find only his clothes and sandals, covered in blood, but no sign of him," Talaemenes explained, pointing at the blood on the sculptor's clothes.

"We too heard this scream and came running," said Euneas.

"Is he murdered then, do you think?" Metron asked.

"We know not, but it does not bode well for Skaios. But if he is, someone took his naked body with them," Talaemenes said, looking around nervously, as the attacker might still be abroad.

"It was one of the Gorgon Sisters, I glimpsed her two streets away," Euneas's other college companion said in fear.

"Yet Metron and I saw nothing but fog. Get a hold of yourself, Demarmenos, or you will never pass muster to be on one of the Sacred Vessels," Euneas chastised his craven companion.

Talaemenes raised his free hand to stop Euneas and laid it gently on Demarmenos's arm. "Do not be so harsh on him, Euneas, for I saw a cloaked and hooded figure earlier when the fog appeared. It had a lolling long tongue, and large teeth like tusks showed on either side of its mouth. I assumed it was a mask."

"You saw her too then? A Gorgon, right here in the streets of Athens." Demarmenos wasn't sure whether to be relieved or more afraid as someone backed up what he had witnessed.

"Then why aren't you turned to stone?" Metron laughed, but his voice died as he looked at the worried faces of the men around him.

"I did not see the creature's eyes, they were hidden by the hood she wore," Talaemenes said, to counter Metron.

"Nor did I. Only the eyes of a Gorgon can turn a man to stone; even little girls at the teat know this." It was Demarmenos's turn to chide his friend.

As one, the group of men turned and looked around them, searching each shadowy corner and the dark ends of the street for this mythical creature Talaemenes and Demarmenos had spotted.

"What do we do now, search the streets for this creature or Skaios?" Euneas tried to sound brave, but he hoped all present would disagree with such an idea.

"I think that would be unwise," Metron said.

"I think we should get back to barracks as swiftly as Hermes himself," Demarmenos suggested.

"What about Skaios? He could be out here somewhere, naked and bleeding to death," Olos said from concern for his mentor.

"What do you say, Talaemenes?" Euneas hoped that the slightly younger man might also suggest they leave.

"Why ask me?"

"Because you have previously faced death and such mysteries that murder can bring. I value your counsel more than anyone I know. I just wish I had realised the good man you were ages ago and not been jealous of your relationship with my uncle and our beloved Kyra. I think we could have been firm friends," Euneas spoke in earnest.

"We still can be good friends, Euneas. I've seen too much death in my life to hold grudges against the living. The only thing I can suggest is to go and see Polydektos, right now," Talaemenes said with a grim, but friendly smile.

"You speak wisely above your years as always, my new friend," Euneas said, and they clasped arms for good measure.

"Look the fog is dissipating," Demarmenos cried, pointing around them. It was true, the fog was turning to faint wisps of mist that clung only in the tightest of corners of the streets.

"Like it was sent this night by Thantos to cover this ungodly deed," Olos stated.

Talaemenes knelt down to examine the ground where he had found Skaios's clothes. Seeing nothing else untoward he stood up and looked from one end of the lane to the other. "Does anyone know where we are and how to get to Polydektos's house?"

"My father always told me as a child that if you ever get

lost in this great polis of ours, just head in one direction until you hit the walls of the city, then work yourself around to the nearest gate and ask for directions," Euneas said, lightening the mood a little.

Metron was the only one to give a brief laugh. The street seemed much less threatening now the fog had lifted.

"Your father Eretmenos is a wise man; we shall follow his lead." Talaemenes patted Euneas on the shoulder and led the group what he hoped was north, towards the nearest outer wall.

"What about Skaios?" Olos asked, following close behind Talaemenes.

"Perhaps we will find him on our travels. If not, there is no better person to solve this mystery in the whole of the city than Polydektos."

"You looked as uncomfortable on that platform amongst the great and the good as I would on a stage at the theatre," Darios cried out in welcome when Polydektos made it back to his friend's home.

"Ha! With your girlish singing voice, they would have you play all the lead female roles. Shave that stubble of yours, and you would make a fine painted Aphrodite," Polydektos said jovially, closing the wooden door to the small home behind him.

Darios raised his cup of watered wine to his former general and took a sip. "Your mood seems improved from this morning. What or who tickled your fancy at the reception tonight?"

"There were fun and games with the unveiling of that peace sculpture by Skaios this evening." Polydektos sat down and poured himself some water. He took off his helm and put it down on the table and rubbed at his hair.

"Intriguing—tell me more. I know Skaios in passing; he seems a decent sort for a sculptor."

"Potters' jealousy, eh?" Polydektos smirked and took a sip of water. He was in a good mood this evening for reasons he could not fathom. Maybe sparring verbally with the Spartans or seeing Skaios brought down a few levels in the social order had cheered his spirit. He knew not which, but he had little time for art.

"They are a pious lot sometimes. Yet you are not telling me what happened at the reception you were dreading to attend."

"Well, I had a run in with Lydos the Spartan ambassador and his wife, which was a good start to the proceedings."

"He looked every inch a man of Sparta. What about his wife? From three rows back in the crowds I did not see much of her. You stuck out like a sore thumb on that raised platform, my general. Did she have hairier pits that a Persian wrestler and more facial hair than most Spartan men can grow? Could you indeed tell which was the ambassador and which was his wife?" Darios joked. It was a long-standing Athenian Army joke that Spartan women were uncomely and lived in kennels amongst the bitches.

"She must be a rare woman. She had more strength, wit, and guile about her than her husband."

"And her looks?"

"You would not kick her out of your cot, Darios, let us say that."

"So you found her pleasing to the eye?"

"Enough, enough. But I will never trust another woman as long as I live, let alone a Spartan woman." Polydektos's voice had lost its jovial edge, and the old anger was building up in him again.

"Well I wasn't thinking about you trusting her. Thrusting her, maybe. But I will let it slip. Tell me more about Skaios and his peace sculpture."

"That is the thing. The faces of the gods were mimicries of Perikles and Lydos. I'm not sure if Skaios thought this would please Perikles's ego, but it did not go down well with either party. Skaios is the laughing stock of all Greece tonight. I deem he will be lucky to escape prison or exile for the embarrassment he caused through his chisel and hammer."

It was Darios's turn to frown. This did not sound like the man he knew at all. "What did Skaios say when his works were unveiled? He is an artist imbued with very little wit and has not a comical thought in his body. He can be an annoying individual at times, full of his own self-worth as sculptors are, but he always takes the utmost pride in his work."

"He claimed another party had altered the statues' faces and painted a red raw end on Ares's member."

Darios raised his eyebrows and took another sip of his wine before he spoke again. "It could be true; several sculptors had their noses smitten because of the importance of this peace sculpture. They were very jealous that Palamon and Perikles chose him above all the others in Athens."

"Like Pheidias, perhaps?"

"Yes, he would be the first on my list of names. Was he there?"

"Yes, braying like a donkey at Skaios's misfortune. Artists— you are an unfathomable lot."

"I'm a potter. There is a difference, you know." Darios smiled back at his former general again.

Polydektos drained his water and stood up. "Well, I can hear the ducks calling me. I've been in this armour far too long for a mere citizen."

He went to pick up his helm and head to Darios's spare room when there came many urgent knocks on his friend's front door. "Are you expecting company?"

"Unless it was those kanephoros virgins I asked Athene to send me, then no," Darios replied.

The insistent knocking continued. Polydektos drew his ceremonial sword, while Darios grabbed a javelin held on hooks high above his cooking-fire pit. Polydektos had a free hand, so went to the door to open it while Darios stood ready with his weapon. The former general nodded at Darios, then unlatched the door and pushed it open.

Several hands grabbed the edge of the door to open it further.

Polydektos and Darios braced themselves for an attack.

The cool night air let in, not foes, but dear friends.

Talaemenes led Euneas, Olos, and Demarmenos inside the warm, light home. Metron had returned to barracks to inform their superiors what had happened and where the rest of the group were now heading. As long as they were back in their cots before dawn, they would suffer no punishment.

Darios and Polydektos immediately lowered their weapons

and sighed with relief.

Polydektos approached Talaemenes and held his arms in a welcoming, tender gesture. "What brings you all here at this time of night? Surely the military colleges have not gotten so lax about their charges since Darios and I were there?"

"It is good to see you so close, Polydektos." Talaemenes smiled, forgetting his urgent reason for coming. He missed the company of his mentor and sharing his bed at night as lovers.

"We are on urgent business, uncle, and did not know where to turn," Euneas had to explain.

"What business?" Darios asked, putting back his javelin above the dying fire.

"There have been foul and murderous deeds happening in the streets of Athens this night. I could not think of anyone better to aid and serve us," Talaemenes said to Polydektos.

"What deeds—what do you mean?" Polydektos frowned, hoping his young friend was not in any kind of trouble, nor his nephew. "And who are these other fellows?"

"I know you, don't I?" Darios pointed at the out-of-breath Olos. The man was much older than the others, and it had been twelve years since he had done his military service. He was carrying a bundle of clothes under one arm.

"I am Olos, apprentice to Skaios, the master sculptor," Olos managed to get out between pants.

Talaemenes spoke for the winded Olos. "It is about Skaios that we come to you this night and bother you so late."

"Then you had better come in and explain." Polydektos turned sidewards to let his young ward past.

"Sit, sit," Darios offered the chairs around the table to the four visitors. "Drink the water and wine; my home is your home, my young friends."

Polydektos let the four men sit and take a drink before pressing them for more information. "Tell why you have sought me out. Are you in some kind of trouble?" He stared at Euneas and Talaemenes, as he did not know the other two men.

"No, not us, but another might be," Talaemenes began, while Euneas looked at the cup in front of him, avoiding his stern uncle's withering gaze.

"My mentor Skaios," Olos clarified. "I fear he has been murdered."

Polydektos exchanged glances with Darios and then returned his gaze to Olos. "I saw Skaios alive and well at the reception tonight. What happened to him after that...embarrassment?"

"Skaios came back to the studio weeping and in a foul mood. He grabbed some coin and took off to a tavern we sometimes frequent. I followed him, worried about his state of mind. He was drinking a lot, and only after his third wine did, he inform me what had befallen him and the peace statue this night." Olos explained.

"I saw the statue. Was Skaios telling the truth that he did not sculpt it in that manner to cause maximum offence to the reception's honoured guests?" Polydektos asked, leaning on the back of Talaemenes's chair.

"I helped him with the base, and those features were of Ares and Athene when we delivered it to the estate of the proxenos, I swear before Almighty Zeus." Olos beat at his left breast to emphasise the truth of his words.

"So what happened at the tavern?" Polydektos urged. His dreams of hitting his duck-feather pillows before dawn were dwindling rapidly.

"We was drinking more and more, blaming Pheidias for all his ills at the reception. I went to relieve myself, and when I returned, I saw him knocking into Talaemenes in the tavern doorway, with Euneas, Demarmenos, and another man, Metron, pursuing him." Olos pointed around the table.

"And why were you chasing Skaios, Euneas, son of Eretmenos?" Polydektos asked his nephew, in a sterner voice than he used for the others. He had forgiven but not forgotten the boy's false accusations that had led to him and Talaemenes being put on trial for the murder of his own family.

"He accosted me at the bar for no reason and punched me when I wasn't looking. Then he ran, so we chased him. We soon lost him in the fog and the narrow streets in that part of town."

"A good soldier should always be on the lookout for unprovoked attacks, nephew. But take heart—most men learn more from their mistakes than their glories." Polydektos paced around the room, circling the table. "I saw no fog when I was in the city."

"It was sent by Khaos to confuse us and hide the evil we saw stalking our very streets," Olos said in an anxious, quivering voice. "A Gorgon took Skaios, I'm sure of it."

"What do you mean?" asked Darios, who was more in tune with the gods and their ways than Polydektos.

"Something was stalking the narrow streets when we were all looking for Skaios for our differing reasons," Olos replied. "I heard hissing sounds but saw nothing. Ask of Demarmenos and Talaemenes—they saw the creature, not I."

"Is this true? What did you witness?" Polydektos's interest was piqued. The mystery unfolding was at least taking his mind off his lost family at this time of night.

Talaemenes spoke first. "I briefly saw a cloaked and hooded figure in the mist. I too heard hissing like many snakes and saw a face caught fleetingly in the torchlight. It was hideous to behold, what I saw of it, anyway. A mouth with two tusks pointing upwards."

Demarmenos backed him up. "I also glimpsed this creature, but heard no sounds at all. With its head mostly covered by a hood and the mouth with tusk-like teeth just as Talaemenes described."

"Could it have been some sort of mask?" Polydektos asked the youths, stroking at the longest part of his beard.

"It was dark and misty, so it could have been. I cannot honestly say yes or no for certain." Talaemenes looked up at his mentor.

"So you chased after the half-drunk Skaios into the narrows? I think I know the area you talk of, from frequenting that tavern of old. An unearthly mist descended, and two of you glimpsed this figure stalking the streets. Then what happened?" Polydektos moved his hand over his mouth to hide a yawn. The night was well into the next day by now.

"It was a very low, unnatural mist, the likes of which I've never seen before," added Euneas, who hadn't spoken for a while. "It barely came up to one's ankles."

"I bumped into Olos, and we both heard a scream of pain

from the next street," Talaemenes explained to Polydektos. "We ran round but saw nobody. Only after a thorough search did we find Skaios's bloody clothes, all of them on the ground, but no sign of Skaios himself. That's when Euneas, Demarmenos, and Metron found us. They had not seen any sign of Skaios either. And then, remarkably, the mist went back to whence it came. We were disorientated by then and headed north to find the wall of the city, then made our way around to the nearest gate to get our bearings."

Polydektos pointed to the sculptor's assistant. "Olos, do you have Skaios's clothes there?"

"Yes." Olos nodded, his eyes glistening like he was on the verge of crying. He placed the bundle of clothes on the edge of the table.

Darios and Polydektos both moved forwards to open the bundle and examine its contents, Darios the chiton tunic and Polydektos the outer blue himation. Both garments had stains of blood on them, yet not copious amounts. Neither item had rents or holes in them, and the sandals had little to give up to the naked eye.

"No blade wounds, and the blood is around the neck and middle parts of the clothing," Darios stated, holding the chiton up to the nearest torch.

"So it appears that Skaios was not stabbed when he was first attacked. The blood indicates he was struck around the head or neck and then stripped of his clothes," Polydektos deduced from where the blood stained both garments.

"So he could have been knocked unconscious and kidnapped?" Talaemenes ventured.

"Or had his head caved in and was killed," Darios grimly added.

Olos gave a little whimper and wiped at his wet eyes.

Polydektos put down the chiton on the table again. "Olos, is anything missing from these clothes? A brooch or a belt or his moneybag?"

Olos spoke in a croak of an upset voice. "He wore his moneybag on a leather strap around his neck. We did not find it, but it could have been hidden in the darkness."

"A robbery, perhaps?" Darios surmised.

"Or revenge meted out for that abominable peace sculpture unveiled earlier tonight," Polydektos said, returning to his pacing of the floor.

"Do you think we should go back and look for the money bag?" Talaemenes asked.

"I think there would be little point now. If it were hidden by the night, someone else would have surely picked it up by now and thanked Tyche for their found fortune. I think you three epheboi should head back to your barracks before you get flogged for not being back before dawn. Olos, you head back to Skaios's home or studio and see if he turns up injured," Polydektos ordered.

"What will you do?" Talaemenes stood and faced Polydektos, concern in his young voice.

"Darios and I will sleep, and at first light we shall visit this tavern in which you met. Olos, when the dawn comes, meet us there and tell us if we still need to search for your mentor. Let us hope he returns home naked and with a sore head, but not too wounded. Agreed?" Polydektos looked around at the other men as they rose from their chairs to leave.

Talaemenes touched Polydektos's arm tenderly. "What shall we do after we get back to barracks?" He nodded back towards Euneas and Demarmenos.

"You do what your instructors tell you to do. You are epheboi now and serve the city, not yourselves." Talaemenes began to protest, but Polydektos raised a hand to silence him. "You have your duty to perform. Darios and I will find out all that is to be learned about this attack and let you know in due course. Now go, all of you, before I get my whip out." Polydektos looked at the others sternly and then kissed Talaemenes on each cheek.

Talaemenes gave such a look of hurt as only the young and naïve could pull off and turned and left with the others, back into the night. They had a long march back to their barracks and would have to run some of the way to get in before dawn's first light. Olos went with them as far the Dipylon Gate. They parted, going east and west to their desired destinations. Talaemenes, Euneas, and Demarmenos heading back to their military college barracks.

"So we try to sleep?" Darios asked, draining the last of his interrupted nightcap.

"Yes," Polydektos replied. "It won't come easy, but we need to rest and have our wits about us at the dawn. I will need your tracking skills again, my old friend."

"I am yours to command as always, my friend and General."

The two old soldiers went to their separate beds and got in as much sleep as the slender hours before dawn would allow.

CHAPTER THREE

A rough shake of Polydektos's shoulder woke him from a near-comical dream of two Titans using tree trunks to hit cattle over the walls of a mighty city. He opened one sleepy eye to see Darios standing over him as the first light of dawn crept through his bedroom window.

"Time we were up, general."

"Time I stopped getting caught up in the affairs and mysteries of others," Polydektos groaned. He sat up in his cot and rubbed at his barely focusing eyes.

"What is life without a little bit of excitement?" Darios yawned and left the room.

"What is life without loved ones," Polydektos murmured to himself, a phrase he thought worthy of his friend Sokrates. Polydektos lowered his face into a bowl of clean water and then brushed it through his hair. With the cold water running down his back, he shook himself awake and dressed quickly. As an afterthought, he fixed and hid his sword under his outer garment.

By the time he had put on his walking sandals, urinated in the piss-pot, and left the guest room, Darios was waiting by the open front door to his simple abode. He had a waterskin and food wrapped in a cloth, for them to eat as they made their way up to the city. The air outside had a slight chill and the dawn was throwing waves of orange and red against the morning clouds.

"Red sky at dawn, sailors be warned," Polydektos said, remembering what his father used to tell him as a boy. His grandfather, who had died before he was born, had been a captain of one of the sacred ships of Athens.

"Blood-red sky does not bode well for our ventures," said the superstitious Darios as they set off towards the city walls. "Red is the colour of Ares."

"And Hestia." Polydektos tapped his gods-fearing friend on the shoulder. "Let us meet Olos outside the tavern and see if we can put this mystery to bed this day and get back to our lives."

Darios smirked at his former General. "What lives?"

Polydektos did not answer. He was a widow now, devoid of children and any hope of heirs to his family. Darios had his pottery, but no wife or children either. They were two lonely old soldiers shacked up together because they had no one else. Who would be around to mourn when death came for them?

The red-tinged clouds had become thicker and grey by the time they had reached the Itonian gate. They still had a long walk across the city, from the southern gate up to the north where the tavern was situated. A cool breeze had risen from the sea and whipped through the city, causing dust-devils to arise in corners as they passed. Both men were glad of their outer woollen himations. Polydektos loved the polis at this time of the morning, before the streets got too hot and packed with people. He wished he and Darios were heading for the gymnasium instead of dealing with other people's problems, but he had promised Talaemenes to look into it, so he would.

They saw Olos outside the closed tavern, hopping from one foot to the next and rubbing his hands together to keep warm. He still sported the chiton he had worn last night and no warmer outer garment. It looked to Polydektos like the man had got little or no sleep at all.

"Good morning, Olos, what news this windy day?" Darios hailed him, in his sometimes tactlessly jovial manner.

"No news, I am afraid. Skaios did not return to the studio last night, and he did not go home to his wife and bed either. She is most anxious about him. She heard of the trouble with the peace statues, and rude and angry graffiti has already been daubed on the walls of their house." Olos was visibly worried about his mentor's whereabouts and state of life.

"We have thousands of citizens with a motive already, it seems, Polydektos."

The older former general looked from Darios to Olos, wondering to himself how any of this was his concern. People were born, died, and went missing every day in such a large city as this; what did he care?

"Can you show us where you found Skaios's clothes?" Polydektos said in a tired voice, wanting to get this over with as quickly as he could. He would look into it, but if nothing came to light, he would be off to the gym at a speed which would make Hermes himself proud.

"Skaios ran this way," Olos pointed.

"Then lead on." Polydektos wrapped his himation tighter around himself and followed after Olos and Darios. Losing weight had brought many benefits, but it also meant he felt the cold more.

It took a few dead ends and several trips back up and down the Narrows to find the right place. Finally, Olos pointed out the corner where he had last seen Skaios alive before he lost him in the fog and narrow streets.

"It looks different in the daylight," Olos explained. "Less threatening." He pointed from the sconce on the wall to the side of the street where he and Talaemenes had found the clothes, muttering to himself under his breath as he did. "We found Skaios's clothes right here."

Polydektos and Darios made their way over to the side of the street where the sculptor pointed. The denizens of this part of the city were not ones to be up and about early, so they had the street virtually to themselves. Polydektos put an arm out to stop Olos trampling over the place where the clothes were found, and let Darios do his thing. A sharper, keener-eyed, and more knowledgeable scout Polydektos was yet to meet in his life.

Darios knelt down on one knee to examine the area. "This strong breeze coming in from the sea does not help our cause, General," he stated, rubbing at his stubble-covered chin.

"Do the best you can, my friend, which is always better than most others."

Darios moved low to the ground and rubbed his right eyebrow. He even put his head down to the dusty ground at one stage, then stood and walked in a stoop along the street.

"Anything?" Olos asked impatiently.

"These cobbles and ruts do not help, neither the strong winds. The place where the clothes were found is a confusion of sandal marks from when you and Talaemenes and the others eventually turned up. There is little to glean from that spot except to corroborate what you all told us last night. It gives us little, General. What I can tell you is what isn't here—signs of a struggle, or blood trails. Nor any signs of a person being dragged away from the spot where the clothes were found," Darios added.

"What does that mean?" Olos's voice had risen to a squeaky tone of anxiousness.

"It could be interpreted in many ways," Polydektos began to answer, hoping to appease the highly-strung sculptor's worries about his mentor. "That Skaios was attacked and stripped someplace else, and his clothes just dumped here for you to find. Or Skaios was attacked here, stripped, and then carried off by a person or a cart, or even a horse. It could also mean Skaios stripped himself naked here, to give the appearance that he was attacked so he could leave the city in disguise." Polydektos touched three fingers of his left hand in a row, as he went through his theories.

"Why would he fake his own attack?" Olos squealed in a pitch almost so high that only the dogs and the alley cats might hear his voice.

"The shame of what happened at the Proxenos's reception. The shame, and fear of a possible court hearing, added to his drinking, might explain these actions. Olos, even you must admit Skaios is a ruined man. His reputation is destroyed. He could easily have fled the city to save his wife or you any further embarrassment."

"I won't hear of it—this is not the man I know. He was attacked, plain and simple. He probably lies dead in a communal well somewhere close by. Not that either of you cares," Olos continued to squawk like a hawk caught in a bird trap by the leg.

"Polydektos and I are only trying to help, Olos," Darios said, trying to placate the sculptor. "It could well be that he was attacked, beaten around the head, and was kidnapped or killed; because of the peace statue or for some other reason we do not know. We are just spitting ideas into the wind. Calm yourself, my friend."

"Did he have any enemies or owe any debts to the wrong kind of people?" Polydektos asked, growing tired of the sculptor's whiny voice.

"He has been paid handsomely by the state and other cities for his work. These past two years have been a boon for him, he has no money worries that I know of. If he had, he never shared any of them with me. On enemies, before last night's fiasco, I would say he had none. He had rivals, jealous of his skills as a sculptor, but none I ever feared would do him harm."

"What about his political views?" Polydektos pressed, walking away from Olos and down the street a little way.

"He was a staunch support of Perikles and his building programme, and a loyal citizen of Athens. Apart from that, he kept his views to himself. He was no lover of wars, I suppose," Olos shrugged.

"Yet he travelled widely and sold his pieces and statues to Sparta, Corinth, and Arcadia?" Polydektos slowed and turned back to face the sculptor.

"He sold pieces to other Greek states, yes, but visited them rarely. He did a lot of his work in this city and exported his wares. We spent a year in Sparta building the temple there. We are not at war with Sparta yet, are we, General? He has broken no laws or covenants?" The whine from Olos's high-pitched voice dulled to something near aggression. Polydektos smiled; aggression he understood, the arts he did not.

"Just Polydektos. Only Darios and the men who served under me in battle get to call me General." Polydektos clapped his hands together and walked further down the lane to a crossroads. He looked left and right, seeing that this part of the city was waking to the new day at last. A few people were emerging from their small homes, and slaves were about their masters' early business. He wasn't sure what else he could do at this stage; searching every street and lane for clues did not appeal to him. He heard footsteps behind him.

"What next, *General?*" Polydektos could almost see the amused smirk on Darios's lips in his mind's eye.

"My stomach votes for breakfast. My mind says to visit Skaios's wife first and then forget the whole thing as a waste of a good morning."

"You are right, we have very little to go on so far. A mysterious cloaked figure from legend and some bloodied clothes, but no corpse." Darios came round to stand next to Polydektos. Olos hung back from the two former soldiers.

"We can inform the Scythian Rod Bearers, and anyone we know, to keep an eye out for the sculptor, but little else can be done unless he turns up alive or dead. We will visit his wife for Talaemenes's and Euneas's peace of mind and then let that be an end to this folly." Polydektos lowered his voice to a whisper as he heard Olos approaching.

"What now—do we search the streets for Skaios or clues to what happened to him last night?" Olos rubbed agitatedly at his left eyebrow as he spoke.

"No. You will take us to Skaios's house, and we will talk to his wife. If he is alive, I'm pretty sure that's the place to which he would return. Lead on, Olos." Polydektos ushered the sculptor before him.

Skaios's home and nearby studio were in Diomea, in the eastern part of the great polis. There were many taverns closer to his home and studio than the one in which he had been drinking in the Skambonidai district, but married men often drank far from home and from the earshot of their wives and family members. It was a good sized home for a sculptor and had a small shop incorporated into the right-hand corner of the front of the house. Today, though, the doors were closed and the windows shuttered. It was situated on a busy street and had an excellent view of the Akropolis from the front entrance.

A metic servant was standing at the entrance, turning away unwanted visitors and answering enquiries on why Skaios's shop was shut.

"Closed for family reasons," they heard the metic say to a

stout, short wife who was out shopping, before she walked off back down the street.

"Any news, Prokrutes?" Olos asked the metic porter as they arrived at the entrance.

"I was hoping that you would have news, Olos—we have not seen the master since yesterday. He hasn't returned to the studio; I got one of the slaves to check not long ago."

"We need to talk to Anthousa," Olos told the metic.

"She has taken to her room and will not come out," Prokrutes replied.

"Then get a slave girl to fetch her. This is important, Prokrutes. She might have some vital knowledge that we men have not thought of, that could help us find Skaios. We will wait in the andron for her. And bring some wine, as we are parched," ordered Olos, who regularly stayed at the house.

"And water," Polydektos added.

Darios put in his two drachmas' worth. "And some food would not go amiss."

Polydektos frowned and patted his old comrade's stomach as they entered the building. The andron was situated in the far left corner of the ground floor of the inner courtyard. Soon after Polydektos and the others lay down, the two slave girls hurried in. One bore jugs of wine and water and cups on a bronze tray, the other some barley cake, eggs, barley porridge, grapes, myrtle berries, sun-dried grapes, and figs.

Polydektos passed on the wine and had a full cup of water and some figs. Olos just had wine. Darios had watered wine and a full plate with some of everything apart from the porridge. He was still eating fifteen minutes later when a puffy-eyed Anthousa entered the andron. Olos immediately stood up to let her sit down. Polydektos and Darios also stood until she was seated. *She may be a widow already*, Polydektos thought, *so we will treat her with the utmost respect.*

"Is there any news of my husband?" Anthousa asked, dabbing her eyes with a square of embroidered cotton. A Syrian slave girl stood behind her, holding more of the fresh, perfumed cotton squares for her mistress.

"Nothing new has come to light, and no one I have talked

to has seen him since last night." Olos stood at the head of the couch, while Polydektos and Darios sat down again. Polydektos was glad that Darios found his manners and put down the tray of food he had been eating. He lived alone and had no wife, so his table manners could sometimes be a little coarse in female company. "This is Polydektos and Darios. They have been helping me look for your beloved husband."

"I know of you, of course, General Polydektos. I met your wife on the odd occasions in the agora. It was a tragedy to lose her and your beautiful daughter in that way. I cannot think of anyone in the whole of Greece more qualified to solve this mystery than you." Anthousa's sad eyes nearly melted Polydektos's strong resolve to drop his investigation in favour of a morning at the gymnasium.

"Thank you for your kind words about my late wife and daughter. My companion and I, with Olos's help, will try to locate your missing husband. But I must warn you to prepare for the worst news. If it is permissible, I would like to ask you a few quick questions, and then we will be on our way."

Darios looked at his former general while his tongue poked at some food in his cheek, and his eyebrows raised. Polydektos raised his bushier eyebrows back at his companion, before returning his attention to the woman who was almost certainly now Skaios's widow.

Anthousa nodded and raised her hand back to her slave to replace the sodden cotton square for a fresh one.

Thoughts of his late wife and daughter filled Polydektos's mind and left little room to find any questions he could ask her. By the Fates, Darios stepped in to aid his faltering mind and break the long pause in proceedings.

"When was the last time you saw your husband, Anthousa, and how was his mood?"

A sudden question instantly shot like an arrow into Polydektos's thought process, but he waited for her answer to Darios's question first.

"Yesterday afternoon. He had just returned from the proxenos's estate after making one final check of his great work, the *Hands Across The Evrotas River* peace sculpture. He came to bathe, eat, and dress in his finest clothes for the night. He left an hour later to see the Spartan ambassador arrive at the Dipylon Gate, and that was the last I saw of him." Anthousa began to weep, realising that might be the last time she would ever see her husband alive again.

"I was wondering, as this was Skaios's greatest night in his sculpting career, why I did not see you by his side at Palamon's reception for the Spartans," Polydektos stated, as absently as he could manage for a man with a suspicious mind of women's motives.

"Skaios thought I might take attention away from his sculpture," she said in a clipped reply.

"In what way? You are a fair-faced woman and beautiful to behold, but why would people take any notice of you, above his statues and the Spartan being in town?" Polydektos pressed.

"Because I am not an Athenian, only married to one. My husband thought Pheidias and his cronies had enough arrows in their quivers against him and his works. He thought parading his Zakynthian wife would harm his big night. I would love to have been there, but I would never go against my husband's wishes." Anthousa spoke towards the mosaic of the naked goddess Aphrodite in the centre of the andron's floor.

"Even though Perikles himself has a foreign-born wife?" Darios interjected.

"Skaios is a very proud Athenian. We have no children, as he can't bear the thought that they would not be full citizens of this great city-state. He loves Athens, even above me," she said sadly and simply.

Polydektos sat with his chin resting on his left hand, deep in thought.

"Does your husband's and Pheidias's rivalry run that deep, that he wished to harm him in any way?" Darios asked as Polydektos pondered. "Or are there any other men who would wish violence against him?"

"I know that Pheidias has Perikles's ear and would get the major works around the city above my husband. I could see him and his friends mutilating the peace statue, but to attack my husband once his works were worthless and mocked around the city...what would be the point?"

"A good and clever point well-made, Anthousa," Olos said and rested his hand on her left shoulder for comfort.

"Of others he clashed with, there was Olagnos the critic. And Boule—he always went out of his way to demean anything my husband did, citing him a friend of the Peloponnesian League and not a true lover of Athens." Anthousa waved her hand for another comfort cloth to dab her wet eyes.

Polydektos nodded. He knew these men to talk to. They hung around his friend Perikles like a bad smell from a dung heap. He had no time or love for such fawning, politically motivated fools. He would be polite to them in his old friend's presence, but he would not seek out their company. He chose his friends for loyalty and not what favours they could bring to the table. Perikles often warned him that associating with Sokrates and his often undemocratic views on Athens would not help him get voted back to being a strategos and leading an Athenian army once more. Polydektos would nod, but would not take the advice. He loved Perikles as a brother, and he was a great leader and general, but his ways were not Polydektos's ways. Like brothers, they would argue and disagree on matters. Perikles spent money on temples, statues, and works around the city and thought the Athenian Navy and the high walls made Athens undefeatable. Polydektos, ever the soldier, would rather have spent the money on a permanent hoplite army to match the Spartans. Only then would they be undefeatable. His ideas got the backing of a few old strategoi, but he had no famous tribes or family behind him anymore, nor was he a political hanger-on. So the idea was borne on the wind like a leaf at the end of autumn—doomed to turn brown and wither to nought.

"We will do all we can to find out what has befallen your husband, Anthousa." Polydektos slapped his knees and stood up. "If you hear anything, or if he returns, or a ransom is asked for, send a runner to Darios's home. Olos knows its location."

Darios glanced mournfully down at his platter of his half-eaten food and stood up beside his friend. "I will help find your husband also."

"We will not rest until you know his fate, one way or the other," Polydektos promised.

Anthousa rushed from her couch and flung her arms around Polydektos, kissing both of his cheeks. He was grateful when she moved onto Darios and did the same. Polydektos did not like the closeness and affections of women anymore, for it reminded him of his terrible fortunes earlier in the year.

Anthousa stepped back from them both. "A thousand thanks from my heart. May Artemis help you hunt down the perpetrators of this crime against my beloved Skaios and hopefully bring his body back to my bosom...whether living or not...and give me peace of mind."

Polydektos nodded, and he and Darios took their leave of the worried wife of Skaios.

Olos followed them out into the open courtyard. "If you need any help, send a runner, and I will come to aid you whatever hour of the day and night."

"You are needed here, Olos. We will contact you if we need any further assistance." Polydektos waved him off and strode out of Skaios's home, back out onto the busy street.

"What misguided Heraklean labour have you gotten us into this time, my old friend?" Darios smirked, clapping Polydektos on the shoulder.

"I'm not really sure," Polydektos said in a soft voice. He had no idea why he wanted to find Skaios. This morning, he had just wanted to go through the motions of looking for him. He had a feeling that the gods, or something else, were behind his stumbling into this mystery, and more than any battlefield defeat, he hated being manipulated. He wanted to live what remained of his life as his own man. He felt a cold and uneasy shiver run down his spine as the wind whipped down the streets, causing others to cover their faces from the rising dust swirls.

Polydektos looked up at the recently completed Parthenon sitting resplendently on the Akropolis hill. The windswept clouds parted a crack to let sunlight in, spearing rays shining down on its painted friezes and giving the columns an almost golden glow.

"By the gods, it's a sign, Polydektos," Darios said, moving close behind his friend.

The clouds shifted, and the sunlight was gone as swiftly as it had arrived. Polydektos looked around the street, but no one else seemed to have noticed the sudden celestial glow on the Parthenon. "A sign of what, though?"

"I know a mantis who lives not more than three streets away from here, we could ask him. I know you don't like soothsayers, but he is really good."

"Let us go then, before I change my mind," Polydektos said, sucking at the hairs under his bottom lip. He felt like he was a stranger in his own skin. Maybe the figs he had eaten were off, but this time, for once, he let the gods guide him.

CHAPTER FOUR

"I fought under you, yes," the shaven-headed mantis nodded. He had a patch over his left eye, and his right arm ended at the elbow. "I should have seen that Persian sword and arrow coming—that's what you are thinking, General."

Polydektos tried not to stare at the slightly older man's scars as the soothsayer cackled away in a high-pitched laughter.

"That was before the gods called to him, and he could understand their whispers on the wind," Darios tried to reassure his sceptical friend.

"Yes, a new calling for the one-armed, one-eyed man. I wish Hermes had come with a message from the gods before the battle, as I may have slept in and stayed in my tent that morning," the soothsayer cackled on.

Polydektos wanted to leave, but for Darios's and the old soldier's sake he sat cross-legged before a low table, behind which the mantis sat. A golden bowl rested in the middle of the table, with a rabbit's foot on one side and an eagle's claw on the other. An incense burner sat to the left of the bowl, and on the right was a large copper goblet filled with small, burning white coals.

Polydektos went to speak, but the soothsayer shushed him. "You seek what all men seek—answers to the imponderable depths of the gods' chosen path for you, Polydektos."

"In truth, I seek only the answer to the riddle of whether Skaios, the sculptor, is dead or alive." Polydektos couldn't help himself. He knew without looking that Darios was frowning at him.

"The two are woven like a tapestry into the story of your existence and purpose on this earth, Polydektos. You seek divination, not for the answer to the mystery you find your-self in, but because you wish to know *why* you are drawn to this, why are you called and led by the gods to find out what has happened. This missing sculptor is but olive oil floating on the surface of a boiling pan of water. To discover the truth, you must plunge your hand into the swirling heat and find what lies deep beneath the tumultuous waters. Only then will your true destiny be revealed. Seek out this mystery, embrace it; it is but the beginning of a journey that will lead you from the safe walls of Athens into a place you never thought you would end up." The mantis moved his hands in front of his face wildly as he spoke.

"And where would that be?" Polydektos asked, knowing that this visit had been a bad idea.

"Via many strange roads and seas to the very heart of Sparta," the soothsayer replied with a wide grin.

"I'm going to Sparta?" Polydektos sighed and look back at Darios dubiously.

"All roads, all fates, and the death of Athens converge in Sparta, General. No one can escape the red storm now. The gods have seen our hubris and have decided to end us all. The ruling family will be plucked like feathers from a diseased goose, one by one, until none remain. Only then will you become a strat-egos, for one last fateful time," the mantis prophesied.

"Now I know you are insane." Polydektos flipped two drach-mas into the golden bowl set before the mantis and hurried from the tiny ramshackle shop, which was squeezed between a fishmonger and a bakery.

Darios caught up with him halfway down the road. "Didn't you believe what he said?"

"He had me, right up to the part when he said I would be voted in as a strategos again. You know all too well they would never again trust me with an army."

"We do not know what the Fates have in store for us, General," Darios rebuked him. "I will see you back at home, after dark." He headed off in haste down another road.

"Darios, wait," Polydektos called after his friend, but did not chase after him. Darios was always like this, even as a young soldier—always saying his life or death was the will of the gods. He let them decide his fate. In battles his faith made him fearless. Polydektos's faith in the gods had been worn down over the years to make him more of a sceptic of their ways. The death of his entire family hadn't helped his beliefs. He wasn't sure why he had visited the mantis today.

He felt suddenly very much alone in the world again. Realising he was standing in the middle of the street, with carts waiting to pass, he headed off around the other side of the Akropolis.

Polydektos pulled his woollen himation tighter around him to keep off the chill wind that swirled at the top of the rise and bit at his exposed skin. *There used to be a home here once, full of love and laughter.* He looked over the area, recognising part of a wall, or a line of brush and dried grass.

His old two-storey home was gone. Even the old olive tree he and Talaemenes used to stealthily climb into the courtyard of his villa had been uprooted and cut down for firewood. On his orders, the place had been levelled along with all the outbuildings and the well. Work had begun on building a small, round temple that would house a statue of Athene when complete. Only the base had been completed, though, and the high winds were whipping up to a gale, tugging at his clothes, seemingly urging him to leave. Dust devils circled around the temple works, but Polydektos stubbornly refused to move. It seemed that Aiolos, the ruler of all the wind gods, was trying to get the former general to leave. Polydektos pulled his himation over his head like a hood to keep most of the dust from his face.

"Do your worst," he muttered through gritted teeth. Polydektos stood his ground until he was ready. He said a silent prayer to Athene to look after his wife and children in the Elysian afterlife. Only when he was ready to leave did he wander down the slope and back along the lower road, slightly out of the wind. Aiolos and his fellow wind gods tried to push him down the Panathenaic Way, buffeting his back with strong gusts, but he moved at his own pace to Darios's house.

Hyllos beat at the slave with a wooden baton until blood appeared in the welts on his back. Seeing the blood, Hyllos roared and kicked the supplicant slave's hip, knocking the poor man to the floor of the former general's bedchamber.

"Let that be a lesson to you to close the shutters of my bedchamber before half the dust of the city blows in and covers the room. I'll have you lick it up next time, you witless dog. This place had better be spotless when I return." Hyllos's face was red and he was breathless with anger. He stomped on the slave's bare foot before leaving the bedchamber and heading down the steps to the andron of his compact Athenian home.

A pretty slave girl was standing by the door of the andron, waiting for him. Hyllos liked to think he was still on campaign and ran his home much like his army camps. He made his slaves stand for hours on end in certain places around his home, just to tend to his needs if he happened to pass. He took pleasure from the knowledge that it caused them pain. Hyllos was a fearsome general to the enemy, but a brute of a man, full of hatred in ordinary life as well. He had only slaves in his house, as no metics would work under his harsh rules for more than a week. His third wife was no more than fifteen summers old and lay in her own chambers, probably still sobbing from the sadistic marital acts he meted out on a nightly basis.

He had divorced his first wife for bearing him no heirs and killed his second for having an affair with a neighbour when he had been away on war duties. She had not been able to bear his children either, so he had acquired a fresh new bride.

Hyllos suddenly grabbed the slave girl by the hair and wrenched her backwards, causing her to whimper with pain. Any screams or shrieks of pain would only bring harder punishment. A familiar smell rose in the room and he looked down to see the slave girl had wet her simple, old tunic. Her urine puddled around her dirty, bare feet. Hyllos laughed in her face and let go of her hair, amused by the hurt and shame he had brought upon her.

"Bring me a fresh jug of wine," he snarled at her and pushed open the door of the andron. Not many Greek homes had inner doors, but Hyllos sometimes liked to entertain his slaves inside the andron with the wooden door shut. It served to intimidate the rest of his household into submission. Screams of pain and anguish from behind a closed door were often more troubling to the other slaves' minds if they could not see the punishment Hyllos dealt out. The mind and its imagination would always conjure worst images of torture if only the wails of the pained were heard through the red-painted door.

Hyllos closed the door behind him, only because it would require the slave to open it again when she returned with his wine. Any chance he had of making their miserable lives more difficult, even in the tiniest form, gave him pleasure. The torches were lit as if night had fallen. None of the ground floor rooms, except the kitchen, had any windows, so there was no chance of dust getting into the andron that way. The slaves were only allowed inside to clean or service him. He had no male friends around, because he had no friends, only equals or soldiers with whom he was acquainted.

Hyllos lay on the single couch in the room and waited for his wine. He smiled cruelly, wondering if the slave had paused to clean herself before returning with his drink. It didn't matter; either way, he would punish her.

He awoke sometime later, from the snap and crackle of one of the torches nearest his head. Hyllos blinked himself into consciousness and yawned until his jaw cracked. He must have fallen asleep on his couch. He sat up and rubbed his large, hairy belly and wondered how late into the night it was. He remembered the cruel punishment he had inflicted on the slave girl with an almost boyish glee. Best she remembered to keep her fluids inside her next time.

Hyllos rolled around the wine jug on the table before him, finding only a little wine left to slosh about the bottom of the jug. He was thirsty, so he called towards the closed red door. "Slave, bring me more wine."

No answer came, and he wondered if the girl had fallen asleep at her duties. He would sew her eyes shut if she had, to teach her and the other slaves a lesson on staying awake to see to his every whim.

"Where are you, girl? Fetch me some wine!" Hyllos thought

she might have scurried off at his first shout without replying to him, so he sat and waited. He heard nothing outside. Frowning, he could wait no longer, the anger rising in him. He stood and walked over to the only entrance to the andron. As he did, he heard footsteps outside his red door.

"About time," he shouted and pulled the door inwards himself. He grinned to himself, already thinking of cruel punishments for the tardy slave girl.

But it wasn't the slave girl in front of him at all. It was a taller figure, cloaked in the darkness from the unlit passage beyond. The figure wore a dark blue or green cloak, with a hood covering the most hideous face Hyllos had ever the misfortune to see. A red tongue lolled from a wide mouth, with tusk-like fangs pointing up from it. Its eyes twinkled like emeralds in the dying torchlight, and vipers hissed and danced from the dark confines of the hood. Hyllos stood petrified to the spot in fear as the creature moved into the andron and fixed him with its glittering, inhuman green eyes.

Hyllos's young bride, Elleni, awoke from her first painless night of uninterrupted sleep since her poor father had married her off to that brute of a man. Night after night she had been forced to endure his rough marital advances. Yet not tonight; perhaps he had fallen asleep in the andron, his drink saving her from his brutish advances. She got out of bed and almost skipped to the window to open the shutters on a new day. She had run back to her parents' house after two weeks of being married to Hyllos; her mother had comforted her, but her father had sent a slave to Hyllos, who had dragged her to the horse and cart by the hair and brought her back home. That night her punishment was tenfold what she usually had to suffer in the marital bed. The punishment served its purpose; any thoughts of running away and divorce were beaten out of her. He never touched her face or arms, but would whip her bare thighs and behind, leaving great welts and scars on her young skin that would never totally heal.

She stood at the open window, where she discovered the winds of the previous day had died down to a warm breeze and the sun was once again shining over Athens. She turned and frowned. Normally her slave girls would have come in to feed and dress her. Pulling on yesterday's yellow chiton, still on the chair where she had left it, she kicked on her sandals and hurried from her bedroom. She leant over the balcony and looked down into the open courtyard below and saw it was empty. Normally a male slave was stationed outside her bedroom door to both protect her and to stop her from fleeing in the night. He wasn't there, nor were any of her slaves. In fact, Elleni could see no slaves anywhere around the silent house.

Elleni made her way down the wooden stairs into the open courtyard, expecting with every step to hear the angry cry of her husband. She reached the courtyard and offered a brief, silent prayer to the altar of Zeus Herkeios before heading for the kitchen. It was normally the heartbeat of the home every morning, with slaves preparing the morning and lunch meals and baking bread, but there were no cooking smells wafting from the kitchen today and no sounds of slaves busy at their work.

She peered inside from the entrance. The room was empty and the cooking pit unlit.

Had the slaves revolted against their cruel master and run off in the night? If they were caught, they faced death or being sent north to some dangerous copper mine. Elleni thought it was worth the risk for them, and wished them the fleetness of Hermes in their escape. Elleni pulled at her tangled bedhair. She missed it being brushed this morning; it was one of her few pleasures in this house of pain. She timidly hurried on her sandaled toes over to the slaves' quarters and peered inside. They were devoid of life and the bed mats on the floor appeared unslept on. Maybe they *had* all run off in the night. So where was her husband?

Had they murdered him in his sleep? She silently rebuked herself for hoping that was the case. It was time to be bold; searching the villa was getting her nowhere.

"Husband?" she croaked out, barely above a whisper. She chided herself; her call would hardly have woken a mouse. "Husband, where are you?" she managed to call in a frail, but louder voice.

A whimper from the storeroom across the courtyard was

the only reply. Elleni moved back to the doorway. The place had
no windows, and a base funk oozed from it. The end of the
room was hard to make out from the limited light filtered in
from the courtyard. "Is someone there?"

"Mistress?" A voice sounding timid and more broken than
her own replied.

"Rakhel, is that you? Where is everyone?" Elleni squinted
through the gloom at the figure hiding behind the urns and
jugs at the far end of the large storeroom.

"Is it gone, mistress?" the slave girl asked, sitting up from
her hiding place so Elleni could see her silhouetted form.

"Has what gone?" Elleni moved a step inside the storeroom.
The slaves had it so much worse than she on a daily bias under
Hyllos's closed, belligerent fist.

"The monster..." The girl swallowed loudly. "It came after
you had taken to your bed chamber. It scared the household to
the hills. I was trapped, so I hid, fearing for my very soul."

"Come into the courtyard and tell me more. Where is your
master, my husband?"

The slave girl paused for a moment and then rose and hurried over to the open doorway, wrapping her arms around her
own body. Elleni sniffed as the girl passed into the courtyard;
she smelled like the piss-pot. Rakhel looked around the courtyard, searching for danger like a frightened rabbit. "I'm not sure,
mistress. The monster came at night—I was in the storeroom
fetching more wine for the master when it arrived. I heard the
other slaves running for the door and then saw it pass, heading
for the andron."

"Saw who pass? What did you see, Rakhel? You aren't making much sense."

"A monster from some nightmare. We have no tales of this
creature where I come from, but it was tall and cloaked and
hooded. It had breasts and the body of a woman, but the face
was hideous to behold, and snakes hissed from under its writhing hood. I was so scared I ran back and hid behind the pots.
Sometime during the night, I must have fallen asleep. Please
forgive my insolence, mistress." Elleni could see the slave girl's
hands trembling with fear. Her heart ached; she knew what it

felt like to be alone and afraid in this house.

"Where was this creature heading?"

"Towards the andron, where the master was."

"Do you think you have enough courage to come and help me look, brave and faithful Rakhel?" Elleni tried to give her a reassuring smile, even though she was also scared. She was the mistress of the house when Hyllos was not there, so he told her every time he left, drumming the knowledge into her head with a finger. She had to act like one when he was absent.

Rakhel nodded, and Elleni took her hand in hers.

Together the two timid girls walked across the courtyard and headed left along the covered corridor to the andron. The red door was closed. Elleni and Rakhel were worlds apart in status, but at that moment they were two young, frightened girls, standing before the door behind which the man they loathed had spent much of his time.

Elleni could have ordered Rakhel to push open the door, but she was the mistress of the house, so she moved a step forward and pushed the red door herself. The door creaked inwards to reveal her husband standing just beyond the reach of the opening door. His hands were up at his face, and he was recoiling from the door in terror. The torches in the andron had long since gone out, and in the gloom, his features looked grey.

"Husband, are you well?" Elleni asked, her voice timid again.

Her husband did not reply, or even move. It was like he was frozen to the spot in fright.

"Hyllos?" Elleni ventured a step closer. Something was very wrong with her husband. He looked petrified and rigid, not moving or even appearing to breathe. Elleni swallowed hard and reached out to touch the nearest part of her husband's body, his covered right elbow. It was cold, hard, and rough like it had been baked in mud for a week under the blazing sun. Elleni reached up and grabbed his hand, but he did not flinch or grab her back. His skin felt cold, like his clothes, and solid – unlike any flesh she had felt before. Rakhel let go of her hand and cowered by the open doorway. Elleni did not blame the girl for being scared.

"Hyllos, talk to me." Once again, her words fell on deaf ears. Elleni moved her hands to touch his face. It too felt cool and unyielding. She recoiled, taking a step back towards the red door. What ailment had befallen her husband, to hold him rigid as he stood like, like...?

She could not see properly in the gloom, so she left the andron to fetch some light. She returned with Rakhel close to her back. Elleni held the lit torch before her and edged closer towards the kyrios of the house.

Both girls screamed as one. Elleni dropped the torch as they fled the andron and the house—mistress and slave, hand in hand, running away from the horrors of their home. Their screams echoed down the streets of Athens.

Hyllos, general and citizen of mighty Athens, had been turned to stone.

CHAPTER FIVE

Polydektos got up the next morning to find Darios was already in his potter's hut outside. He let his friend be and made himself a simple breakfast. He left the house early, heading towards the city, as the gymnasium beckoned to him. His thoughts turned to finding himself a new home. A property in or outside of the city? He wondered, or perhaps even both. He had outstayed his welcome with Darios, though his war comrade would never say so. The last thing he wanted was to damage their friendship irrevocably.

He would work out his thoughts on the matter and then check on Olos to see if he or Anthousa had heard anything. At the gymnasium, Polydektos kept himself to himself as he ran and then used the punchbags. It was only when he was relaxing in the cool water afterwards that he picked up the conversations around the baths from some of the other men.

"His poor wife, running down the street in fear, I heard," said one man to his companion.

"So, the rumours of his death are true then? Well, that's a turn up for the scribes, eh," said another man, talking to two others who were sitting on a bench to the side of the room, behind Polydektos.

"They are saying Medousa herself visited the general's house last night."

"Turned him to stone while he was making mud," his companion, who was lounging back in the baths, replied with a smirk, pinching his nose.

"Paopeos please, it is wrong to speak ill of the dead."

"Well, he was a frightful bore and brute of a man. The

caterers for his funeral will not make many drachmas that day, I tell you," Paopeos told his companion with open candour.

"Excuse the intrusion, my friends, but who is this general that you speak of?" Polydektos interrupted their not-so-private-conversation.

"You should know him well, being a fellow strategos," Paopeos, a man with thin, wet large lips replied. "General Hyllos was murdered last night."

"We don't know it was murder. We've only heard the rumours," his companion added.

"He was turned to stone, Loxias. Petrified by Medousa or one of her sisters—I can never recall their names," Paopeos went on, glad to have another ear to his story.

"Hyllos," Polydektos whispered. He was a great and fearful soldier and dreaded throughout the lands, including by the men that served under him.

"Stheno and Euryale," said Loxias.

"What?" Paopeos replied, bemused.

"Medousa's immortal sisters," Loxias said, shaking his head. "You never studied."

Polydektos had heard enough of the two men prattling on beside him, so he left the baths to get dressed.

Polydektos made straight for Skaios's dwelling. One of the metics there informed him that Anthousa had taken to her bed and was not to be disturbed. He had no new news of his master at all, and Olos was over at his studio.

Polydektos nodded and headed off to the studio. Maybe the studio held some vital clue to the missing sculptor's whereabouts, but he doubted it. The trail was getting colder than a week-old campfire. Unless Skaios turned up alive, or most probably dead, he had little more to go on at the moment.

Polydektos was only a street corner away from Skaios's studio when an official messenger ran up to him.

"Can I help you?" Polydektos asked the man.

"General Polydektos! Perikles, First Citizen of Athens, requires you to attend to him at the Odeon that bears his name, as a matter of all urgency on official state business," the well-rehearsed messenger related.

"Tell our esteemed long-headed leader to hold his chariot horses, and I will be there presently." Polydektos walked off towards Skaios's studio with a smirk under his beard.

The shocked young messenger was taken aback for a moment and then raced after Polydektos again. "The First Citizen was insistent that you attend him immediately. Without delay. He was very specific on this point." The young messenger, caught between two famed generals, cleared his throat.

"Tell him I've received your message and will be there presently."

Polydektos almost felt sorry for toying with the poor lad. Yet, it did not stop him walking the long way around the corner to Skaios's studio. The messenger hurried after him, worried that he might get into trouble for not relaying the urgency Perikles himself had expressed on the order. He feared both men, but Perikles was the unofficial leader of the Athenian Empire.

"He was very insistent," the messenger continued.

"Shut up," Polydektos barked as he saw the front of the studio.

Olos and two other men were outside scrubbing away at red painted graffiti on the front of the studio. Polydektos frowned and could still read the words, even though Olos and the other men were scrubbing at them with brushes and water: *Spartan Lover, Traitor,* and *Archidamus's man-whore.*

Polydektos walked briskly over to stand behind the upset-looking Olos. "I suggest you paint the whole wall red and then white wash tomorrow, or those words will seep through again."

"Who would do such a thing?" Olos replied, waving his arms in front of him.

"The same people who daubed the word 'murderer' on my home earlier in the year. Cowards." Polydektos laid a hand on the sculptor's shoulder. "Any news of Skaios?"

"Nothing," Olos shook his head. "No sighting, no ransom demands, no corpse. Only this!"

Polydektos nodded. Skaios was almost certainly buried a long way outside the city in an unmarked grave. Not that he would say that to Olos or Anthousa. They still had hope for his safe return. He did not want to upset Olos anymore than he already was. The poor metic looked close to tears already. "I will leave you to clear up this mess. If I hear anything, I will let you know swiftly in person."

"May the gods aid you, Polydektos," Olos cried, suddenly hugging the former general for a few seconds.

Polydektos nodded and backed away from the sculptor's embarrassing embrace. It would take the aid of the gods to find Skaios, he deemed.

"General?" The messenger was still behind him. He cleared his throat again.

"To the dogs with you, boy," Polydektos barked at him, but hurried off towards the Akropolis at last.

The Odeon of Perikles was a huge square theatre covered with an orange tiled roof in the shadow of the Akropolis. To reach it, Polydektos had to walk past the now fully redecorated Theatre of Dionysos. Seeing the theatre brought back bad memories of the events of half a year ago. His mouth felt dry, and he swallowed hard and increased his walking pace. He hurried up the steps to the Odeon's entrance, just as two armed Athenian soldiers stepped out from behind separate columns to challenge him.

"Isn't pointing spears at an Athenian general a flogging offence?" Polydektos asked as he approached the crossed spears of the soldiers. He tapped the shafts of their weapons for good measure.

They immediately withdrew back to their hidden guarding positions, without an apologetic reply. Polydektos smiled at them both as he passed out of the heat of the day and into the cooler confines of the vast indoor theatre. There were seats for three thousand around the straight walls, and the large roof was held up by many load-bearing columns. Light flooded in from a raised roof in the centre, casting a lattice of bright sunlight and shadow on the first five rows of the western seating area.

Sitting in that sunlight was Perikles: First Citizen of Athens, strategos, unofficial ruler of the Athenian Empire, and Polydektos's friend.

"You took your time." Perikles smiled at him as Polydektos crossed the floor to greet him.

"I'm neither young nor Hermes," Polydektos replied.

"Then I'm glad your old legs made it up the hill," Perikles laughed as they embraced like brothers.

"So why was I summoned to your theatre? To juggle or put on an act?" Polydektos asked as they separated.

"Oh, stop being so melodramatic and sit with me. We need to talk." Perikles gathered up his himation and chiton to make it easier for him to sit down again.

"Well, I surmised you did not send for me for my comedy skills, for they are sadly lacking these days." Polydektos sat down on the long marble bench next to his old friend, but one person's width apart.

"No, that would be a waste of your talents, Polydektos. It is others skills that I require of you. Athens needs you."

"Urgent messengers, secret meetings...I am intrigued. Though I must confess, I didn't think Athens had much use for my talents anymore." Polydektos picked at some dirt under his thumbnail.

"This time last year, you would have been the last person I would have asked, my old friend. But life and events have sobered you up, it seems, and you are talked about in the assembly for good reasons. I've missed my old friend, and Athens has missed you, General Polydektos."

"Talked about in the assembly, eh? Should I be worried? You know I hate politics, Perikles. It is your arena, not mine, and you excel in it. I just want to be left in peace."

"Just because you do not take an interest in politics, that doesn't mean politics won't take an interest in you. I need you to do a couple of things for me, for the love of Athens and for old times' sake. I need someone I can trust. Before, I couldn't say that was you, but now I think I can."

Polydektos's face flashed briefly with anger. "Only a couple of things, eh? The old whoring drunk who let his family get murdered by a mere slave girl has sobered up enough to be of some use, eh, First Citizen?"

"I don't blame you for your harsh words. I could have been

more of a friend to you, but as you always say, I am a political beast. You, though, have skills I need, General. You are a stout, brave soldier, an excellent tactician, and from your dark times of half a year ago, I see you will leave no stone unturned to find the truth."

"What truths do you need seeking out?" Polydektos wasn't sure if he was asking in order to aid Perikles or to hasten the moment of his refusal of the request. His thoughts wandered to the task of finding a new home. and he toyed with a new home outside the city or maybe even farther afield, to the north of Attica.

"Ever to the sharp point of the spear, my worthy friend. I've missed our conversations. Compared to the long, turgid oratory of the Assembly, they are like a welcome swift sea breeze on a stifling hot day. Too long have the fawning masses surrounded me, wanting to be dragged towards power on the back of my himation. Every one of them wants a piece of me to polish and glimmer next to their dull lives. Can you imagine what that is like, my old friend?"

"I can only imagine," Polydektos said, not looking up from his sandal-covered feet.

"But not you, Polydektos, you never ask me favours. You never put yourself before Athens. You surround yourself with men you like and not ones that can be bought. In the past you could have asked to get your old command back, and I would have owed you enough to grant that request, even though it would have been a disaster. But you know your worth and your limits, and that is what makes you a great Athenian." Perikles patted Polydektos hard on the shoulder, making him look at the First Citizen's face and deep, calculating eyes.

"To be honest my friend, I am nothing but a shell of a man now. Living for what, I know not. What do you need of me?"

"Your losses have been greater than even Herakles could bear on his broad shoulders, yet still you live and fight to see another day in this glorious of cities. I will get to my points, my friend. You have heard of the untimely and macabre death of your fellow general, Hyllos?"

"I heard men gossiping like old slave women in the baths.

Some wild tale that one of the Gorgon Sisters had visited him last night and turned him to stone."

Perikles raised his eyebrows up his high forehead and continued. "They are no wild tales, my friend. The slaves that we've caught from his house all say that Medousa herself entered the General's home and sent them running for their lives. One slave girl saw the creature head for the andron where the general was drinking alone. When his young wife, Elleni, awoke she came downstairs and found her husband petrified and stone cold dead."

"A mystery indeed, but no great loss to the Strategoi," Polydektos had lost too many people he loved to worry about an old soldier that he had never liked in life.

"True," Perikles nodded, before rising from the long bench, hoping to get his old friend's attention better from a standing position.

"Restless legs?" Polydektos pointed at the First Citizen's knees.

"I feel more alert standing. More like I'm at the Assembly. It helps me to think when I pace."

"Then pace off, as far as you require, Perikles," Polydektos smirked.

"You would like that," Perikles smiled back at him. "I left you alone to grieve, but now Athens, nay *I*, need you again."

"To do what?" Polydektos asked, with a guarded edge to his voice now. He was tired of Perikles's political way of skirting around a subject rather than going for the jugular.

"A famous general like Hyllos killed in our own polis is an inconvenience to me. But added to the fact that the Spartan ambassador is here at this moment, it makes us look weak. We are about a dōron away from a war that will ignite the whole of Greece." Perikles showed Polydektos his splayed left hand to illustrate the measurement.

Polydektos stared at his friend's hand. He knew what he wanted. He had known before he had even stepped inside the theatre, but he wasn't going to volunteer. Perikles would have to ask him outright and give him no choice but to do it for the good of Athens.

"I need you to help me investigate this most unusual murder. You have the nose of a bloodhound and aren't afraid to stick your oar in any unwanted waters, however dangerous. The culprit must be caught will all haste, Polydektos. I know you are the right man for this task. What say you?" Perikles reached out his arm towards Polydektos.

"That rather than being the right man, I am the only man for the job. Nobody else would do this, knowing it might go against the will of the gods that decreed cruel Hyllos the death so many think he deserved. I will do this for the good of Athens and the strength of our friendship." Polydektos stood and clasped the First Citizen's arm like the old comrades they were.

"Good man, I know you will find the truth swiftly. You can ask of me any resources you need. A company of Rod Bearers, perhaps, to lend a little muscle? And any expense, plus a retainer from the public purse, will be given each day to you in gold until this unpleasant situation is ended to my satisfaction."

"I need no help, just to be left alone to do things my way, unhindered." Polydektos turned half away from his friend and then back again. "What would be a satisfactory conclusion to my investigations into Hyllos's death, if he is dead?"

"As you wish, you will have as much or as little aid as you require of me. My only thought is to catch Hyllos's killer and put an end to all this scaremongering around the polis. Why do you question if Hyllos is dead?"

"I question everything now, my friend. Even death, especially ones that apparently turn a man to stone. I will visit Elleni, Hyllos's wife, and report back to you what I discover." Polydektos turned and walked towards the exit.

"Wait!" Perikles almost shouted to the back of Polydektos's head. The word echoed slightly and was amplified around the enclosed Odeon. "I did not give you leave to depart. We are not yet finished talking, my old friend."

Polydektos noted the anger leave Perikles voice as he spoke, returning to his more political sounding oratory tones. Polydektos stopped, but waited a few moments before he turned to face the First Citizen of Athens again. "I have nothing more to say, so you have the floor, my old friend."

Perikles swallowed a laugh and circled Polydektos, making his old comrade turn his head this way and that to keep him in his line of vision. "I hear on the grapevine that you are looking into the disappearance of the sculptor, Skaios."

Polydektos just nodded, his lips pressed tightly together.

"I would not want this to get in the way of your investigation of the murder of General Hyllos. His strange death takes precedence over everything else, do you understand?"

"I understand that the unveiling of the peace sculpture caused great embarrassment to Skaios, ending his career in this city. I also understand many people close to you would revel in his fall from grace. I understand many things, Perikles, except why this most important piece was given to Skaios to carve, ahead of others such as Pheidias. A peace offering of goodwill and trust between Athens and Sparta defaced in such a crude manner does not aid peace, does it?"

"I forgot how good you used to be before the drink, fornication, and the death of Sokos took the life and wits from you." Perikles's voiced had a cruel edge to it.

"Don't mention his name in this. You have given me leave to investigate every corner and crack in this city; don't bind my hands at the same time, Perikles. I do what I must to find the truth. Or does the truth scare you?" Polydektos spat back.

"Whose truth, though, Polydektos? Yours? You will find truth lies with great leaders, kings, and the victors of conquests."

"I find slaves and common men speak the truth more often than the rich and powerful. Is that all, First Citizen? I am eager to depart this place and begin my investigations."

"Skaios is such a small pebble in a great sea. Hyllos's death is like a rock in a puddle. Find me his killer, Polydektos, my old friend," Perikles said with open arms.

"I will do what I must. Do I have your leave to depart now?"

"Of course—the days aren't as long at this time of year." Perikles ushered him towards the exit.

Polydektos kept his friend's gaze for a few moments and then strode across the Odeon floor towards the doorway he had entered through.

"May Athene swiftly guide you on your quest, my worthy

friend," were Perikles's parting words.

Polydektos's reply was muttered under his breath as he left Perikles and the Odeon that bore his name. He made straight for Hyllos's place of residence in the city. He wasn't eager to begin the investigation into the mysterious death of the general, but he knew he had to speak to witnesses quickly before the facts became misty in their minds. He knew where the general had lived, having spent two or three turgid nights at the man's home years ago when Polydektos had more of a military career and a care for politics.

CHAPTER SIX

Polydektos had a thirst on, and beads of sweat crossed his brow and gathered under his armpits by the time he reached Hyllos's city residence. He had been living a quiet existence outside the city walls, and now in the space of two days, he had been drawn into the cesspit at the heart of the polis once more. He wasn't sure if he was investigating two murders or two disappearances. One thing he didn't believe was that some mythical Gorgon had turned one of his former strategoi colleagues to stone.

Two Athenian city guards were standing outside the entrance to Hyllos's home. They recognised Polydektos immediately and unbarred the doorway, retracting their spears.

"Is the lady of the oikos inside?" he asked the guards. Polydektos needed to see the wife and head of the household first to show his respects for her loss and question her as much as decency would allow at such time.

"General Hyllos's widow waits inside for you, General Polydektos, in the women's quarters," the left-hand guard replied.

Polydektos nodded and went into the cooler, shaded courtyard. Unless a swift messenger or Hermes himself had been sent before him, Perikles had obviously assumed he would do his bidding on this matter and informed Hyllos's household before their morning meeting at the Odeon.

The place looked devoid of people. Polydektos recalled Hyllos telling him that he had trouble retaining metics in his employ. He had only slaves who had no choice but to serve him. No one would be willing to work for such a cruel, twisted brute of a man by choice. He was about to call out when a slave girl rushed out of the kitchen area to greet him. The smell of flatbreads and porridge wafted on the air, making Polydektos's stomach rumble.

"I am sorry to have kept you waiting, oh great General. The other slaves ran off in fright last night. I am the only one left to tend to the whole house." The slave girl had long, strawberry-blond hair, her eyes were deeper-set and ringed, most likely from abuse and a lack of sleep.

"Where is your mistress?" Polydektos looked around the house, then remembered the andron lay behind a closed door to the left of the corridor. He held in a yawn, suddenly feeling very tired. He had successfully avoided talking to people in whom he had no interest for months. Now, in the space of a couple of days, all he seemed to be doing was conversing with strangers and old friends.

"She has taken to her bed, my Lord General," the slave girl replied, not making eye contact with him.

"Will you show me to where you found General Hyllos, then?" Polydektos felt fatigued of the mind, but tried not to take out his grumpiness on the poor slave girl. It looked like she had already suffered enough abuse under Hyllos.

The girl just nodded and extended her right arm across the open courtyard towards the covered areas of the house. Polydektos forced a smile, which seemed to confuse the girl, and he followed her through an archway to a corridor, before reaching the closed red door of the andron. The slave girl's face took on a look of total fear as she approached the red door. Polydektos wondered if it was the sight of her petrified master that scared her, or bad memories of torment inside this very room. He had heard and seen the cruelty Hyllos inflicted on the enemy and his own men on the battlefield, it didn't take much of a leap to wonder what he did to the slaves of his household.

"I will need to question you later, but for now attend to your porridge before it spoils. I did not catch your name?" Polydektos asked as kindly as he could.

"My name is Rakhel, and I give thanks for your kindness, Lord General." The girl bowed and then hurried off back to the kitchen before her food burnt.

Polydektos waited for her to leave before taking a deep breath and pushing the red door inwards. The door creaked and the stone remains of General Hyllos were revealed to him.

"By the gods, it's true," Polydektos whispered and entered the room. He hadn't been sure what he had expected, but definitely not this. "Hyllos," he whispered and reached out to the lifelike figure. He touched one of the figure's hands, held up to ward off some evil encroachment. The hand was cold and hard like rock. This seemed like no statue he had ever seen before. There was no base, no obvious carved lines. It had spots and scars. Polydektos moved around to get a better look at Hyllos's face. It was his, all right, or least the truest likeness he had ever seen in sculpture before. "How is this possible?"

Polydektos touched the petrified man's back, but put too much pressure and the stone Hyllos toppled towards the corner and broke into many large broken pieces on the mosaic tiled floor. "Oh, Polydektos, you sack of wine, what have you done?"

Rakhel came running to the andron, stopped at the doorway, saw the remains of Hyllos on the floor, and screamed. This brought the two guards from outside running in, followed by Elleni, Hyllos's wife, from her sleep upstairs.

It took a small while for everyone to calm down and leave the andron. They closed the red door with the stone remains of Hyllos inside and went to the dining room to talk and escape the fragments of stone scattered across the floor. Luckily for Polydektos, the two guards had seen the remains of the general intact, and Elleni did not blame him for accidentally toppling over her husband's petrified body. Apart from the shock of it all, Elleni and Rakhel seemed to be holding up pretty well in the circumstances. Polydektos wondered if this was because of their torment under their overbearing tyrant of a kyrios. As a widow, Elleni might be free of a much older husband but had no immediate claim to the house in which he had died. Hyllos had no sons, so it would become the property of any living relative, or of the state, before her. Elleni faced a time of mourning, then having to live with her parents again, before being married off for a second time.

He questioned Elleni and Rakhel together as they held each other's hands in comfort—either in grief for their loss or just in fear of what uncertain future lay ahead for them both now that Hyllos was dead. Elleni had little to tell, as she had missed all that had happened until she had woken to the sight of her husband turned to unliving rock.

Rakhel had more information of what had occurred when one of the Gorgon Sisters had apparently visited the house of Hyllos. She, trapped in the storeroom, had hidden from this ghastly creature from the time of heroes, lucky to glimpse its hideous face but not its petrifying evil eyes. The rest of the small slave household had fled into the night in fright for their lives.

"So everyone, apart from yourself and your mistress who was sleeping upstairs, fled the household? You saw this creature enter the courtyard—"

"—Medousa," Rakhel added and then shrunk her head down into her shoulders, expecting a slap for interrupting him.

"Why are you sure it was Medousa and not one of her immortal sisters?" Polydektos pressed. "Surely she is slain, it is told?"

"She did not have brass hands like her sisters. I have seen the carvings and mosaics, my Lord General—Medousa has normal hands. This creature had hands like you or me."

Polydektos nodded. He could not fault the scared slave girl's belief or knowledge. Hunting murderers and enemy soldiers were where his skills lay, not seeking monsters from the heroic past in the streets of Athens. "So you hid in the storeroom until the next morning when your mistress's cries awoke you. Did you see or hear anything else after Medousa entered the courtyard?"

"I heard my master cry out briefly and then I heard Medousa's sisters enter the house a little after that."

"Did you see them?"

"No, but I heard the shuffling of more than one set of feet and the hissing sounds of the snakes they have instead of hair. I was too scared to look, so I hid behind the grain sacks and stayed there until they left. I must have fallen asleep."

Polydektos nodded and smiled. It was well known that the

least educated in Athenian society were more likely to believe every myth and heroic legend they heard, unlike the more well-educated critics.

"Did you hear any words at all? How long did the creatures that invaded the kleros spend inside?"

"No words, only hisses. They were not here long at all, less than a quarter of one hour and then gone."

"Did you notice anything else? Smells or other sounds at all?"

The slave girl looked at her lap, thought for a moment and then shook her head. "I'm sorry, I was very scared. I don't recall any smells. I hope I haven't let you down, Lord General."

Elleni squeezed the slave girl's hand. "Don't be silly, Rakhel. You have been very brave and more loyal than any other slave in this household." Before her husband's strange death, she would never have dared to praise a slave so openly and in front of male company.

"Your mistress is right," Polydektos agreed. "You have done well and did not run like the other slaves. Now I must take your leave, Elleni, and I am sorry for your loss." Polydektos stood up and took the widow's hand in his and then bent and kissed it. He thought of praising Hyllos's great war deeds, but he was no hypocrite, even before his widow. Athens was probably a better place now that he was dead, truth be told. "I may return and speak with you again if I find anything out."

"Please do, and thank you again for your kind words and help, General Polydektos." Elleni stood proudly and bowed her head to him once.

Polydektos left them and headed outside. One of the city guards by the entrance addressed him. "General, a messenger came when you were inside. They have caught one of the fleeing male slaves."

"Where is he being held?"

"The Rod Bearers have him in custody, sir."

"You have the praise of Zeus himself today, guard." Polydektos nodded and headed off on tired legs to the prison to interview the slave.

The state prison was southwest of the agora, near the law

courts. It was a low, grim building by abject design, not a place any citizen of Athens would like to end up. Two Scythians were guarding the entrance. They seemed relaxed to the point of boredom, chatting amongst themselves. Their tipped hats pointed forwards over their ruddy faces. Their coloured jackets and trouser-covered legs made them stand out from any Greek in the city. They rose to attention when Polydektos approached them.

"Hail, General Polydektos," the nearest one greeted him with reverence.

"You know me?" Polydektos asked, followed by an elongated yawn. It had been a long day already and it wasn't finished yet.

"The whole of the empire and beyond knows of your deeds, General," the Scythian replied in his accented Greek.

"And we were forewarned that you would probably come to interrogate the prisoner we caught this morning," replied his fellow.

Polydektos could not help but laugh at the second Scythian's remark. "So you captured the fleeing, frightened slave then?"

"Yes, we killed two who would not heed our warnings. The last one got the message all right." The Rod Bearer smirked at his comrade, who gave a nodding smile.

"You killed two frightened, unarmed slaves?"

"They were slaves on the run without their master's leave. They have no rights to clemency," stated the first Rod Bearer matter-of-factly.

"They had a chance to stop, but they ran and we shot them down with arrows. A good quick death," the second Rod Bearer replied.

"Who is in charge here?" Polydektos asked wearily. He wasn't happy with the itchy release fingers of these two Scythians, but they had done nothing outside of their city remit for him to castigate them. He should be glad they had left at least one slave alive.

"Nikodromos is the captain of the Prison. His office is through the gates in the two-storey building directly to your left as you go inside, General," the first Rod Bearer said. He turned and gave a special four-rap knock on the high thick gates. One of the gates was pulled inwards enough for Polydektos to go inside.

"So that was the great general, the Maenad and Persian-killer Polydektos," the first Rod Bearer said to his comrade as the gate was shut and locked once more.

"I expected him to be taller," commented the second.

Polydektos was making for the only two-storey building in the prison when its door opened. An Athenian citizen with a milky, blind left eye appeared. His black beard was bisected on one side by an old scar that marked his features, and the two smallest fingers of his left hand were missing. He was dressed in a simple loincloth and stank of old sweat and wine; he looked and smelled more like a prisoner than a gaoler.

"I was expecting you, Polydektos, but not this swiftly. A messenger arrived from the First Citizen himself, a rare honour for this establishment, informing me that you would be coming to interrogate the prisoner."

"I wish to talk to a frightened slave about the tragic death of his master," Polydektos replied. It seemed that Nikodromos had spent so much time with the Scythians that he had picked up some of their crueller foreign traits.

"Well, he is certainly frightened now, I can tell you that." The prison captain guffawed and began walking in an odd gaited waddle towards the prison cell blocks.

"Aren't you going to get more suitably attired?" Polydektos slowly walked after the prison captain, trying to breathe through his mouth lest he gets a whiff of the ugly smells emanating from the gaoler.

"Why would I dress to see a slave? If he were a worthy and wealthy citizen of this great polis, then maybe I'd even wash and dab perfumed oils behind each ear." Again, the prison captain cackled with spittle-filled laughter.

Polydektos just shook his head and followed after the odious citizen. They passed a squad of Scythians practising their renowned archery skills in an inner courtyard, before passing through the gates of a wooden stockade into the prison proper. A long prison block on the right-hand side ran from the walls of the main gate three quarters of the way down the prison yard. To the left, under the two-storey office and guard tower, was a second cell block. This was totally different and older than the one to the right. It had been carved into the rock of the hillside and looked a darker and more foreboding place to be imprisoned. The prison ended at a yard far beyond the ends of both cell blocks, where the prisoners could exercise and see the sun at least once a day.

"Your escaped slave is in here." Nikodromos pointed to a door at the far end of the rocked-carved prison.

"Of course he is," Polydektos barely whispered. He followed Nikodromos past another guard who unlocked the door for them. The smell inside was worse than Nikodromos and a war campaign latrine trench after a long siege, together. A small antechamber led to a gate set into a low, round opening in the rock walls.

Two torches fluttered and spat, attached to sconces on the antechamber walls. Beyond the reach of the light, the cell extended an undeterminable distance into the rocky hillside and was as dark as a Stygian Witch's eyesight. Nikodromos took one torch from its sconce and thrust it towards the bars of the cell. "The slave belonging to Hyllos! Come forward into the light. I have someone who wants to talk to you."

Polydektos bent his back to peer inside what surely must be the worst of the cells in the State Prison, or at least he hoped it was. He was aghast to see many shadowy shapes caught in the circle of light from the torch. Most animals in pens had more freedoms than these poor unfortunates. One shadow detached itself from the masses and made his way towards the bars of the cell. He was blinking and, apart from taking a few cuts to the nose and lips, looked in good health.

Polydektos snatched the torch from the prison captain's hand and knelt on one knee to be at the same level at the prisoner. "I will speak to this prisoner alone and outside in the daylight."

"I am the captain of this prison, Citizen, and I deem this worthless piece of scum too dangerous and unworthy to be let out of his cell," Nikodromos said, with a proudness that

Polydektos had not detected before in his appearance and wit. *Citizens and their little titles and petty powers of control,* he thought.

Polydektos raised his voice to the commanding shout of a general giving orders to the rank and file. "By order of the First Citizen Perikles, who is a close personal friend of mine, I order you to release this prisoner into my care so I can talk to him without gagging on the smell of shit!"

Nikodromos opened his mouth to speak and then closed it again. He knew that Polydektos was indeed a close friend of Perikles and that the First Citizen had instructed the captain to give him all the help he could. The prison captain had little recourse but to call in the guard from outside to unlock the metal gate set in the bars and hand the prisoner into Polydektos's care.

Polydektos ushered the poor man down to the empty court-yard and sat him under the shade of the lone tree there.

"I thank you, General Polydektos, for getting me out of there," the slave said, gasping at the outside fresh air.

"Don't thank me yet, slave. What is your name?"

"Bruton, Master. Bruton of Phrygia."

"I am not your master. Your master Hyllos is dead. I want you to tell me what happened last night in the general's home. Every and any detail you can recall." Polydektos stood over the slave. Even though the sun was harsh and hot on his back, it was more tolerable than being inside that dank prison.

"I will tell you everything, General, but what will happen to me?" the man asked in a timid, broken voice.

"If you tell me everything, I will put in a good word for you, Bruton of Phrygia. You have been punished enough in my eyes, but I am not the prison captain or a lawmaker. The best that you can hope for is to be resold to another, kinder owner at some point. You have committed only the crime of cowardice, but after what has happened to your master, even that seems harsh to my ears. Tell me: what happened to frighten you to run from your master's home last night?" Polydektos did not water the wine with his words to the slave. He would be taken from his prison to another life of little freedom—hopefully with a kinder master than Hyllos.

"We were making for the Shrine of Theseus before they cut

us down with arrows." Burton pointed to a dark red line across the meat of his lower leg, which Polydektos had not spotted before because of the layer of dirt covering the slave. "The other two were not so lucky as I. Or maybe they were…maybe they are in a gentler resting place."

"I see. If you made it to the shrine, they would have to offer you refuge and sell you to another owner." Polydektos nodded. "But what made you flee in the first place—can you tell me that?"

"General Hyllos had only ten slaves and no metics in his household. We were all in the kitchen trying to grab some food while we could. The general kept us *on watch*, as he liked to call it, for long hours, and we could not sleep until he did. One of the girls, Rakhel, was serving him in his private andron, but the rest of us slaves were in the kitchen when it happened.

"It appeared from nowhere at the kitchen doorway, tall and hideous to behold. I remember little except seeing large teeth, a big tongue and snakes, live snakes, where there should have been hair poking out from under its low-pulled hood. *Medousa*, screamed one of the cooks. Lucky for us, the kitchen has two exits, and we all fled like scared sheep out the other door and into the night. We had no choice, you see—we are slaves, not warriors. The general kept us in a constant state of fear of his sudden punishments: we were broken men well before the Gorgon visited us in the kitchen. We split up. I and two others hid in an abandoned perfumery until we decided to head for the Shrine of Theseus. The Scythians found us and told us to halt, but we were so scared of Hyllos's terrible retribution that we would not stop. Not until the arrows started to fell my companions, that is." Bruton stared down at his hands. His body slumped. Any remaining will to fight had left him.

"When did you find out about Hyllos?" Polydektos asked, feeling sorry for the slave. In his sandals, he would have probably made the same choices.

"When the Scythians brought me here and not back to General Hyllos's home. The prison captain informed me while he punched information out of me that I would have given readily." Bruton rubbed at the dark red marks on his lips and cheeks.

"Can you remember anything else odd about the creature?

Were the streets empty when you fled? Where there any strange sounds or smells in the air?"

"There was a low mist, I just remembered, around the entrance to the villa when we fled. I don't recall any smells as I was running. I did hear a horse bray somewhere close to the villa, but I did not look round to see where the noise was coming from. That is all—I'm sorry, General." Bruton looked up at Polydektos, with puffy, dark-ringed and bruised eyes full of apology.

"You have nothing to apologise for, Bruton of Phrygia. You did what many fine citizens of Athens would also do: run for your very life. It is time to go back to your cell, I'm afraid." Polydektos reached down and offered the man his hand.

Bruton the slave looked up at Polydektos with astonishment and tentatively raised his hand, so the former general could pull him to his feet. "If I had been your slave, I'm sure I would have stood and fought to the end for such a man as you."

"A man who is leading you back to a squalid, dank cell."

"A man who let me talk like a free man in the sunlight, under the shade of a tree," Bruton replied as they walked side-by-side back to the cells.

A Scythian guard took him inside as Nikodromos ambled up to Polydektos on his bandy legs. "Did the dog bark?"

"The man spoke to me, yes," Polydektos replied, pulling his money purse from inside his robes. He pressed two drachmas into the three-fingered hand of the surprised prison captain. "Move him to a better cell with sunlight and treat him well. I may need to talk to him again."

"As you wish." The prison captain stuck out his bottom lip, confused by Polydektos's generosity. He had plans for each coin. One would go towards some illegal Persian wine a trader could procure for him, the other to a certain doxy at the House of Javelins. He could now afford one night of pleasure. He ordered his guard to take the slave to another cell, just as grotty, but it did have a tiny high window and a pot to piss in.

CHAPTER SEVEN

Polydektos bought a leg of lamb and a jug of ewe's milk on the way back to Darios's home. He downed the milk to quench his thirst from talking so much in a single day. He couldn't recall speaking so much in years, he thought as he wearily trudged down the rutted cart track to his temporary home. It had been a long day, and the sun was low on his back and neck. He wondered what type of mood Darios was in now.

They made an odd couple of house-sharing comrades, and Polydektos hoped his comments on their last parting hadn't upset their friendship. He hadn't that many people in the world he loved and trusted anymore; he couldn't afford to lose the few he had left.

Polydektos needn't have worried. When he rounded the stone boundary wall of Darios's small homestead and passed a line of lemon trees, he saw the welcoming sight of the house. As he neared, he could hear the unmistakable sound of a lyre being playing loudly inside, accompanied by the sounds of revelry. He knew only one person who played that loudly and badly.

He opened the door to find his old war comrade, Alkmaion, attempting to play the lyre. Standing with one foot on a stool, Darios was singing his heart out about meeting a pretty Kretan girl on the road to Phalerum. Sitting opposite, drinking and laughing, was Trekhos of Krete—one of his old drinking companions, who had been away from the city for many months.

"I haven't forgotten a festival or a Heroes' Day, have I?" Polydektos closed the door behind him as he entered. He hung the leg of lamb on a hook by the shuttered window.

"No, but Trekhos has returned to Athens from Krete and

brought wine and exotic victuals with him," Darios explained, lifting a half-drunk jug and a plate of food to show his former general. From the gaiety in Darios's speech, Polydektos had no problems in guessing who had drunk half of the wine.

"Well met, Polydektos, my old friend." Trekhos stood and opened his arms wide. He looked like he had put on even more weight around his middle since Polydektos had seen him last. That had been just after the fateful night Polydektos's wife, daughter, and household had been murdered. Megas, the Athenian simpleton and business partner of Trekhos, had aided Polydektos and his ward Talaemenes at their trial and helped them both get off the murder charges brought against them. Both had left the next day to visit Krete while Trekhos had gone home to see his dying mother. That had been six months ago.

"I heard from my shop that you wanted to see me," Trekhos said.

To his shame, at one point Polydektos had considered Trekhos to be part of the murder plot until the truth was discovered. "I fear I owe you an Olympian-sized apology, my old friend." Polydektos wrung his hands and approached the Kretan humbly.

"There is nothing to say, Polydektos. Your war companions have explained it all to me. A terrible injustice was done to your loved ones by someone you trusted. I, too, would have looked under every rock and in every corner of the world for answers. The only apology I require is for you to sit down and join the celebrations of my return to Athens." Trekhos hugged him tightly until Polydektos patted his back to be released.

"I thank you for your kind words and understanding, Trekhos. I will sit and rest my weary feet and partake of one cup of your wine. I hope it is the fine stuff." Polydektos sat down between Alkmaion and Trekhos and took off his sandals.

"Only the best for the great General Polydektos. All the way from my own vineyard in Krete. Plus some aged cheese from Egypt, pungent enough to mask the stench from your feet, I think." Trekhos laughed heartily and so did everyone around the table.

Polydektos picked up a clean cup and took some of the

Kretan wine and added a little water to it. They all toasted Trekhos's return to Athens. The wine was as good as Trekhos promised. Polydektos felt good, having the distraction of company to forget the taxing day he'd had.

"With wine as fine as this, why did you stay away so long, Trekhos?" Polydektos touched his cup to the merchant's cup and then savoured some more of the drink.

"I went to see my dying mother, as they said she had only weeks left in this world," Trekhos replied, putting on a sad face.

"We are sorry for your loss, Trekhos," Alkmaion said, putting aside his lyre for the time being to eat more delicacies from the merchant's travels.

"Not as sorry as I was. The old bat took four months to die in the end," Trekhos burst out laughing loudly, causing Alkmaion to spit out the wine he had just drunk.

"You will go to Hades for that one," Darios commented with a smirk.

"As long as mother isn't there, it will be like living on Olympus and bedding Aphrodite every night," Trekhos chuckled.

Polydektos smiled. He had missed evenings like this. He missed the taste of wine also, but he vowed this one cupful would be the only one passing his lips that night. So he tucked into the food Trekhos had brought instead.

"How goes the day, General? Darios tells me you have another mystery on your hands?" Alkmaion asked, wiping his lips on the sleeve of his himation.

"Well, there is more news to add since I saw Darios last, my friends. Due to Perikles, I now have two mysteries to solve before I can get some peace and quiet, it seems."

Alkmaion looked at Polydektos warily. "Perikles? What did he want?" He did not trust a politician as far as he could throw one.

"He has tasked me to investigate the strange death of General Hyllos last night."

"The Medousa Murder!" Trekhos exclaimed, nearly choking on his own wine.

"Is that what they are calling it?" Polydektos looked at the merchant as he ate.

"From the docks to the city, all I've heard on my return today is that Medousa stalks the city at night, turning people to stone."

"In that case, yes," Polydektos nodded.

"Surely they are the wild rumours of the mob," Alkmaion said, eating a hardboiled egg.

"Are they true, Polydektos? Did you see Hyllos for your-self?" Darios asked, putting down his wine cup.

"I talked to his wife and slaves and saw what looked like Hyllos, petrified with fear and his body as hard as rock, yes." Polydektos eyed his drinking companions closely. "No word of this leaves this room."

"We understand," Trekhos nodded, as well as Darios and Alkmaion silently.

"So, what are you saying? That Medousa has come back to life to stalk the living of Athens and turn them to stone?" Darios, the most superstitious of the men, asked.

"I'm saying nothing, nor ruling anything out at this time. The facts are, Hyllos is gone and what remains of him is a stone likeness that brings more questions than answers. What that means, one way or the other, is my job to find out."

"What about Skaios's disappearance?" Darios said.

"Not on the top of the First Citizen's agenda. I will say no more. And no more of mysteries, deaths, and the like; I've had my fill of it today. What I haven't had my fill of is this delicious wine, Trekhos." Polydektos poured himself some more but watered it down by half. He wanted to enjoy himself and be sociable, without returning to the old drunk he used to be.

Polydektos's night with his old friends cheered his soul but did nothing to aid the mental and physical fatigue he was feeling. Alkmaion and Trekhos did not leave until an hour before dawn, so Polydektos slept in until noon, something he had not done in six months. He was glad of the sleep, but missed the gymnasium and vowed to be up with the lark and back at his training routine tomorrow.

Darios was still sleeping as Polydektos stumbled naked and yawning from his bed in search of water and the piss-pot. His war companion had been putting away the wine quicker than Trekhos could pour it. He wondered what Alkmaion's formidable wife was barking at him right now. Smiling to himself, Polydektos grabbed a jug of water and went to sit outside on the porch area, which was still mostly shaded from the harsh morning sunlight. Blinking his eyes to slits, he sat down naked and greedily drank half of the water. The sunlight shone on his aching feet, enlivening them with Helios's grace. He passed wind, scratched himself, and then used water on his fingers to dampen down his wild morning hair.

Polydektos looked out on the lemon trees that Darios had brought back from a Persian campaign; they had grown well and fruitful in Attica. He really loved it here, but knew he had to find a new home soon. A farm outside the city or further north away from Athens itself might suit him, but he'd miss his friends.

War was coming. Like the old soldier he was, he felt it in his bones, so perhaps a small townhouse inside the city would be better. Or perhaps both a farm and a townhouse. He could afford that. He tried to clear his mind and just enjoy the simple pleasures of life. At times like these, he missed Talaemenes, but the boy was beginning his own adventures at the Ephebeia.

Polydektos closed his eyes against the glare of the sun and leant back on his stool. He rested the back of his head against the side of the small house and tried to forget his vagabond life, the Gorgon Sisters, and politics for the time being. Sadly, that did not last long.

Polydektos was half-woken from the nap he had not intended to take by someone clearing their throat. He opened one watery eye to see a messenger standing before him, staring at his nakedness.

"What do you want?" he croaked out, searching for the water jug. He found it by the side of the stool and drank as the messenger shuffled closer.

"General Polydektos?" the messenger inquired.

"You must be the only person in Athens who does not know me by sight. Yes, I am he, the one and only." Polydektos finished off the now warm water in the jug.

"My apologies, General Polydektos. Are we alone?" The

nervous-looking messenger edged a little closer, not wanting to get too close to the naked general.

"Apart from the lemon trees and birds, I deem yes, don't you?" Polydektos replied wearily. The cat nap had done little to aid his tiredness, it only seemed to make him feel sleepier.

"I have a most private message from the Lady Eione of Sparta. Her husband the ambassador and her son will be at the stadium this afternoon on a state visit, and she wishes to speak with you most urgently on a very private matter," the messenger whispered, even though there was no one else about. Darios was still sleeping off the night before in his cot.

"On what matter?" Polydektos wiped at his wet chin.

"On a matter so secret she did not trust even me to hear of it, General. All I can convey is the urgency and secrecy she impressed on me to bring this message to you."

"Hmmm, and who do you work for?"

"I am Keyx from Skyros. I am employed by Palamon the proxenos, but am loyal to Athens, my General."

"Yet you bring messages from a Spartan woman to my door?" *Technically, Darios's door,* Polydektos idly thought.

"I do as my employer asks of me. He put me at the Lady Eione's disposal. I just pass the messages on, General, not worry what they mean."

"I worry though, young man," Polydektos stated, mainly to himself. "Where does the Ambassador's wife want me to meet her?"

"At Palamon's estate, where they are staying. She says to come to the servants' entrance and one of her handmaidens will let you in."

"Sounds like a trap—what do you think, Keyx from Skyros?" Polydektos stood naked before the messenger, hands on his hips. He, at the moment at least, had nothing to hide, nor any place to hide it.

"I am not paid to think, only to keep my mouth shut," Keyx smiled knowingly at Polydektos.

"Wise words. Tell her I shall be there when I've made myself more presentable," Polydektos turned and headed for the open door to Darios's home.

"Wiser words," Keyx replied, as he turned to walk back up the lane.

Smiling, Polydektos entered the cooler shade of the house to wash and dress and to wake Darios from the dead.

"Hey, what? Where? Are you going somewhere?" Darios woke at Polydektos's first shake of his shoulder. He groaned and sat up in his cot, smelling like a ripe old mule after a long trek.

"No, *we* are. Now get washed and dressed up smart, we are off to visit the Spartans," Polydektos half-explained as he got up off his friend's bed.

"Are we at war, then?" Darios yawned loudly and rubbed at his face, trying to wake it up.

"Time will tell, my friend. Come on—best not keep a lady waiting, even a Spartan one." Polydektos left the bedroom to pour some water for his friend and get some bread for his sour belly.

"A lady?" Darios stood and instantly regretted it. He ran over to the piss-pot and vomited into it.

"I feel awful," Darios moaned as they passed under the shade of the Itonian Gate and into the city.

"Your looks match how you feel, my friend." Polydektos could not help but laugh at Darios. He had his chiton pulled up over his head like a hood, topped with a straw hat to keep off the blazing afternoon sun. He hadn't been sick again, but his head felt like it had been used as a battering ram. "I will find a stall and buy us both an apple juice before we reach our destination."

"Perikles one day, Spartans the next; you do keep interesting company from one extreme to the other, my friend."

"Be quiet, even Athenian walls have ears," Polydektos shushed him, and adjusted his short sword under his chiton, looking behind at the tall thick wall that surrounded the city.

"A command I can easily adhere to, my General," Darios replied. The walk up to the city had left him parched.

It took them another half an hour to walk from the south of the city to the northern Skambonidai district where the proxenos Palamon had his estate.

"How do I look?" Polydektos raised his chin and rubbed his throat. He needed a shave.

"A lot better than I do," Darios remarked, as they approached the merchant's entrance to the vast villa estate.

Keyx, the messenger, was nowhere to be seen, but a veiled Spartan woman, no more than twenty summers old, ushered them inside with a frantic wave of her hand.

"I thought you would come alone," the girl said as she led them around a large open courtyard to the separate guest accommodation. This, in turn, was as large as Polydektos's old villa. Politics obviously paid better than warfare.

"My friend is a deaf-mute, so he hardly counts at all, really." Polydektos smiled and winked at Darios, who threw him back an evil look. He had noted how his friend was staring at the shapely figure of the Spartan handmaiden as they followed her past a line of imported palm trees to the guest residency.

"He has no hearing or speech? Does he have a tongue in his head?" the girl asked, looking Darios up and down.

Polydektos looked at his friend, and took pity on him, having played a cruel joke on him. "Yes, his tongue and other parts are in fine working condition," Polydektos smiled back to the girl, his hands behind his back.

"Good," the girl replied as they slipped seemingly unnoticed into a side entrance to the residency. "Your companion can stay here and keep me company, my mistress is through here." The handmaiden pointed to a red-curtained doorway seven strides down a mosaic corridor. "What is your handsome companion's name?"

"His name is unknown, as he cannot tell us, but we call him Kerberos." Polydektos walked off, swinging his arm back and forth from his groin area.

Darios groaned, from his old friend's antics and his massive hangover.

"There, there…come with me, my pet dog, and I will give you a bowl of wine to sup on." The Spartan handmaiden stroked his bare arm seductively.

Maybe the deaf-mute ruse was a winning ploy after all.

Polydektos smiled at his friend and winked. Then grabbing

his short sword under his chiton, he pulled aside the red curtain and stepped into the warm and barely lit room. If this was some sort of Spartan trap, it wasn't the one he was expecting. A small corridor led to a curtained rail above the humid room beyond. The curtains were green and sheer so he could see the room beyond. It was a bathroom, lit by flower-scented lamps sunk into the foundations of the residency, in each corner of the square bath.

The bath had but one occupant: Eione, the wife of the Spartan ambassador, Lydos. Her beauty was on full show, from her high, full breasts that had not lost the shape of youth to her taut, exercised stomach that most Athenian men would be proud of. Her arms were tanned and wiry; this was no pale Athenian undertrod wife before him. It was always said in Attica that the Spartan women were only discernable from their male counterpart by their longer hair, but this strong woman had a defined beauty all of her own. Polydektos could not help but stare at her as she poured warm water over her chest.

"Are you going to stand there watching all day or come and join me?" she spoke without turning her head towards him.

Polydektos straightened his clothes, gripped the pommel of his sword, and pushed himself through the sheer curtains. He had hoped for a proud, strong entrance, but the thin curtains caught on one sandal, and he had to hop twice to clear them. This brought a frown to his face and an amused laugh from the Spartan lady in the water.

"Careful now, you wouldn't want to topple in and get your clothes wet, would you?" she said in a light, amused tone. She turned her back to him, showing she had no fear of attack, and poured more water from the bath over her shoulders and back.

"You sent a messenger, Eione of Sparta. As your husband is an honoured guest of our city, I was obliged to come." Polydektos kept his words simple and his eyes on the nearest lamp.

Eione turned to face him once again, with no shame of showing off her naked form to a near-stranger. "So very formal are your words, General Polydektos. And I thought we were old friends now, you and I."

"We have met once, at a reception. I hardly call us more

than passing acquaintances," Polydektos replied, still gazing at the flickering lamp.

"Maybe we have met before, and you have just forgotten? Perhaps if you look at me more closely you might remember. Or maybe you've seen me in your wildest dreams, General?" Eione said in a confident voice he rarely heard coming from an Athenian woman's lips. Her words were strong, but she purred seductively like a great cat.

"I think I would have remembered if I had seen such a rare jewel in that rock wasteland of Sparta," he said, staring into her eyes for the first time.

"A compliment inside a barbed remark, I will take that." Eione smiled up at him. "My request was true and honest; will you not join me? The water is lovely, and as you can see, I am unarmed."

"I bathed this morning," he lied for some reason. The water looked tempting for his aching legs and feet, but only if she was not in the bath also.

"Then as a host, I must come to you," she replied, moving slowly through the water to reach the steps leading up one side to help her exit. She got out and sauntered up to him with a seductive swing of her hips, not looking for a towel to dry herself. She had firm but not too muscular legs, and was shaved between them. She stopped a foot's length in front of him, slightly taller than he. He found it hard not to notice the water rivulets dripping down the length of her tanned body.

He thought of his dead wife, of Gala his lover and her ultimate betrayal of him. This was a Spartan woman before him, a married one and not to be trusted. Eione reached out and put a slick wet hand under his clothes. She grabbed the hilt of his sword. "Are you Athenian men so afraid of a mere naked Spartan woman who knows her own mind?"

"What is on that mind, I wonder? Why am I here, Eione of Sparta?" Polydektos said, regaining some control over himself.

"Do you not find me beautiful to look upon, Athenian?" She said, gripping his hilt harder.

"You are a rare beauty indeed, Eione, but you belong to another," Polydektos said, placing his hand on hers before slowly pulling her from the folds of his clothes.

"I belong to Sparta, and no man," she smiled, eyeing him up and down. "Do you not desire me?"

"I desire only to know why you sent for me."

"Down to business and no play—who said the Athenians are not strong of will and resolve? It is a shame; of all the Athenian men I've met, I've only desired three worthy of such attention, and only you have turned such an offer down. Is it because you still mourn your poor departed wife, or do you yearn for your young male lover instead?"

Polydektos gripped her wrist harder for a moment and then released her. She had played him at little, but he would not give in to her games. "I say again, wife of Lydos of Sparta, why am I here?"

Eione looked at him and nodded. She turned and pulled on a red himation and tied it loosely around her waist with a golden cord. "You are stronger than I thought. I've picked well to call on your aid, Polydektos of Athens. Come sit next to me and have some wine."

"I'll have some water, if you please," he said, coming over to sit next to her at a small round table in the corner of the room. It had a white cover, atop which rested a jug of wine, a smaller jug of water, two cups, and a bowl of mixed grapes.

"So you cannot be tempted, eh? I cannot help but feel a little spurned, General," she said, pouring them both cups of clear water.

"Your feelings are your husband's concern, not mine. Enough of these games; why am I here?" Polydektos had appreciated the show but was getting tired of her seduction and mind games. Any more and he would get up and leave.

"Very well. Many things have come to my attention these past couple of days since our arrival in your fair city," she began, before sipping her water. "I worry about the safety of my husband and son, and of Sparta and her many friends. Creatures out of history stalk the streets turning people to stone."

Seeing her drink relaxed Polydektos sufficiently to drink his own water. "If you are concerned, I'm sure Perikles and Palamon would have the guard around the estate doubled."

"It's not Gorgons I fear, Polydektos, nor death. I fear betrayal. I know you are looking into the disappearance of Skaios the sculptor and that certain parties wish you to desist your investigation." Polydektos started to protest, but Eione raised a still slightly damp hand to stop him. "I have many friends in Athens, and this is not my first visit here either. Skaios was a good Greek—he took no sides and was a fine artist. I wish to see him found, dead or alive."

Something else flashed in her eyes, not desire, but actual concern for Skaios's fate.

"Was he a lover of yours?"

"No, but his wife is. He was also a friend of Greece itself and I am one of his patrons. Perikles and his pets Olagnos and Pheidias threw him to the dogs out of sheer spite and jealousy of his talents and his fame around the whole of Greece, not just Athens. I want you to find him for me, Polydektos. Learn his fate, whether the news be good or ill." Eione was showing a new side to herself. A more honest representation of who she really was under her strong Spartan façade.

"I will try and find out his fate—not for you, Eione of Sparta, but because he was an Athenian citizen, mistreated and attacked in his own city where he should have been safe." Polydektos stood up from the table. "Thank you for the water."

"Are you sure you do not want to stay and taste more than water?" Eione smiled coyly, her forefinger circling the wet lip of her golden cup.

"Some things are more dangerous to taste than even hemlock. I will take your leave, Eione of Sparta, for it appears I am a very busy man once more." Polydektos turned and left the bathroom before she could speak again. It took a lot of inner resolve to do so. Seven months ago, he would have taken her in the bath, on the cushions, and then over the table. But he had lost much since then and gained at least some self-respect.

She spoke no farewell at his leaving, nor bade him to return. He thought more of her because of that. He heard grunts and groans from a nearby storeroom, which did not help his wanting libido. He knocked three times on the doorframe but kept his eyes averted from the writhing naked coupled forms inside.

"I shall meet you outside, my friend." Polydektos picked his words carefully, not wanting to blow Darios's cover, and left them to it. He went out into a small walled-off courtyard with a fountain and waited there under the shade of a line of almond trees.

Darios was longer than he hoped finishing off his dalliance with the Spartan handmaiden. Polydektos had stood to go back inside to fetch him, or maybe talk to Eione again, when his friend came out, adjusting his clothes. At least it had given him time to think over the two crimes he had been tasked to look into. Skaios and Hyllos; two men unconnected and poles apart in social circles, but both seemingly entwined with the hooded Gorgon Sisters haunting the city. Was Skaios's disappearance related to Hyllos's death by petrification, or was it mere coincidence? The figure Euneas and his comrades had seen might not have anything to do with Skaios at all. Until he found the sculptor, alive or dead, he had little hope of answering that conundrum.

Darios smiled widely at his friend as they left the residency together and set about returning to the Agora to have something to eat.

"So how did you get on?" Polydektos asked when he deemed they were sufficiently far away from Palamon's estate.

Darios smiled back and just patted his ears and mouth with both hands, continuing on the ruse that Polydektos had begun.

"I deserve that," Polydektos smiled thinly and patted his friend's back. "But seriously, did you find anything out from the girl?"

"Only that a deaf-mute has just the same amount of fun as the speaking and hearing. She was a comely girl for a Spartan and knew a trick or two that nearly had me praying to Aphrodite for a love potion to keep me in the game," Darios replied, having had enough of his forced silence for one day.

"Did she let anything slip about her and her mistress?"

"Her name was Lyto, and tonight I will make up a love song for her that she will sadly never hear from my mute lips. Of her mistress and herself, she said very little, though she did let slip she and Eione sometimes shared a bed when Lydos was not around. Not that I could question her, but at least I could not give any secrets away either." It was Darios's turn to clap Polydektos on the back. "How did you fair my friend/ You were not *in there* long."

"I was not in anyone, let alone the Spartan ambassador's wife. She was in her bath, as naked as the day she was born, and though she did offer more, I declined her advances. Yet she did tell me also that she had a taste for female company in her bed, including Anthousa, wife of Skaios."

"These Spartan women are not as manly or reserved as we Athenians like to make out then," Darios answered. "So do you think Eione is connected with Skaios's disappearance?"

"She claimed to be Skaios's patron and friend, so I don't think so. And why would she ask my help to find him, if she'd had him done away with?"

"What about Lydos though?"

"What about him?" Polydektos and Darios had made it to the edge of the Agora by the Painted Stoa.

"Perhaps, and I am just loosing arrows into the wind now, perhaps Lydos found out about his wife licking lips with a certain sculptor's wife and decided to teach them a lesson." Darios looked around him and spoke softer as they entered the busy Agora.

"Why not have Anthousa killed if he was slighted?"

"What would hurt her more? Losing her husband means she loses her rights to his home and she has to return to her home island of Zakynthos. It is much closer to Sparta and he could easily do away with her then."

"Possible, but unlikely. Spartan women are not like our gentle Athenian wives and daughters. From what I can glean from my brief conversation with Eione they have a more independent lifestyle and more freedoms than here in Athens. Eione is not slighting Lydos's manhood by sleeping with women, thus he has no reason to be bothered. Maybe he enjoys watching or joining in, who knows. All this thinking and conjecture is making me hungry, I could murder an eel or two," Polydektos said, rubbing at his flat empty stomach.

They found a table at the rear of a shop that serves all types of fish and seafood. Polydektos ordered two eels, the most expensive dish on sale, and his meal arrived with bread and olives. Darios had salted swordfish, which came with bread and two quartered, baked figs. They ate with gusto and swallowed down their food with apple juice.

"So, do you have any idea where to start to search for either Skaios, his kidnappers or murderers, or in fact *the Medousa*?" Darios said the mortal Gorgon Sister's name in a low whisper from behind his hand raised to his lips, so no one else in the shop could hear him.

"I have no idea where to look my friend, nor the real reasons for these two murders or disappearances."

"Skaios is missing; he might have fled the city in shame after what happened at the Proxenos's reception. Yet, surely General Hyllos was murdered? However terrifying and mysterious his death?"

"Who is to say someone did not kidnap him also and replace him with a stone sculpture, so as to lay blame on Medousa and cause panic throughout the city as it sits on the edge of a sword blade between peace and war with Sparta?" Polydektos wiped his mouth and pushed back his wooden bowl.

"Why go to all that trouble? Hyllos wasn't loved even in his own household; he would not have been missed if he had his throat slit in his own andron."

"Fear," Polydektos stated, staring directly at Darios's pupils. "One death of a highly regarded, but loathed, General would do little to upset daily Athenian life. A creature from history coming back from the dead to turn the living into stone...a creature that could strike anywhere in the city at night...such a creature would foster terror. We've both seen it before in battle—fear kills more men than swords, spears, or arrows."

"Then you think it is a Spartan plot?"

"Perhaps, but many Athenians also want war in these troubled times. A war to end all wars. A war where Athens takes over all Greece. What we need are more eyes and ears on the ground, Darios." Polydektos prodded the wooden table with his forefinger three times.

"We could ask Alkmaion, Talaemenes, Trekhos, and even

that weasel Euneas to help us out."

"Yes, but we need to get the word out in quiet to every beggar, metic, and bought slave in the city without drawing attention to ourselves. If a crime has been committed, who is best to ask?"

"A criminal?" Darios shrugged, not sure he had given the answer his comrade was looking for.

"Exactly." Polydektos tapped the table excitedly.

"I am a retired soldier and a part-time potter. I do not associate with thieves and the lower lives of this polis."

"Nor do I, but Trekhos has many dealings at the dock in Pireás, he might know someone."

"We shall pop into his shop on the way home and ask him. We can offer a reward for any valid information on the disappearance of Skaios and any information on what happened to Hyllos too."

"What else can we do before then? Speak with Anthousa again, about her sapphist relationship with Eione?"

"Would that help us in any way?" Polydektos scratched at his beard-covered chin.

"Maybe if we tell her we knew of it and would inform the whole of Athens, she might reveal something. Put the fear of Zeus into her. Tell she will be carted off in exile to Lesbos."

"Threaten a woman who is most probably a widow? I didn't think we had stooped as low as that yet, Darios. I need time to relax my mind and think. We will speak to Trekhos on the way home, and if we do not come up with anything new in a couple of days, I will speak to Anthousa again."

"That is why you are the famous strategos and I a mere humble scout." Darios bowed as he stood up, and they paid and left the fish shop.

CHAPTER EIGHT

Trekhos of Krete wasn't at home or in his pottery shop. The metic servant, who knew Polydektos by sight after a run-in earlier in the year, physically cowered at the general's mere presence. Trekhos and Megas, his simple-minded Athenian business partner, had gone north for the day to Phyla to discuss a business deal there and would not be back until tomorrow. Polydektos had told the man to get Trekhos to contact him on his return. The metic had nodded so much that he thought the man's head might fall off.

They returned to Darios's humble abode outside of the city walls. Darios was in an upbeat chatty mood after his coupling with the Spartan handmaiden, while Polydektos was sullen and reflective.

"I'm off to pot," Darios informed his friend, as the ex-general sat on the porch area of the house, thinking. Darios knew his comrade well and knew he needed time alone to think, and he had several pots to finish. Polydektos gave him a vague wave to say that he had heard him, so Darios left him to it. The retired soldier-turned-potter chuckled to himself as he walked around back to his studio kiln. Perhaps he would immortalise the Spartan handmaiden for all eternity on the side of a pot.

Polydektos tugged at his beard, trying to piece together all the random facts and events that had happened in the city over the last few days. He missed Talaemenes's youthful mind and skill for remembering details and bouncing ideas off. Yet Talaemenes had his duties to the City-State, and Polydektos only saw him when he had leave from the Ephebeia. *Every man must do his duty to make Athens the greatest power in the region*, he thought wistfully.

Thinking of Talaemenes made his mind wander from the two crimes he had been tasked to investigate. He thought of his dead family. Of Sokos, his son who had died in battle. He thought of his wife, Kephissa, and his daughter, Kyra, who had been brutally killed half a year ago. He missed them all dearly and hated himself for not spending more time with them before they were murdered.

Then he thought of her: their murderer and the ultimate betrayer.

"No, you will not haunt my thoughts like this," Polydektos cursed to himself and stomped inside. He grabbed a polished bronze mirror that Darios would often gaze into lovingly to trim his beard and nostrils. Narkissos had nothing on Darios and his love of preening. He stared at his copper-tinted reflection in an attempt to take his mind off other things. His face was thinner than it has been in years, but there were piebald patches of white in his beard now. Maybe it was time to shave it off, a clean face for a clean slate. Yet he was too old and had too much auxiliary equipment on his back to forget. Wars, death, scars old and new, he carried them all with him. *They are a part of you, so use them,* Sokrates would often tell him.

Polydektos put down the mirror and went to fetch himself some fresh water from the well outside. It was to the left-hand side of the house and would not disturb Darios at his wheel. He tried to put his mind to his investigations again. If Medousa or one of her immortal sisters had slain Hyllos, there was little he could do about it. If someone had murdered or kidnapped the General and replaced him with a stone carving, then he would have culprits to find.

As he lowered the bucket down the well to the water, he turned his mind to Skaios's sudden fall from grace and disappearance. Bloodied clothes dumped on a fog-shrouded street, but no body or ransom asked for?

Polydektos let the bucket splash to the bottom and clicked his fingers as a sudden thought entered his open mind. What if Skaios had been kidnapped and forced under duress to sculpt an exact likeness of Hyllos, to replace the murdered or kidnapped general? It might connect the two crimes and the sightings of Medousa in the vicinity at the time.

"How long would it take to carve such a matching statue and make if so lifelike?" Polydektos left the bucket at the bottom of the well and hurried over to Darios's studio outbuilding, which housed his wheel and kiln. His friend was working some clay as he entered.

Darios turned to him, his face full of joy and a trace of post-coital remembrance. "I was trying to remember every curve and feature of that Spartan girl, as to immortalise her naked form onto the side of a pot."

"How long would it take to carve a statue from head to foot, from start to finish?" Polydektos asked.

"I'm no expert. You should ask Olos, perhaps."

"Could you make a guess?" His voice grew insistent.

"Depends on the details. Months or even years." Darios shrugged; he was no expert.

"Not in a day, then?" Polydektos frowned as his theory fell apart before his eyes.

"Ah, you are thinking of Skaios and Hyllos," Darios realized. "No, even with ten assistants working on it you could not do such a thing. Did Skaios even know General Hyllos in person? To memorise his every feature and translate onto rock would take hours upon hours of work."

"You make a valid point there. Would you be able to make an image of Hyllos just from memory in your pots?"

"I've only seen Hyllos up-close twice, years ago. I know roughly what he looks like and would recognise him in the street, but to carve such an exact representation of his face I would need hours in his company, or at least to see him many times over a period of weeks. Faces have several basic shapes, but you would need to size up his ears, nose, mouth, and how deep-set or open his eyes were to make it look just like a living man. I am having to do a pot of the Spartan girl today before her exquisite beauty dims in my mind's eye."

"So, if someone needed to sculpt a face, let alone an entire body, to match a victim he would need to have been at close quarters with Hyllos for hours or weeks beforehand?"

"Maybe even months." Darios shrugged again. "Unless

they were one of the great sculptors like Pheidias who can see something once and then recall it in every detail later, then yes, they would need access to Hyllos on a few separate occasions. If a man and not Medousa did this act to Hyllos, it would take months of planning beforehand."

Polydektos came inside the small outbuilding and sat on a clay-stained stool by the unlit kiln. "And then a means to transport said stone likeness to Hyllos's villa, unseen by anyone. Unless the attacker was built like a brute or had the strength of Herakles himself, he would need help to bring the statue inside. The slave girl at Hyllos's villa, hiding unseen in the storeroom, thought she heard more than one Gorgon Sister enter after all the rest of the household was scared off."

"We have many theories, but little evidence to confirm it either way. Unless someone was passing Hyllos's villa in the dead of night and saw men carrying in the stone likeness of the General, you can't confirm anything."

"You are right, but what can we do now—wait?"

"We need to find Skaios, whether he is alive and held captive or a cold corpse," Darios said, putting his clay down onto the wheel.

"Easier said than done, my friend. We have so little a trail to follow."

"Then like good soldiers we wait for our enemy to move again or make a mistake," Darios advised.

"And wait for Trekhos to return." Polydektos slapped his bare knees and stood up. "I have water to fetch."

"Menial tasks often free the mind and let in other possibilities."

"You sound like Sokrates," Polydektos said, moving to the open doorway.

"Then slay me now, for I am from simple stock and do not have the time or capacity for such amounts of learned knowledge in me." Darios laughed as Polydektos left him again to return to the well.

He decided tomorrow he would visit both Anthousa and Elleni, the two widows in waiting, to ask if Skaios and Hyllos knew each other at all and if anyone they knew had been taking an overt interest in their husbands lately. Polydektos drew up the water and put all thoughts of Gorgon Sisters and kidnappings to bed for a while. He could do little more until tomorrow and going over the bare facts again and again would only bring on a sleepless night. He carried the water inside to put it on to boil, before letting it cool and decant it into earthenware jugs in the coolest part of the house.

Night fell over the city, and so did the temperature. A cold northern wind blew down from Macedonia, sending citizens scurrying to their warm homes. Fires were lit and warm meals cooked and an extra layer of blankets added to beds from chests unopened since the early days of spring. A horse whined in a deserted street, and people gave praise to Zeus for another fine day of life and took to their beds. The tavernas were long closed, and only a few brothels and drinking places stayed open for men to go about their insalubrious business under cover of darkness. A dog bark, an owl hoot, or the cry of a robbery victim might break the silent hours of Athens, but most slept the darkest hours of the night away safe in their cots and beds.

The widow-in-waiting turned over to the cold, empty side of the bed. Her sleepy pawing for her husband woke her from endless dreams of chasing shadows through the labyrinth streets of a great maze. On waking she realised the maze was Athens and that her husband was no longer with her.

A sudden noise from somewhere in the courtyard below made her sit bolt upright and strain her hearing, waiting for a repeat of the alien sound below. Her bedroom felt cold and she shivered, rubbing at the goosebumps on her arms. She was about to get back under the warm covers again when she heard movement on the landing outside her curtain-covered doorway.

"Who's there?" The widow-in-waiting was shocked how quietly the words squeaked from her lips, like the cry of a mouse.

The only reply was a hiss, like a snake would make.

The widow froze in her bed. Her blood turned to ice inside her.

The curtain was drawn aside, and a figure entered the unlit

room. A tall, dark, hooded shape moved swiftly towards her on the bed with its long fingers reaching for her face. Her jaw seemed locked open and not a sound but expelled air left her lips. The last thing she heard was the hiss of several snakes as darkness took her.

Polydektos loved the isolation of the small strip of land outside the city on which Darios's home was set. The quiet had served him well in the past couple of months, but it also meant they were the last to hear any gossip or news from inside Athens itself.

He was inside Darios's pottery studio, drinking apple juice and admiring the new pot that featured the naked Spartan handmaiden in all her exotic glory.

"I've done a fair job in catching her likeness," Darios said, turning the pot from left to right in his hand as he gave it his potter's eye.

"I think you have her likeness exactly. Not that I can comment on what lay underneath her garments," Polydektos said, raising his wooden cup in salute.

Darios grinned and put down his pot. He was about to reply when they heard a crashing and a knocking from the house. Both rushed out and past the well to the front of the house to see Olos, Skaios's apprentice, in a ragged state and bashing on the front door with his fists. He seemed out of breath and in distress.

"Olos?" Polydektos said to stop the man's hammering.

"She came for her, by Zeus, what are we to do?" Olos ran at Polydektos and grabbed and twisted the older man's tunic in his fists. His hair was sweaty and unkempt, his eyes wide and unblinking. He was panting hard, like he had run all the way from the city, making it hard for him to get out any lucid words.

"Get hold of yourself, man," Polydektos said, untwisting the sculptor's hand from his tunic before guiding him to a stool on the porch, out of the bright morning sunshine. "Sit down and catch your breath and tell us what has happened."

Olos manage two short ragged breaths in and out before he yammered on at the same speed as before. "She came again and claimed her. In the bed, she lies, cold as ice and hard as rock.

Woe is my life, that everything around me turns to ashes and all light is extinguished by Hades's cloak."

"He isn't making much sense," Darios said as he knelt beside the babbling sculptor.

"Drink this and then slow your words." Polydektos offered up the remaining half of his cup of apple juice to the over-wrought man. Olos drank the juice quickly, spilling a lot of it down his chin and onto his dirty himation. "Now, slowly, what has happened to put you in this state?"

"Medousa," Olus uttered, dropping the wooden cup to the boards of the shaded porch at the front of Darios's house. His eyes stared out at the lemon grove, beyond the two men before him.

"Has she struck again?" Darios got in before Polydektos could ask the same question.

Olos kept staring at the lemon trees until Polydektos took the sculptor's face in his hands and turned it towards his own. Olos's cheeks were awash with tears.

"Olos, what of Medousa? Has she struck again?" Polydektos kept his words soft and spoke slowly as if to a young child.

"She has more than killed. She has turned the lovely Anthousa to stone. She lies in her bed right now, her petrified death scream on her lips for all eternity, and I wasn't there to save her. I fell asleep in Skaios's studio, hoping he would sud-denly return, when I should have been at his wife's side protect-ing her from this creature that haunts the darkness. I have failed the family that fed me and gave me purpose in life. I deserve death, if only that she could live and breathe once more."

Polydektos knew the hopelessness that Olos was feeling—the despair of being in the wrong place at the wrong time and not being able to save someone you cared for. He stood and pat-ted Olos on the shoulder.

"What do we do now?" Darios asked, looking from his friend to the distraught Olos.

"Keep Olos here with you. I must hasten to Skaios's house and see this for myself."

Olos stood up and shouted through his tears. "No, I'm com-ing with you!"

"What use will you be to poor Anthousa, the state you are in?"

"What use am I here? It is my duty to my friend Skaios to take care of her in death, as in life," Olos said, beating at his chest twice.

"Spoken like a true Greek." Polydektos laid a tender hand on the grieving man's shoulder. "All three of us shall go to Skaios's house together, then."

"I need to ask you a delicate question," Polydektos said to Olos as they headed through the countryside towards the Itonian Gate.

Olos's eyes were dry now, but looked dark and full of loss and worry. "Ask away," he replied in a distant voice. Darios walked silently behind the two chatting men.

"Did you travel with Skaios and Anthousa far and wide around Greece?"

Olos nodded. "Yes, for most of the trips to Corinth, Thrace, and even Sparta."

"Did Skaios have any special patrons in Sparta during your time there?"

"He did three major works there, including a piece for one of their many kings."

"Did he do any works for Lydos?"

"Yes, well, his wife really was the art lover. Lydos worships her and gave her everything she ever asked for, such was his devotion to such a rare beauty in that drab state. We stayed with them one summer three years hence, working on a statue of Lydos in bronze for a change. It was a new challenge that Skaios welcomed."

"Did the ambassador's wife and Anthousa get on well, do you recall?" Polydektos asked, as casually as he could.

"Yes, they became firm friends, as Anthousa is...was from close by Zakynthos. You know the way of the world—the men would be in one room and the women in another, talking about what matters to wives and mothers. They spent many happy hours together while Skaios and I worked on the bronze statue."

Polydektos felt it wasn't the time to press his questioning

towards the gutter at this time. He had probably learnt enough. While the men had worked, drunk, and played dice, the two women left to their own company had become close and then lovers. Lydos may or may not have turned a blind eye to it, as he wasn't being cuckolded. Olos had said he would indulge her anything. Lydos may be a mighty General, but one arrow from Eros's bow and he was as weak and helpless as a toddling child, like many men in love.

They reached the gate and the conversation died. The city was awash with the chatter of the next Medousa Murder. From the lowest of slaves to the highest patriarch of the ruling families, every citizen, soldier, and metic alike was talking in hushed tones about the latest horrific murder in the city. Athens, with its high, strong, thick walls, could not keep out the wave of fear that flooded the city.

Olos was distraught once more when they reached Skaios's home. A crowd of curious but also nervous people were gathered outside. A company of Scythian Rod Bearers had been posted by the building to keep the peace. Polydektos recognised their captain immediately; he had been the one that had brought him home when his own family had been murdered in the spring.

Polydektos walked right up to the imposing Scythian captain. "I must get through, on Perikles's orders."

The captain of the Rod Bearers nodded and turned to two of his men who were nearby, holding back the scared mob. "Let these citizens through," he barked.

The two Rod Bearers pushed and parted the crowds enough for the three men to jostle through. The metic that Polydektos had seen previously was at the front entrance to the house with a slave. They both had clubs in their hands, in case things got ugly.

"Olos, it is good to see you again. We were worried the mob might break in to steal a morbid glance at our poor mistress on her deathbed," the metic explained as he let them pass inside.

"Keep to the door. General Polydektos has come to examine her." Olos's words, hitched in his throat, were followed by an outpouring of raw emotion and tears.

"Stay at the door also, Olos; you are more use to her here," Polydektos said as he and Darios moved towards the stairs.

Olos just nodded, grateful he did not again have to see the fair Anthousa in death.

The two men moved up the stairs and round the landing to where a sobbing slave girl and a priestess of the temple of Athene Polias stood outside. The priestess was daubing the curtained-off entrance with holy water squeezed from owl droppings and crushed holly leaves. She half-spoke, half-sang. "Pallas Athene, our city's protector, queen of a land supreme in piety, mighty in war, rich in poets, come to us. Aid us in our time of need against the evil that stalks the streets of your mighty polis."

Polydektos walked the long way around the priestess to pull back the curtain to the master bedroom, followed by a rather sheepish Darios. It was where the two close friends and comrades differed. Darios always quoted the Fates and the gods in leading him through life, while Polydektos felt his life was constantly manipulated by scheming men and women and the spectre of death, rather than the will of the gods. All thoughts of gods left their minds and the prayers of the priestess dimmed in their ears as they saw what lay under the covers of the bed.

There lay the once beautiful Anthousa, with the sun streaming over her body from the unshuttered window: her soft skin turned to hard stone. Her delicate fingers were half raised to her face like she was caught before she could cover her eyes. Her mouth was wide open in a silent, now eternal, scream. Her lips were drawn back, baring her teeth. Lines of terror etched forever on her brow. This was a most terrible way to die, Polydektos thought.

"Darios, help me pull down the covers carefully." Polydektos approached the bed and grabbed the covers. The likeness between the stone Anthousa and the living one was so true, it had to be her. Yet, he had to prove one way or the other whether this was her or just some statue that someone had carved and left here for them to find. He turned to see Darios had not moved; his friend stood at the foot of the bed, just staring into the unblinking eyes of Anthousa, as if some residue of Medousa's power had frozen him in his tracks.

"Darios, I need your aid here."

Darios blinked and then turned his head slowly to his friend. He hadn't seen Hyllos's petrified body, so it was much more of a shock to him. "By the gods, it's true, isn't it, Polydektos? One of the Gorgon Sisters stalks this polis at night, turning people to stone."

"It appears so, but sometimes we know as men of war that appearances can be deceiving. The tallest brute of a soldier may appear the best, but gets hit by many more arrows. The largest army might look unbeatable, but it is the measure and courage of the men you have with you that can sometimes turn the tide of a battle. We must look at this objectively, like planning a battle, and not assume anything until proven. Help me pull back the covers, my old friend," Polydektos urged in a soft, encouraging voice.

Darios nodded and moved around to the other side of the bed. He looked down at his hands and not into the fixed, terrified face of Skaios's poor wife. Slowly and carefully they pulled down the covers and skins to reveal that Anthousa was completely stone from her toes to the tip of her nose.

"Her night clothes have turned to stone, but not the bed or her sheets," Polydektos pointed out.

"A creature from the Age of Heroes has turned this poor woman to stone, and you are worried about her bedclothes? Surely there are more important things to worry about now? Like how this happened and how we can stop it happening again." Darios's voice had gone high pitched and had much fear in it. It was something that Polydektos had rarely seen before—well, not on the battlefield, anyway. There was no braver man than Darios in a fight; he feared no man. But this was totally out of his depth.

"I understand that, but why aren't the sheets turned to stone, when they touch her bare skin too?"

"Did Hyllos's clothes also get turned to stone?"

"Yes, but he was standing and not in contact with anything. Until I knocked him over." Polydektos's voice lowered to a lip-mutter at the end.

"We are dealing with a woman with tusks for teeth, snakes

for hair, and the ability to petrify people with her gaze. How are we mere mortals supposed to fathom the whys and wherefores of her abilities? Who knows what a Gorgon Sister can or can't do—they have not been seen in Greece for an age beyond reckoning."

"We do not have a hero here to aid us, so we must do the best we can as mortal men." Polydektos swallowed hard and forced himself to examine Anthousa's stone corpse. Inside her open mouth he noted her tongue and teeth as he examined her from top to bottom. He could see no chisel marks or signs that this was a carved statue, but he had seen works before that looked lifelike.

Polydektos exhaled loudly, perplexed. He could find nothing to disprove that this indeed was Anthousa, turned to stone by Medousa or one of her sisters. He found a chair in the corner of the room and sat down to think. He rubbed at his bearded chin, trying to coax any other thoughts from his mind beyond a Gorgon attack on Skaios's wife.

"Well, what do we do now?" Darios asked after a while.

Polydektos rubbed his hand across his mouth and back down his bearded jawline. He looked around the bed. The place was swept clean on a daily basis and no marks covered the floorboards. Apart from the puzzlement in his mind about why her night clothes had turned to stone but not the sheet, he could think of nothing. There were no clues to be found in the bedroom, it seemed, so it was time to leave and talk to the metics and slaves.

"We leave poor Anthousa in peace. Never will she find out the truth of her husband's disappearance, unless they are now both dead and together again once more. We need to find out how this creature got inside and did this to her." Polydektos blew out his cheeks, patted his knees, and stood up. Darios covered Anthousa with her own sheet and followed Polydektos out of the room. The priestess and the teary slave girl were still outside.

Polydektos pointed at the upset slave girl. "You, come with me."

With intensified fear in her already scared eyes, she followed the two Athenian citizens down the stairs to the courtyard below. Seeing them return, Olos rushed over.

"Well?"

Polydektos wasn't sure what the man expected him to say. That it was a ruse and that it wasn't Anthousa upstairs? He could not prove or disprove anything at this stage. Polydektos ignored his question.

"We need to see everyone in this kleros and talk to them all one by one. Darios and I will be in the andron. I need you, Olos, to send in every citizen, metic, or slave that was here last night, one by one until we have questioned them all. Do you understand?" Polydektos put a comforting hand on the sculptor's shoulder.

"Yes," the unsettled man answered.

"We will start with this one," Polydektos thumbed over his shoulder to the slave girl who had dutifully followed them downstairs.

She gave an audible squeak of fright, then hurried after the two former soldiers as they strode off to the andron.

It took an hour to talk to all the metics and slaves present. Only Olos and another metic who was at Skaios's studio with him were exempt. No one had come into the house via the front door, the only entrance. A metic or slave had been outside on guard duty at all hours, with no exceptions. Most of the other slaves or metics who lived inside had been asleep and had heard nothing untoward.

"Nothing came in or out. Surely you must believe that Medousa is behind this?" Darios said to his friend as the last slave left the andron.

"Medousa was beheaded by Perseus, was she not?" Polydektos raised his eyebrows at his friend sitting on the next couch.

"It is the work of Stheno or Euryale, then? Men cannot turn people to stone; only a Gorgon Sister could have done this," Darios shot back, with a frown.

"That remains to be seen."

"Why are you being so stubborn on this? Are you a critic? Will you deny the gods exist next?" Darios stood and flapped his arms in frustration at his friend's stance.

"I do not deny anything; that is the problem here. You and everyone sees the stone woman upstairs and believes that Medousa is the culprit. I will keep my mind open to this and all possibilities until it is proven one way or the other." Polydektos found he was shouting now and on his feet.

"Then what can we do to prove it one way or the other? Tell me that, Polydektos!"

"By eliminating all other explanations. If I cannot prove that mortal men are behind these murders, then we have a problem on our hands which even I am too frightened to contemplate. If the Gorgon Sisters have returned to haunt Athens, then this city is doomed."

Darios looked at his old General, and the anger left his face as he saw the fear on Polydektos's. "Then what now, my old friend?"

"We search the house from top to bottom." Polydektos clicked his fingers at his friend as a thought came to him suddenly. He headed for the open doorway.

"Why?" Darios asked, in his wake.

"If someone did not come through the main entrance, maybe they came through a tunnel, or through a window."

"That sounds more like the general I know," Darios said, clapping his back as they entered the courtyard.

They found no tunnels, and the windows to the ground floor were too tiny for anyone but a child to enter. The sides of the house were within a horse's stride of each side, but the back was different. It was less of a garden and more of a dumping ground for old and unsellable works by Skaios and his studio. Ivy and scrub grass covered some of the older works, while some just lay in ruins around the few wildflowers that grew amongst the statues.

"Any other time and I would admire some of the abandoned works here, but now it gives me the shivers. It's like Medousa's been here on a killing spree," Darios whispered into his friend's ear.

Polydektos nodded. It was an eerie place indeed under the current circumstances. They looked up at the rear upper windows. Most were too small for someone to enter. There was one large window that led to the women's gynaikonitis rooms. The ground was stony, with banks of grasses, flowers, and ivy. Someone could have easily put a ladder up to the large gynaikonitis window without leaving any tracks on the hard terrain below. They could have climbed up, killed Anthousa, and taken the body out the same way. Getting a stone statue up there without breaking it would be much more of a Heraklean task. They would need a block and tackle hoist, as least, and that would surely have been be noticed.

Polydektos looked behind him. The brush would be a perfect place to hide a statue of Anthousa if needed. He didn't want to be in the eerie garden any longer than required. He forced himself to look at as many of the statues as possible. The ones covered with ivy and weathered by years outside seemed much older and of a different style to the newer ones closer to the house.

Polydektos crouched down and pulled the ivy and grasses from a statue that seemed to have been half buried by vegetation during the years it had been outside. He recognised the face at once: it was his late father, Praxilios. It was very lifelike in features, though pitted with rain and covered with dirt on one cheek and green stains on the upward facing cheek. His father had been dead a decade now, and he wondered how he and Skaios had met, and whether he had sat for such a sculpture to be made. Praxilios, like his son, had had little time for the arts and even less time for the gods. He had been called a critic and sent into exile by Cimon's youngest son, Thessalus— one of Perikles's old rivals—after a long, unfounded campaign against him. He died a year later on the island of Melos after he had taken hemlock to end his life.

Polydektos had been away fighting at the time and had not heard of his ostracised father's death until his return to Athens almost five months afterward. He had plotted with Perikles, and a year later, Thessalus, like Polydektos's late father, had lost all his power and had been exiled. It had been a fitting revenge.

Polydektos used the end of his himation to wipe the green slime from his father's marble countenance. He stood up and exhaled through his nose and strode quickly from the rear of the house without speaking to Darios.

"Where are we going?" Darios called after him as his friend pushed passed the dwindling crowds outside the front entrance to Skaios's house. He did not try to re-enter the house, but set off down the street in the direction of the Akropolis.

"I am going to the Parthenon to sacrifice a pig to Athene in the memory of all those that have gone before, and ask for guidance in our endeavours. Then you and I will find a quiet little taverna to eat, drink a little wine, and try and put our heads together and work out this mystery we've become embroiled in. Are you with me, Darios?"

"You had me at wine, my good friend," Darios laughed and caught up with Polydektos as they headed through the city to the limestone edifice that was the Akropolis.

CHAPTER NINE

They were in the Parthenon for over an hour in the presence of the imposing figure of Athene. Polydektos spent most of his time in silent reflection, thinking about his father, mother, wife, and children: all separated from him by death. He bought a pig at the entrance to the Akropolis and sacrificed the animal to gain favour with Athene and ask for her divine help with the mysteries that surrounded him like the Labyrinth of Minos. Any help, from any form, would be welcome.

His head was splitting from the bright low sunlight of late afternoon, and the thoughts whizzing around his mind caused him pain. He was glad when he and his companion left the hillside and walked down to the streets near the Agora, which offered more shade. They entered a taverna where Darios knew the owner, an old campaigner like themselves. He had served under Hyllos ten years ago and told them loudly that he would not dare go to the state funeral for his former general in two days' time as he would be too tempted to piss on the man's grave afterwards.

He gave Darios and Polydektos his best table. It was by the entrance and looked from the north-west corner of the Agora, with the odd stoa and temple to block the view. The table was shaded from the late afternoon sunshine and caught any breeze that might dare to twirl down the street. The owner, still cursing Hyllos even in death for his treatment of his own men, came over with bread and olive oil, plus jugs of water and wine for starters. He wandered off to scold some diners who had been taking too long to eat their meals, giving the pair time to think what they wanted to eat.

They were just deciding when Trekhos of Krete entered the taverna with Megas, his simpleton business partner. Polydektos could not see the Akropolis from the taverna, but he wondered if his request for aid from Athene had been heard.

"Polydektos and Darios, my friends, I've been looking all over the city for you today. I hear you need the help of Trekhos of Krete. As a great friend of Athens I will readily oblige you anything." The pot merchant bowed low and then joined the two men at the table.

"I, Megas, King of Athens, will help you too," Trekhos's companion slobbered from one side of his mouth.

"Sit down Megas. And what have I told you about saying you are a king?" Trekhos grabbed the young man's tunic and pulled him gently down into a chair next to him in the corner.

"That kings should be regal and silent. But mostly silent," Megas repeated something he had heard many times before.

Polydektos and Darios laughed with Trekhos at the simpleton's amusing words, but not at the youth. A stray discus had addled his mind and frozen half of his face. His lips were always wet, and he had his face fixed in a permanent squint. Yet he was a good lad, and an Athenian citizen that Polydektos and Talaemenes owed their lives to. It was his testimony at the law courts six months ago that had saved them from exile or even death.

"Here, Megas, my good friend, have some watered wine," Polydektos passed spare cups over to the new arrivals.

"A king should have a loyal general," Megas said. He poured himself some wine, splashing the table with his unsteady hands. Polydektos smiled at him; it was hard not to like the unfortunate young man.

"So, to business, then, my fine Athenian friends," Trekhos said in a low voice, and he bent over the table towards Polydektos and Darios. "You want my help, and here I am."

"We need your help to get the word out to the streets, to the beggars, prostitutes, thieves, and other unsavoury people. We need to find Skaios, or at least his body if there is one to found still," Polydektos whispered.

"And you ask me. I do not know whether to be flattered or offended, General." Trekhos shrugged.

"Flattered," Darios nodded, pursing his lips.

"Flattered," Megas mimicked.

"You know the ways of the docks at Pireás. You know whose palms to grease to get things unloaded first, which tolls to pay to make sure your goods get to your shop unstolen. We need to talk to the leader of such people and put out a small reward for any information leading to Skaios or his body being recovered. You are a smart businessman, with contacts in every port in every major city. What do you say, Trekhos, will you help?" Polydektos opened his hands and showed his empty palms to the pot merchant.

"I know of such cutthroats, yes, but they are not men to be trifled with. They earn their reputations well, through fear and murder."

"As do I," Polydektos whispered back at Trekhos.

Trekhos rubbed his chin and looked from Darios to Polydektos, reading their resolute faces. "I can try and arrange a meeting if this is what you truly want. I warn you, even meeting with them usually comes at a price, let alone any further reward they require. Their time will cost you in drachmas, Polydektos."

"That is not a problem, I assure you."

Trekhos leant back in his chair. "Then if it is what you need of me, I will arrange it and send word to you at Darios's home."

Just then the owner returned to the table. "What do you want to eat?" he asked grumpily.

"Nothing, as my friend and I are just leaving," Trekhos stood, tugged at Megas's sleeve, causing the youth to spill the dregs of his wine cup.

"Sad," Megas said, getting up and leaving the table without a farewell to the two men who remained seated.

"I will be in touch soon, farewell," Trekhos said, as he and Megas left the taverna and hurried off down the street.

"So?" The taverna owner asked again.

"More wine," Darios offered up the near empty jug, a resigned tone to his voice. "And as this could well be our last meal, bring us lots of your finest food, my friend."

Polydektos watched Trekhos and Megas disappear around a corner and wondered if he had made the right choice in enlisting the help of petty criminals to aid him. He hoped Zeus would reveal all eventually, but only time would tell.

Polydektos and Darios took their time with their meal and wine. After they left the tavern they waited until they had put the city walls behind them before continuing their talk about the recent murders and the events surrounding them.

"So, what does this new Medousa Murder mean, Polydektos?" Darios asked, picking up a fallen branch from a nearby tree as they walked and talked. "Why Anthousa?"

"That is what I have been cogitating on, my friend. Eione asks me to continue my search for Skaios, she admits that she and Anthousa were lovers, then Anthousa is killed."

"Killed? She was turned to stone in her own bed." Darios raised his voice and eyebrows as he stripped the branch of side twigs.

"She is dead, whatever the means, Darios. Why kill her? Did she know the killer or some piece of vital information that needed her to be silenced?"

"Or, is this a list of people someone has given to the Medousa to petrify?" Darios stripped off the last side branch of his long stick.

"I wish you wouldn't keep saying that name. Do you really believe that Medousa's body has found her head again and has come back to life to kill only a few certain people in the city?"

"Gorgon Sister, if it makes you happier. The gods can do anything, you know that. Maybe Zeus or Athene are using her as a warning to Athenians to trust no one and not let our enemies inside the city walls."

"What could poor Anthousa have done to anger the gods?"

"Slept with the Spartan ambassador's wife," Darios replied, scything through some tall grass with his stick.

Polydektos exhaled loudly. "I don't think the gods are too bothered about two women kissing, do you? We are getting off the beaten track here. Let us talk of mortal men and why they murder. Eione asked us to help find Skaios, and then Anthousa dies. What connection does she have to Hyllos in all this?"

"Thinking along your tracks, who gains from Skaios's disappearance and Hyllos's and Anthousa's deaths?" Darios whacked his stick into a bush, breaking part of it off.

Polydektos shrugged, getting annoyed at his companion hitting every trackside piece of vegetation with his stick. "Olos is a metic, so has nothing to gain. Elleni, Hyllos's wife, gains her freedom for half a year perhaps, before she is married off again to some relative. She does not get Hyllos's house or monies. Skaios is missing, presumed dead. He could be hiding out and behind these deaths. He could have carved the stone statues. Maybe he found out about Eione and Anthousa and felt it was an abomination before the gods. Faked his own death and murdered his wife?"

"He would need help. But what of Hyllos? I'm pretty sure they did not share the same social circles. The connection between Hyllos and Anthousa has to be found before we can solve this mystery." Darios clobbered the overhanging branch of a lone olive tree, sending a shower of ten or so green fruits onto the track. He caught two and popped them into his mouth.

"Perhaps Skaios served under Hyllos as an ephebos. Hyllos was a cruel man, even to his own men."

"For argument's sake, say Skaios is the one taking revenge on people who slighted him. Then who is his next victim?" Darios hit a solid old bush this time, causing his stick to snap in half. Polydektos was both silently amused and relieved as his friend threw away the remains of his temporary wooden weapon.

"If we are guessing correctly here, and not just pissing into a squall wind, the next target must be someone who has hurt Skaios during his life. Perhaps Pheidias and his cronies, for allegedly ruining his peace sculpture, or the Spartan woman Eione, for sleeping with his wife?"

"If the Spartan ambassador's wife is slain on Athenian soil, it could start a war," Darios prophesied darkly.

"That's if it is Skaios, and if he is still alive somewhere. What if it's Lydos, the ambassador himself? He is a general in their army. He, too, could have a war agenda."

"My head hurts, and I've not even drunk enough wine to make it a pleasurable experience," Darios wailed and put his hands into his neat curly hair.

"You are right. We have many theories and no facts at all," Polydektos exhaled again. They rounded a corner and could see Darios's lemon grove a little way ahead. They were nearly home, at least.

Polydektos was woken from his late afternoon nap by Darios. "A cart is coming down the track," he warned, shaking his houseguest awake.

Polydektos's old army training kicked in; he grabbed his short sword and followed Darios out to his front porch. The sun was nearly setting and the birds in the lemon trees were singing loudly to each other.

They were relieved to see that it was only Trekhos and Megas on the seat of the cart, leading the donkey attached to its reins. Darios and Polydektos walked out to greet them.

"Good evening," Darios said to his visitors.

"Good to see you both again, my old friends, and so soon," Trekhos called down from his cart seat. "Yet as you wanted, this is no mere social call."

"Will you come inside for food and drink?" Darios offered.

"Wine," Megas cried happily from the working side of his face.

"No, not tonight, my friends. We have deliveries, remember, Megas—oil for the lamps of the Odeon.

"You have your meeting, Polydektos, but I warn you not to go; it will be dangerous even for a famous general like yourself. These villains have no qualms about killing prominent Athenians, no more than the most lowborn slave."

"Where and when?" Polydektos said resolutely.

"The Blue Shrimp tavern in Zea Harbour tonight, once darkness has gained its hold," Trekhos replied. "The Pitch Tunics are a deadly gang of the most hardened criminals in the whole of Attica. Go armed, but with a mild voice and your eyes wide open at all times."

"Who should we seek—do you have a name?"

"They will seek you out, Polydektos; everyone in the city knows you by sight, my friend. Now we must be off and have this oil delivered before dusk settles into night. Good luck, my friends, and enter into no bargains that you cannot get out of easily." Trekhos geed his donkey to turn and head back down the track to the turning that led to the Odeon.

"We will be on our guard." Polydektos waved them off.

"It will soon be dusk; we'd better get ready, then," Darios said matter-of-factly. He would walk into a hydra's den if Polydektos was leading him.

"Yes, we have a bit of a walk," Polydektos said as they returned inside to ready themselves for their liaison.

Darios insisted that Polydektos wear a hood, as they dressed in some old worn clothes with concealed weapons under them. Dusk was settling over Attica as they left the house and headed back to the city. At night, the only way down to the port of Pireás was via the city. They had to head through the Itonian Gate, up the Kollytos Road, to exit through the Piraean Gate. This gate led to a well maintained wide road leading down to the port. Even though it was dark now, it was well-lit by staked torches and brasiers, as it was an important trade thoroughfare from the outside world to the city of Athens.

Every import and export had to come up or down this road at some point. The walls here were high and impressive and manned night and day by the best archers and hoplites. When Polydektos walked down to the two ports, old and new, he always felt a comforting safety to be between such imposing structures. They showed the might of Athens in defence of what it had earned, making it the greatest of all Greek states.

Polydektos just wished the city-state had a bigger standing army to match their naval power and impressive defences. He had spoken until he was blue in the face in years gone past to increase the army and match the might of the Spartans. His pleas for a permanent, large, paid force had fallen on the deaf ears of the wealthy families. Even Perikles, his good friend, was against it, preferring that it be spent on beautifying the city and making sure its defences were strong.

"*Who will pay for this army of yours, Polydektos?*" Perikles would always retreat to the same defence.

"*We will, if we don't match our hoplites spear for spear against the Spartans and her allies,*" Polydektos always retorted. In the end, they always agreed to disagree.

There were empty stalls along the road down to the port, with only a few places open after dark to serve refreshments and snacks. The walk took them a while, but a straight road led them to the curved harbour of Zea. The Blue Shrimp tavern was well-lit outside, and many of its inebriated clients had spilt out onto the curved road around the docks. The air smelled of salt, fish, exotic spices, vomit, and piss, and the atmosphere outside was loud and raucous.

The two men exchanged a quick *Is this a good idea?* glance and then entered the seedy tavern on the quayside. The inside of the tavern was remarkably different from the outside. It was dark to the point of inky gloom. Small lamps were lit high in the ceiling but did not illuminate the clientele too much. It was only moderately quieter inside, with many men talking among themselves or playing dice on wine crusted tables.

A table against one wall became free when a sailor and an ebony-skinned male pornos left together heading for a cheap, paid-for-the-hour room or a dark alleyway. Darios squeezed himself through the tightly packed-in tables and chairs to claim it. Polydektos slowly followed, eyeing the tavern drinkers from under his hood. He kept the cover up as he sat opposite Darios, but did not look out of place at all. Many of the predominantly male drinkers in the tavern wore hoods, hats, scarves, and even a Corinthian helmet to hide their identities from prying eyes. Darios caught the wrist of a tired-looking serving girl in a short blue tunic, and she turned to face him with a worn smile that seemed to convey disdain at the same time as welcome.

"A jug of your better wine and two cups," he ordered gruffly, pushing a drachma into her hand.

Her smile widened but did not infuse any added warmth to her face. She nodded and headed off to the bar. Darios watched her ease her way between the tables and chairs and the groping hands of the drinkers to reach the bar with a measure of speed and grace.

Polydektos watched his friend's wandering eye. "We are here on business, remember."

Darios turned his head and body towards Polydektos and gave a smile that women had often swooned over. "Just playing my part."

"Hmmm," Polydektos replied, scanning the dark confines of the drinking establishment for signs of anyone watching them. Nobody apart from the serving girl was paying them any attention at all. "I wonder what we are supposed to do now."

"Sit and wait. Oh, and drink." Darios spotted the girl in the blue tunic on her way back from the bar with their wine order. "I'm sure one of these men is keeping a watchful sly eye on us at all times."

Polydektos looked around the rough clientele of the tavern, but it didn't give him a feeling of confidence. He looked from one coarse, bearded and scarred, half-hidden face to the next, wondering which one of these ruffians was their contact.

The girl in blue set down a jug of wine and three cups.

"Are we expecting a guest?" he queried.

The serving girl said nothing and poured wine out for three, then sat down on the empty chair between Darios and Polydektos. "What does Polydektos, famed General of Athens and delver into terrible mysteries, want in the Blue Shrimp tonight?"

"Not what you are offering under that." Darios pointed to her low-cut dress, which showed off a hint of small cleavage.

"Who's the monkey?" the girl sneered, thumbing towards Darios.

"I'm Dari-"

"-I know who you are, Darios the famed scout, *and* I know the looks you were giving me. Believe me when I tell you that you do not have enough coin in that ramshackle potter's hut of yours to buy even the briefest of kisses from me, if they were even offered. I wish to talk to your general. You can look all you want, but if you speak or touch me again, I will stab out your eyes before your companion can even draw that sword he has concealed under his clothes."

Darios went to speak, but a quick sign from Polydektos's hand made him close his mouth again without uttering the many swear words and threats he had readied.

"You seem to know our names; may we have yours? Only in order to converse with you in a polite and equal manner." Polydektos kept his voice neutral and even.

"You can call me what my men called me: the Blue Shrimp. Sometimes delicious to eat; sometimes I give you a stabbing pain in the guts and the death-shits."

Polydektos watched the cruel smile on the woman's lips. He saw beneath the make-up and perfumed oils in her hair that she was probably in her early thirties, rather than her late teens as he had initially assumed. It was an act, a ruse to make lustful men see someone who wasn't a threat—probably right before she cut their throats and stole their coin purses.

Darios wanted to butt in, but instead he took a long sip of the wine the woman had poured. The Blue Shrimp did the same, but Polydektos decided to keep a clear head with such a devious female criminal mind before him.

Polydektos stared deep into her green eyes. "Are you the leader of such men we seek, or just their pretty mouthpiece, I wonder?"

"Does it matter to you that I am a woman, then, General Polydektos? Does it concern you that once again a female might have the edge over you? Does it matter either way if I am a spokeswoman for the Pitch Tunics, their leader, or their whore, as long as you get what you need? Which is what, great strategos of Attica?" The Blue Shrimp laid her nearest hand idly over his, caressing the hairs on his wrist with her blue painted nails.

Polydektos pulled his hand away and under the table a bit too quickly for his own liking and self-control.

"Not going to kill me with that sword you have under your himation, are you, General? I was only playing. No point cutting off your nose to spite your face, eh?" She gave him a knowing wink that made his blood run cold for a moment.

Polydektos breathed hard and controlled his anger, forcing himself not to rise to her baiting.

"The Pitch Tunics control much that comes in and out of

this port. This is our city and our empire, General. Nothing of importance gets past me or gets onboard ship without me knowing first." The Blue Shrimp let her words linger across the table, like the black smoke from the lamp on the wooden rafters above them.

"I need the help of the Pitch Tunics. Paid help," Polydektos began, trying not to lose his temper and storm out of the tavern. He knew any sudden movement might end badly for him and Darios. This Blue Shrimp woman could have five, twenty, or all the men in this tavern at her beck and call. They would never make it to the door alive, let alone out of Pireás, if he angered her.

"We do little for free in Pireás. Our God is Ploutos, and he expects a sacrifice of coin rather than a pig or goat. What do you seek from us?" she asked, her green eyes slitted at Polydektos while she drank her under-watered wine.

Polydektos was finally allowed to get to the point of their visit. "I need to find out the whereabouts of the sculptor Skaios, whether he be dead or alive; in hiding or a corpse in a shallow grave somewhere. I need to know where he drank, who his friends were, if he had a lover or a prostitute he favoured above others. If he had any enemies or other properties around the polis."

"This will be done. We will tell you the price, depending on what information is out there to be found. It won't be cheap, General; we will need a certain amount of danger money."

"Danger money for a gang of cutthroats and thieves?" Darios blurted out, unable to help himself.

A thin stiletto dagger flashed from its concealment against the Blue Shrimp's inner thigh. It was at Darios's temple before he could blink. "It may not look much, but one push into your thick skull would end your carousing days forever."

"Put the knife away," Polydektos said. "I have money. How much do you need?" He pulled his coin purse from under his clothes and dropped it with a chink on the table.

The sound of the coin purse brought looks from the nearby tables, rather than the sight of a serving girl with a blade to a patron's head. Seeing who was holding the thin spike of a dagger, they all returned to their own business rather quickly. The Blue Shrimp took her dagger from Darios's temple and used it to pick up the coin purse and weigh it. She slipped it down the edge of the blade and then hid both between her thighs.

"Call that a tariff for your friend speaking out of turn, and us having the goodwill in meeting you. Don't worry, I won't hold it against you, Darios. A lot of men have done worse than interrupt me or touch me in the wrong way; they have ended up in the sea, feeding the swordfish. And you are pretty, in an obvious, old man warrior type of way. Shame that your younger vital days are behind you. There is danger on the streets for all my men these dark nights. You, Polydektos, know this more than any of us. A monster, beyond any fear that the Pitch Tunics can render in a man's heart, is on the loose. I hope you catch the Gorgon soon, it's driving down business. Men with large coin sacks and timid hearts are likely to stay indoors with their wives rather than venture out and risk being turned to stone."

"If you hear whispers or confirmed sightings of this supposed Medousa, I want to know this also," Polydektos demanded, leaning closer to the woman without any fear in his grim face.

"These rumours I will pass on for free, Gorgon Hunter," she replied, stroking his leg.

Polydektos stood up quickly. The eyes of the tavern were on him, as the feet of his chair squealed loudly along the sawdust covered floor. "By your leave, we will let you get to the task I'm paying you for," Polydektos said to her sternly.

"I like you, General, and your pet monkey. So I will let your abruptness slide on this occasion. I may be charging you for my information, but common courtesy costs nothing at the Blue Shrimp. I will tell you, go into the night and hunt whatever foul creatures hide amongst the darkness. I will send word around the city that in these endeavours you are under protection from the Pitch Tunics. So the only thing you have to worry about is dangerous women with snakes for hair." The woman waved her hand and the men on the two nearest tables stood up and quickly moved out of the way to let Polydektos and Darios through.

Warily, they made their way through the crowded tavern to the exit. Darios dared one glance back at the woman leaning back on her chair and smiling. She waved at him and briefly pulled back her blue tunic to expose her small right breast at him. Darios hurried after Polydektos, back out into the night. He could hear the Blue Shrimp laughing at him as they left the tavern behind.

"What have we got ourselves into?" Darios hissed at his friend as they headed through the dockside towards the long walls again.

"Deep into the muddy mire of trouble, I fear," Polydektos replied as they left the Blue Shrimp behind. Polydektos wondered if the tavern was named after her, or if she had taken the name of the tavern as a pseudonym for her own true identity. He neither knew if she was just the mouthpiece for the Pitch Tunics or their leader. Wars were sometimes won on military might and sometimes on deception. If you kept your enemy guessing, they were more likely were to make mistakes.

CHAPTER TEN

"Why are they called the Pitch Tunics, do you think?" Darios asked the next day over breakfast in his home. He had had a fitful night of interrupted sleep, interspersed with vivid erotic dreams about the Blue Shrimp woman, in which coitus was ended with her satisfied cries as she cut his throat. Parched and sleepy, he drank a mixture of sharp lemon and apple juice to wake him up.

"It's a badge of honour, or a snub to the punishment they receive if caught," Polydektos answered. "Their tunics are covered in pitch and they are set alight for their crimes. A horrible way to die; I've seen it too often. Life is full of pain," he finished in a mournful tone.

Darios grimaced at the thought and ate some porridge.

Both men were quiet, thinking over the events of the last few days, trying to make sense out of chaos.

"Do you think that Hyllos's and Anthousa's souls will find rest because of their deaths?" Darios asked after a long silent pause as they finished up their breakfast. "They will have funerals of a sort. Straight burials, I assume, but there will be no coin between their lips to pay the ferryman over the river Styx."

Polydektos shrugged. He was taught, like all Greek boys, that if you could not pay Kharon, the ferryman of the dead, you would wander the shoreline for a hundred years before you gained free passage into the world beyond death. But he would rather be thinking about the living now, not the dead. He wasn't sure what to do next. Wait and see if the Blue Shrimp and her Pitch Tunics turned up any information on the missing Skaios? Or go visit Eione again and see if the grief over Anthousa's death was in her eyes? Even though Perikles had given him permission to go anywhere in the city to solve the Medousa Murders, did that include bothering the Spartan ambassador's wife at the proxenos's residency?

After a while, he got up, dressed, and put on his walking sandals.

"Are you off somewhere? Do you need me to come along?" Darios asked as Polydektos came out of his guest bedroom.

"Just to the gymnasium to exercise my body, instead of my mind. The only company I want is my own placid thoughts." Polydektos walked over to the front door.

"Understood," his loyal friend said. "I will be at my pots then."

"Have a good morning." Polydektos grabbed his straw hat and put it on. He left his sword, but hid a dagger under his clothes. The weather was putting on a show of warmth, even with the cooler seasons approaching. It would soon be the festival of Oskophoria, he recalled as he walked past the lemon grove. He remembered it only because Sokos, his late son, had led the procession through the streets of Athens up the Panathenaic Way to the Akropolis. With the son of another noble, they had carried branches laden with grapes to honour Theseus and Ariadne. Polydektos remembered that he and his wife had been so proud of him.

Polydektos smiled, even though the happy recollections of that distant festival brought sadness to his heart. Sokos, Kephissa, and his daughter Kyra were all gone. With the sun beating down on his hat, he thought of good times they had together as a young family and tried to block out the bad.

A sudden idea came to him and he changed direction. He had had enough of Athens for the time being, so he took the long road around the east side of the walls. A long walk was as good as any sprint. He recalled the forced marches of his youth and leading his men into battle. He had raised a good sweat and developed a nice walking rhythm by the time he rejoined the road on the northwest, outside the walls. It led to the Ephebeia, the military gymnasium outside of the city. Polydektos had turned off the road before the gates of the Ephebeia, where youths trained for two years as epheboi, learning tactics, leadership, and comradeship; how to fight; and how to survive on the land if at war on foreign soil. Polydektos wandered up a path used by rabbits and other small animals to reach the top of the hill, where a copse of trees brought shade to the former general's overheating body. He sat under the deep shade of the first walnut tree and looked down from the hillside onto the Ephebeia below.

He could see some young epheboi at their training in the vast, open dusty courtyard to the side of the barracks. Either naked or wearing leather kilts, they trained and sparred with spears, swords, and shields. Polydektos watched from afar and smiled again as he remembered his days training with his friends and new comrades-in-arms—the gruelling tasks and long endurance runs he was sent on, into these very hills. He rubbed at his much older, aching calves and took off his straw hat, laying it on the dried grass beside him.

He had spent twenty minutes or so watching the drills and hearing the faint barks of the instructors when a horn blew somewhere below. He stood up, but could not see anything untoward. Then the double-wide wooden gates opened and twelve riders trotted out from inside the training facility. They wore wide-brimmed and domed riding hats of boiled leather, but all were bare-chested and had on kilts or wrappings around their middles. Each rode their steed bareback. They turned off the road and quickened into a canter as they gathered speed into a half-gallop towards where Polydektos was now standing, just in front of the copse of thick walnut trees.

These youth were the wealthiest of the epheboi in the gymnasium, rich enough to afford horses and become the elite cavalry of the Athenian army. Polydektos looked through their number and his hope turned to joy as he saw the young figure of Talaemenes at the rear right of the two-abreast column. An older-looking youth, with a blue armband on his right bicep, wheeled the young cavalry unit towards where Polydektos was standing.

"Hail, stranger! What brings you to the Ephebeia this fine morning?"

Polydektos recognised the type instantly: brave-voiced beyond the point of rich youthful arrogance, from an entitled family as he had been. His nose pointed to the sky like his own shits didn't stink.

"That is no stranger, Aesculapios; that is General Polydektos of Athens, Persian killer and slayer of the Maenad threat." It was Talaemenes, of course, who spoke up for Polydektos.

"My apologies, General," Aesculapios said, trying not to look too embarrassed in front of the unit he was leading.

"Then you can be on your way and let me speak with Talaemenes here on an urgent matter," Polydektos said in his most commanding general's voice.

The youthful leader of the unit squirmed on his horse, not sure how to proceed. He had been given the honour of leading this unit on its daily gallop into the hills, and he wasn't sure what other authority it gave him. Surely not to challenge a famed general of Athens and known friend to First Citizen Perikles.

"On my leave, I will spare Talaemenes and pick him up on our return," he replied with as much haughty confidence as he could muster.

"I neither care for nor need your leave to talk to a witness in an ongoing murder investigation assigned to me by the First Citizen himself. On your way, lads," Polydektos said with a wink towards his young ward. Embarrassment spread over Aesculapios's face as some of the other hippeis under his charge giggled openly behind him. With an angry look, he goaded his horse into a gallop, with the rest of his laughing troop behind him. They were round the hill and out of sight before Talaemenes could even slip off his horse and lead it over to tie to a low branch.

"It is good to see you, Polydektos, but why are you here? Have you found Skaios, or need my help with the Medousa Murders? Everyone in the barracks is talking about them and you," Talaemenes said, his words rushing from his full lips like water poured quickly from a jug.

Polydektos pulled the bare-chested young man into a tight embrace. He noticed the boy's chest and abdomen had become harder and more defined since he had started his military train-ing. "I just wanted to see you," he said into the young man's ear.

Talaemenes pulled his head back, looked deep into Polydektos's eyes, and then kissed him hard on the lips. He pulled his older lover free of his clothing, and they lay down in the grass and did not speak again for some time.

"Was this the only reason you sought me out today?" Talaemenes asked as they lay naked, facing each other under the shade of the walnut trees. "Not that I am complaining."

Polydektos reached out and touched the youth's face, feeling the first signs of stubble on his once alabaster-smooth cheeks. "I needed to be with someone I love, who is still in the mortal world. I needed to be close to you. I'm sorry to have interrupted your ride."

"One ride is much like the other," Talaemenes joked bawdily.

Polydektos grinned and picked at the grass in front of him. "I needed to get away from the city and the murders and the constant conversations with people about death. I hope you don't mind."

"Why would I mind? I've missed you so much while I've been here, including what we just did," Talaemenes reached out and squeezed the older man's hand quickly. "How are the investigations going?"

"Aha, no escape even here," Polydektos laughed. "I'm not quite sure myself what is going on with these so-called Medousa Murders, as the mob has named them. I fear there is something grander and more sinister behind them than I can grasp at the moment."

"You will win out, Polydektos—you always do," Talaemenes said, leaning down to kiss his older lover's hand.

"Yes, but at what cost this time?"

The distant sound of approaching horses ended their tryst and had them hurrying into their clothes. They were just walk-ing out of the walnut wood on the crest of the hill, Polydektos leading his ward's horse, when Talaemenes's troop returned from their ride.

"Are you ready to rejoin us, Talaemenes?" Aesculapios

could hardly keep the scorn from his voice as he pulled up near the two lovers.

Talaemenes just gave his biggest youthful grin and leapt onto his horse. Polydektos passed up the reigns, and Talaemenes took them with a wink. Polydektos had missed that near-innocent smile. A smile of the young, to whom everything and anything was possible.

"Yah," Aesculapios cried and kicked his heels into the flanks of his horse to start a gallop down the hill towards the Ephebeia. His fellow riders charged after him. With a whoop and a wave back to Polydektos, Talaemenes rode off, charging after his comrades.

Polydektos watched him ride off with swelling pride in his chest and just an ounce of jealousy for the adventures his young lover had to come in life. After a year here, he might be posted to some far-flung part of Attica or the Athenian Empire. That was part of life; setting the young free to escape the nest and live and die by their own mistakes. Polydektos knew he would slowly lose him little by little as his training went along, but he took vigour from their meeting today. Talaemenes's youthful excitement and lust for life had been the tonic his jaded mind required.

He watched the horse troop ride through the gates of the Ephebeia and out of sight and then turned and headed back towards the city walls.

Polydektos made directly for the proxenos's residency. He had hoped to have a word with Eione, or at least her handmaiden who had taken such a shine to Darios. He could see neither as a slave led him through the rear courtyard to a different, more open, garden than he had been in before. Palamon was there, with Lydos and the Spartan ambassador's son. Isandros was stripped to the waist and throwing javelins across the garden into man-shaped straw targets on the far side against the garden wall. Palamon's son and another man that Polydektos only knew by sight were challenging him. They were both losing badly.

"Well done once more, Isandros," Palamon called, clapping politely.

Isandros's competitors were both breathing hard and had less than polite looks for the ambassador's son behind his back.

"Once again Sparta triumphs against both Athens and Thessaly," Isandros roared into the clear blue sky.

"If only wars could be resolved so easily, without having to resort to all that unnecessary bloodshed," Polydektos said, increasing his pace to overtake the slave that was leading him through the garden.

"General Polydektos, what an unexpected pleasure." Palamon swept an arm out towards the approaching new guest in welcome.

"I have bested Palamon's son, Palaechthon of Athens, and I have bested Neokles the Olympian from Thessaly. Do you care to take a throw against my strong Spartan arm, General?" Isandros goaded. He picked up two javelins from where they had been stuck into the dirt and offered one to Polydektos.

"Isandros, be quiet," the ambassador said. "An old general like Polydektos has no urge or the strength left in his arm to thrown javelins with young men. Be about your contest and leave us men to speak." Lydos managed to insult both his son and Polydektos in a most uncharacteristic way for a Spartan, a people well known throughout Greece for their plain, direct words.

"I give thanks to Athene for your kind concern for my arm, ambassador. It is good to see you and your family enjoying your stay in our great city. Is your wife not joining us this afternoon?" Polydektos smiled serenely back at the Spartan, his hands behind his back to show he wasn't afraid of the man or his words.

"She is tired and has taken to her bed today," Lydos replied gruffly, eyeing Polydektos with suspicion.

"I hope she is feeling better soon. Her beauty is much missed here today."

Lydos took a menacing step towards Polydektos, who stood his ground. Palamon, sensing danger, diplomatically stepped in front of the Spartan to address his unexpected guest face-to-face. "Is there something I can help you with this day, my friend Polydektos?"

"You will have heard of the terrible fate of the wife of Skaios." Polydektos let the words hang in the sizzling afternoon air.

"An awful thing to happen inside Athens. I knew her well. It is such a terrible thing to happen after Skaios's disappearance, too. I pray to Zeus that they are reunited on some distant shore and are in peace with each other." Palamon said, his face giving a good impression of grief.

"You and your wife knew her well, Ambassador. Will you be attending her funeral?" Polydektos pressed, seeing what information he could squeeze out by angry accident.

"I fear that it might not be safe enough for us to do so. Athens is not the mighty stronghold that Perikles would like the rest of Greece to believe. The daughters of Phorcys and Ceto roam the streets of the city at night, petrifying whom they wish, with no one to stop them. Anthousa was a good wife to my friend Skaios; it is worrying that Perikles can find no one to stop these creatures."

"I will stop them," Polydektos replied in a soft, matter-of-fact voice.

"Then I wish you well on your quest, Polydektos, though Athens can ill afford to lose another of its famed generals to the Gorgons."

"I thank you for your concern, Ambassador. I can arrange more guards for the residency if you are feeling worried about your safety," Polydektos jibed.

"I, unlike some, can look after my family," Lydos struck back.

"I do hope so, Lydos, for I would not wish that pain on even my vilest enemy. I give thanks for your hospitality, Proxenos." Polydektos walked over to where Isandros was beating the other two young men. He grabbed Palaechthon's next javelin from the dirt and hefted it towards the Spartan's target. It hit the red circle painted on the straw target's head, knocking it off its shoulders.

Polydektos left the stunned men in his wake, turned on his heel, and left the residency. He walked back down through the Agora with a sense of deep unease at his back. He wasn't sure if his visit to the proxenos's residency had helped much. It suggested that Eione was probably telling the truth about herself and Anthousa and was now deep in grief at her loss. Lydos, though annoyed by Polydektos's carefully balanced tone of veiled confrontation, did not give himself away as connected to the Medousa Murders or Skaios's disappearance.

As he left the Agora and the busier street behind, he had the feeling again that he was being followed. He caught sight of a thin, red-hooded and caped figure trailing him at some distance. As he neared the edge of a butcher's, he ducked quickly down an alleyway to wait and surprise his new shadow. He waited, but no one in a red cloak went past his hiding position.

Polydektos waited a little while longer, then peeked out from behind the mud-brick wall. He could see no one in a red cloak in the main street or the side streets beyond. He continued on to the southern walls of the polis. The feeling of being trailed had left him. Perhaps the person following him had sensed that he or she had been noticed and had left off the pursuit.

Polydektos was glad to pass through the gates into the open countryside, where his feelings of unease lessened with every step back to Darios's house.

Darios was still in his separate potter's shed, stoking up the wood fire at the bottom of his kiln. The heat of the kiln, plus the heat of the day, nearly made the already hot and sweaty Polydektos swoon.

"Warm enough in here for you?" he asked his friend, who was stripped to the waist and had an old leather kilt on, splattered with old and new clay stains.

"Might throw a few more logs on the fire." Darios smiled back, rubbed his bare arms and pretended to shiver. "How was your walk?"

"Very therapeutic in parts," Polydektos said, stripping off his sweaty himation as he stood in the doorway. He fondly recalled the last time he had taken it off.

"Something has put a spring in your step. Any progress on solving the murders?" Darios caught the gleam in his former general's eye.

"Not really. I popped in unannounced on the proxenos

and the Spartan ambassador," Polydektos replied, holding his clothes to his side.

"And were you well received?"

"I wouldn't go that far. The ambassador's wife has taken to her bed, ill, and I can't see Lydos behind these mysterious murders either. Even if he did have cause to wish Skaios and his wife ill, why not send an assassin?"

"It would not be easy for the Spartan ambassador to arrange such murders in Athens without a good citizen spotting him or one of his entourage."

"Then where does that leave us? Another dead end in a labyrinth of dead-ends." Polydektos sighed and leant on the doorframe. He wasn't sure if Perikles's faith in him was justified. He didn't appear to be getting anywhere in solving the mystery behind the Medousa Murders or finding the missing Skaios.

"With the help of the gods, perhaps. This still points towards the Gorgon Sisters, and you have found no evidence to disprove this yet, my friend." With his pots in the kiln, Darios washed his hands and forearms in a bucket of water he had raised from the well just before Polydektos had returned home.

"I still think this is the work of evil mortal hands, but I will take any help I can get at the moment. Perhaps the Pitch Tunics will dig up some gem of information that we would never find."

"Perhaps." Darios took the bucket and poured it over his head. He shivered and shook his wet hair around. "I need a drink."

"I second that motion, citizen." Polydektos nodded in agreement with his old friend as they padded back to the house together.

From behind a jagged line of bushes and strawberry trees a pair of keen eyes watched intently as the two men entered the house.

CHAPTER ELEVEN

A chill wind, dark foreboding clouds, and heavy rain had swept up from Persia and hovered over the city of Athens like a giant roc, making even the white marble look gloomy and dim. The funeral procession of Hyllos, infamous general of Athens, made its way slowly up the Panathenaic Way towards the Dipylon Gate.

Two sleek black steeds with crowns of black feathers and bridles of dark leather and copper pulled the funeral waggon through the driving rain. Perikles walked next to Elleni, the widow of Hyllos, with his Corinthian helmet back off his head, dressed for the occasion in his general's attire. Hyllos had no children or living relatives, so Elleni's family and other high ranking officials, priests, and generals followed behind. A military band played a drowned lament for his soul, as best the weather would allow. A phalanx of hoplites in full uniform and black armbands, to mark the colours of Hyllos's army, followed after. At the rear walked some paid wailing women mourners.

Polydektos was there amongst the strategoi. It was not because he had any regard for the callous Hyllos, but just in case his murderer showed him or herself at the funeral for some morbid reason. Earlier in the morning Darios and Alkmaion had gone ahead to stake out the cemetery at Kerameikos. The more drenched he became, the less he thought of his own bright idea.

With everyone soaked to their skin, they finally made it to the cemetery. Hyllos's stone remains had been wrapped in two heavy shrouds and had his old worn campaign cloak over them to hide the fact that his petrified dead body was in pieces. His

helm and his entirely black shield, with no family or state sym-
bols on it, were laid over the body also. The only blessing was
that, because of the stone state of his remains, there would be
no cremation on a pyre, just a hasty burial. Polydektos looked to
the grey sky above, the rain making him blink rapidly. No fire,
save perhaps the fire of Hephaistos's forge, would light today.

Perikles gave a short speech over the grave, telling of all
the battles that Hyllos had won for Athens over his time as a
general. Elleni came forward afterwards and laid the general's
sword and whip next to his corpse. Polydektos could not help
but smile inwardly at the fortitude of the young widow. He
knew what she meant by burying the whip he had often used
upon her and the servants of his house: his cruelty would die
with him.

Polydektos looked amongst the mourners gathered in a
semicircle around the grave. Palamon was present, but no
members of the Spartan delegation were with him. He didn't
blame them, as feelings towards the Spartans and their allies
were running high throughout Attica. If you took away the hoplites, band, and paid mourners, it was a poor turnout for a man's
life. It also reminded Polydektos that how you lived your mortal
life would either repay you in the afterlife or sting you on the
behind like a giant scorpion.

He saw no one out of place. Nor could he see his friends
hidden out around the boundaries of the cemetery. Yet gloom of
the day was like dusk and the rain both blurred his vision and
shielded anyone too far away like a mist.

Polydektos went over to Hyllos's widow as the funeral party
began to break up and the gravediggers piled muddy earth over
his shrouded, tainted corpse. "You have been stronger than any
hoplite today, Elleni. I swear by almighty Zeus and the goddess
Athene that I will find who did this to your husband."

"I thank you for your kind words," was all she said in reply
as her parents led her away.

"The gods have spoken without words about the earthly
deeds of Hyllos this day," a familiar voice said from behind him.

"Indeed, they have." Polydektos turned, his sandals squelch-
ing in the muddy ground to face the First Citizen of Athens.

"I have not seen you since we spoke at the Odeon, my old friend." Perikles moved closer and grasped Polydektos's wet arm in greeting.

"I have nothing to report, First Citizen."

"Come now, Polydektos, you must have discovered something. I know you of old. You do not leave any rock or pebble unturned to seek out the truth. Even though crabs might hide under such rocks, down by the coast." Perikles smiled, but it wasn't a warm friendly one of old.

Polydektos smiled back, his lips wet from the hammering rain. "I am using all the means I can muster to find out the truth of these murders, from the lowest thief to the highest official."

"But to ally yourself with the dregs of the docks...is that wise, Polydektos?" Perikles asked, moving closer so only his old friend could hear.

"This is the strangest of circumstances, and the murders are not natural. So, I must seek the most unnatural of allies to complete this quest you have laid upon me, Perikles." Polydektos raised his voice, causing the First Citizen of Athens to flinch back a little.

"Only the quest I laid upon you?" Perikles's eyes narrowed and he fixed a withering gaze upon Polydektos.

"I must do everything to find the person or creature who killed both Hyllos and Skaios's wife, Anthousa. Would you have me undertake this with one hand tied behind my back, Perikles? I will investigate where the facts lead me and to whoever is responsible for these heinous acts against Athens and her people. If you are displeased with my progress, feel free to find another to take up this task."

"This task was made for you and you alone, Polydektos. The gods have special things in mind for us both. I have my continued faith that you will find the culprit and end these murders sooner rather than later. You are one of my oldest friends and allies, Polydektos; you will do what is right and just."

"I will do what is right for Elleni and the families of both victims, First Citizen," Polydektos said sternly, standing his muddy ground.

"I am sure you will do them and me proud, General

Polydektos. Let Hermes swiftly bring you to the answers you seek." Perikles turned to rejoin his flunkies and head back to the city.

When only Polydektos and the gravediggers remained, his two old soldiering friends left their separate hiding places around the cemetery to join him by the now-filled grave.

"Did you spot anything or anyone untoward?"

"In this blasted weather it was difficult to see anything at all with my old eyes," Alkmaion complained. He wasn't happy about being drenched, for it made his old war wounds ache.

"We saw nothing." Darios shrugged, wiping the rivulets of rain from his face.

"Then let us leave this accursed place, until the morrow anyway." Polydektos led the way back to Alkmaion's farm, the closest place to find a warm fire to dry themselves off. Alkmaion's wife served them hot soup and gave them a change of clothes, but did so strictly out of duty to her husband. She had no love for either of Alkmaion's friends, as they brought him close to mortal danger all the time. The following day would be the burial of Anthousa, without any pomp or ceremony.

The next morning could not have been more different than the last. A change of wind direction had blown the clouds away overnight, and the burning sun was drying the puddles outside Darios's house into round, plate-like crusts of clay.

Polydektos went out under the porch, drinking a cup of mixed juice, and simply stared at the gently sloping countryside and blue cloudless skies. Darios was still sleeping, and Polydektos felt suddenly small and alone in the world. Another day, another funeral. He hadn't thought of the Medousa Murders up until that point. He began to wonder how he had been drawn back into the intrigue of Athens once more, after so long avoiding it.

He cursed his mind. Now all he could think of were murder and death once more.

"Is there no peace in Athens for an old soldier, who has served his state well and given everything to the cause?" he lamented. Polydektos drained his cup and turned back to the open doorway to make breakfast for Darios.

An arrow hit the post holding up the overhanging porch roof by his left shoulder. The thud of the arrowhead embedding deep into the wood caused him to drop his cup and he half dived, half rolled into the safety of the house. He kept low and peered through the open door to see if he could spot his attacker. The angle of the arrow implied it had come from somewhere around the lemon tree grove.

A loud yawn from his right startled him again. He looked over to see a sleepy, naked Darios enter the main room of the house, scratching himself. "What are you doing down there on the floor?"

"Get down—we are under attack from an archer!"

Darios, his chief scout, had learnt many years ago to listen when General Polydektos yelled. He dove onto his knees and wiggled himself closer to the prone Polydektos.

"Where?"

"Somewhere around the lemon grove."

Darios leapt and rolled over his former general like a Thracian acrobat, keeping low to the floor at all times. Polydektos suddenly gave a stifled laugh.

"What is it?" Darios asked while peering out to see if he could spot the attacker with his keen eyes.

"Is this how Polydektos, General of Athens, meets his doom? Scrabbling on the floor next to a naked man."

A breathless laugh burst from Darios's mouth in an instant. "What would our neighbours the Spartans and Persians make of that, eh? But your fears are unfounded, I think, for today at least." Darios laughed again, dryly, and pointed to the arrow stuck on his porch post.

Polydektos followed the line of his friend's finger up to the black painted arrow, and saw it had a message scrolled around it and tied in two places with cord.

"Could be a trap to lure us both outside," Polydektos said, getting to his knees.

"Then they would have shot you down while you were drinking your fruit juice, my friend," Darios stood up and walked proudly out of his doorway and rocked the arrow from his post. "Good morning," he yelled towards the lemon grove, waving the black arrow in his hand. He returned inside and handed the arrow over to Polydektos. "I believe this message is for you."

Polydektos felt a little foolish, and he stood up to his full height and received the arrow from the bold and naked Darios. Apart from the gods, and live chickens for some reason, his friend feared little in the mortal world. Polydektos unknotted the cords and handed the arrow to Darios, then unrolled the black painted scroll. The inside was cream parchment with black edges where the paint had seeped over.

"What does it say?"

"It says that the Pitch Tunics wish to meet with us today and will see us at Anthousa's funeral at the Kerameikos."

"They must have found something out."

"Let us hope so—we need all the help we can get."

"I better get dressed in my second finest clothes, then," Darios stated, glancing at the fireplace where the clothes he wore yesterday still looked damp.

"Yes." Polydektos read the simple note again.

"Here." Darios handed back the black arrow and then padded off to his bedroom to make himself look presentable.

Polydektos read the message scroll for a third time, trying to glean any hidden information from it. He couldn't, so he tossed it and the arrow on the table and went to wash and get dressed.

There was no state funeral for Anthousa of Zakynthos, murdered wife of Skaios. No band, no hoplite escort through the city, and no paid mourners wailing for her untimely loss. She arrived on one donkey-pulled cart, followed by Olos, the student sculptors from Skaios's studio, and the few metics and slaves from her humble household.

Polydektos and Darios were also more humbly dressed today, in full himations with no military regalia. Olos had daubed his forehead with ash as he followed the cart taking Anthousa to her final resting place at the poorer side of the cemetery. Alkmaion was somewhere around the outskirts of the cemetery posing as a relative come to visit an ancestor's grave.

The surprise mourners, who joined the funeral a little late, were Eione and her handmaiden dressed in dark grey himations with black shawls over their ash-covered faces to hide their identities from the rest of the onlookers. The other was the woman they knew as the Blue Shrimp, in a black tunic with her face uncovered for the world to see. Polydektos noticed she had a fine, finger-length scar to the right of her neck, which her long dark hair nearly covered.

He also noted the lines on Eione's stern but attractive face, where her tears had made the ash run down her cheeks. Polydektos was in no doubt that her love for Anthousa had been as real as any love he had felt in his life. To risk coming to the funeral without an escort showed the bravery and devotion of the Spartan woman. If their wives were so fierce, what would a war with their menfolk be like? Polydektos hoped the war that Perikles so desperately wanted with the Spartans and their allies did not happen. His friend's hubris could toll the death knell for Athens.

Without the need for a pyre, the funeral was over quickly. Olos, with tears in his eyes, thanked them for coming. He did not ask about the investigations into the bizarre murder, but Eione did. He could see from the corner of his eye that the Pitch Tunic woman had made a step towards him, but had been frustrated by Eione and her handmaiden getting to him first.

Eione gripped Polydektos's arm, her painted red nails painfully scratching at his skin. "All love has gone from my body this day. Only hate and revenge remain. I want the head of the person or creature that did this to fair and innocent Anthousa so I can mount it on a Spartan spear and carry it around the streets of Athens and then Sparta, to show my enemies that I am no frail woman to be trifled with. Will you do this for me, Polydektos, man of Greece; man of honour, man of his word?" He had never seen such anger and fury in a woman's face in all his days.

He bowed his head slightly. "I will do this thing for you." He had felt grief such as this so many times in the past few years.

"I trust you, like I have trusted no man ever in my life, Polydektos." She patted and then rubbed at the bleeding marks on his arms.

"Let my blood be our contract," Polydektos said proudly.

Eione rubbed his scratches, letting his pinpricks of blood paint her fingertips. She brought them to her full lips and rubbed his blood over them. Then with another last sob for her lost love, she turned and hurried away. Her handmaiden nodded at Darios and rushed after her mistress as they made towards the Dipylon Gate. Olos and the rest of the household stayed to fill in the grave and set a small headstone at the end of it.

The Blue Shrimp waited until Olos and the rest of the mourners had left to approach Polydektos and Darios.

"You seem to have a way with the ladies, even Spartan ones," she teased, her head cocked to one side as she sidled up to face Polydektos.

"What have you found out?" he asked gruffly, covering his bleeding arm with his tunic.

"Not Skaios, sadly. He seems to have vanished from Gaia. And even Atlas, who holds the heavens on his shoulders, cannot find his trail." The Blue Shrimp looked up to the sky as she spoke.

Darios gesticulated angrily at the Pitch Tunic gang member. "Enough of your riddles, bitch. If you haven't found Skaios, why are you here? Why did you nearly take Polydektos's head off with that message this morning?"

"I will let you off for that remark, as funerals bring out the worst in people's tempers. If I am a bitch, then call off your dog, Polydektos, before my friends do something unpleasant to your elderly friend we found sulking around the gravestones." She whistled twice, and two ruffians in black tunics popped up from the long grass near the olive trees, holding a knife to Alkmaion's neck. He had a bloodied lip, but apart from that did not seem harmed in any way, except for his soldier's pride.

"Leave him alone—he is an old soldier and deserves your respect," Polydektos almost snarled, trying to control his anger. "Now tell me, woman, what do you know?"

"It is said that when Skaios went missing and the Medousa was seen around the city, and on the nights that Hyllos and Anthousa were turned to stone, that a black waggon surrounded by the mists of Hades was seen in the streets near each attack. Some say it was drawn by two nightmares, black as the abyss with fire in their eyes and nostrils. Others say two skeletal winged steeds pulled the Gorgon sisters from their home in the west to wreak revenge on Athens and the heirs of Perseus. Others say they are water horses that bring the mists of Poseidon's depths with them. And others just say that they saw two black horses pulling a long black waggon through the city, near where the murders happened." She finished her embellished tale with open palms.

"You tell long tales like a wet nurse, trying to scare children into their beds at night," Darios shot back.

"If you want to suck on my teats, it will cost you, dog." Blue Shrimp tilted her head briefly towards Darios and then back to Polydektos. "I only relay what I have heard. Make of it what you will—it is freely given, my new friends. Two horses and a waggon seen near or about these attacks might mean something in the end. Let us hope there are no more deaths to scare my potential customers away." With that, she clicked her fingers and walked away. Her men released the embarrassed looking Alkmaion and followed a short distance after her.

The three old soldiers came together, Alkmaion rubbing at his neck where the Pitch Tunic ruffians had held him. "Was her information any good?" Alkmaion asked Polydektos grumpily.

"Not at the moment, but you need more than one spoke to make a wheel." Polydektos groomed his beard with his fingers. It needed a trim. He had no women left in his life to help or advise him on his appearance, and he hardly saw Talaemenes. He wondered what the significance of the horses and waggon might be. It could be in a polis like Athens that every other street had a horse or a waggon close by.

"What do we do now?" Darios asked, wiping the sweat from the collar at the back of his neck.

"Get out of this place," Alkmaion grumbled.

"You two go home. I'm going to visit the graves of my family."

Both men were silenced swiftly. Their petty grumblings were nothing compared to the loss and hurt their general had suffered in the past few years. They nodded to him and both men turned to head back to the city.

Pheidias, dressed in a green chiton with yellow floral patterns around the edges, dusted off the flowers he was carrying as he stepped up to the meagre townhouse of his friend Olagnos. They had bonded over their mutual hate of Skaios and other great artists of Greece that were, frankly, not Pheidias. They were both sharp-witted and their remarks were often cutting to new artists, potters, and sculptors on the scene. Pheidias was top-dog in Athens and intended to remain that way. Having the favour of the First Citizen and half of the major ruling families always helped, but his critic friend and occasional lover Olagnos was always good to keep onside.

Olagnos's townhouse was a small affair in the Diomea Quarter, though he had a much larger farm estate on the eastern coast near Araphen. His wife and children lived there, while Olagnos essentially lived a single man's life in Athens. He had only a metic servant and two male slaves to look after him; Pheidias wasn't sure how the man coped.

He had brought flowers to thank Olagnos for his recent help as a parting gift before his friend wintered with his family. Olagnos always found the city sterile and dull during the cooler months and retreated to the warm bosom of his family until spring. Sidestepping some horse dung, the famous sculptor went into the porch entrance of the house. The metic porter's room was empty, and the place was as quiet as a mausoleum. This wasn't anything new for Olagnos's townhouse. Pheidias had often found the place deserted, until a search of his friend's large bedroom located all of the household naked in his bed, sleeping off the excesses of the night before.

Pheidias skipped up the internal steps to the first floor and round to his friend's bedroom. He pulled back the lilac curtain covering the door and entered the room. "Wake up, sleepyhead, the day is waxing towards mid-afternoon," Pheidias sang out, his eyes adjusting to the dim light. The shutters were still closed, and overnight the lamps had burnt away to nothing.

Pheidias blinked, then slowly approached the foot of the

large master bed. "Olagnos?" His voice was timid now and had lost the joy that he had bounded in with. He repeated his friend's name, looking at the forms of four men lying entwined on the bed. As his eyes became more accustomed to the gloom, he saw that there was something terribly wrong with the naked men.

None of them seemed to be breathing. Two had their eyes wide open and their tongues lolling out between their teeth. Pheidias gulped loudly and inched closer, looking from the naked, seemingly dead servants to his friend entwined in their embrace. Olagnos's eyes and mouth were open, and a questioning look sat upon his pale looking countenance.

"Olagnos," Pheidias barely squeaked out as he reached over the seemingly dead slave to touch the nearest hand of the critic.

Pheidias retreated hastily from his touch, flailing back in fright, knocking into the window with his back and breaking one side of the shutter. Bright daylight flooded the head of the bed like a long, sharp triangle, showing Pheidias's eyes what his hand had felt: Olagnos had been turned to stone.

It took Polydektos until he reached the Agora, on his return inside the city walls, to hear the first rumour of the death of Olagnos. At first all he heard was *Medousa this* and *Pheidias that*. He was worried that the most famed artist, sculptor, and builder of Athens was dead. He gathered information and tossed aside the wilder rumours. So, by the time he reached Olagnos's townhouse in the eastern side of the city, he had a pretty good idea of what had happened to the critic. Both Scythian Rod Bearers and Athenian city guard were outside the house, forming a tight circle to keep out the frightened mob. Fear turned the normally placid citizens of Athens into baying thugs; they were shouting, crying, and screaming at the guard to let them in or to save the city from such terrors.

"Polydektos is here to save us," a woman cried, and knelt down to grab him around the thigh in a tight, quivering embrace. Others were not so glad to see him as he pushed and pulled himself through the crowd towards the guards.

"General Polydektos couldn't catch a chill in a frozen lake," a man with terrible breath screamed in his ear.

"What are you going to do to save us from the Medousa?" another man shouted.

"Save us, save us, please," a well-dressed woman from a rich family cried as she clawed at his bare forearm, drawing blood. Polydektos looked at his arm with dismay. It wasn't having a very good time of it today. With the help of the guards and Rod Bearers, he finally made it through into the defensive semi-circle around the front entrance to Olagnos's house. He thanked the men holding back the near-riotous mob and went inside, glad to be able to breathe easily away from the noise and mayhem of the street.

"Up here," a familiar voice called from upstairs.

Polydektos hurried up to the first floor to find Perikles, a captain of the Athenian guard, and a red-eyed Pheidias standing outside the entrance to Olagnos's bedchamber.

"What has happened here, First Citizen?" Polydektos asked, giving his friend's title in front of the captain of the guard.

"It appears that even with you investigating, General Polydektos, the Medousa has struck again right into our inner circle. No loathed general or woman has died this day, but a man I called a friend." Perikles looked shocked, and his face was full of anger, seemingly aimed at Polydektos. "Olagnos lies inside, surrounded by his dead servants, turned into solid rock. I can hardly believe it. What do you say to that, my old friend?"

"That I am sorry for your loss, and I will enter and take a look for myself." Polydektos did not wait for more barbed remarks from his oldest friend. He pulled aside the curtain and entered the bedroom. Even after what he had seen in his life, he was shocked. The shutter over the large window was now hanging down by one broken hinge. Full sunlight angled in over the bed showing the corpses of the three servants and the petrified body of Olagnos in the centre of the bed. Flies had already found their way to the three flesh corpses.

The scene was puzzling. The metic porter and the two male slaves were dead, but not turned to stone like their master. Polydektos held his breath and moved around the side of the bed to the first of the naked men. Polydektos bent closer to

examine the man's face. The colour of life were already draining away from his cheeks and neck. The tongue was protrud-
ing; he had seen this before, so he looked at the man's neck and
throat. Sure enough, there were signs of red pulled skin and
crushing injuries. This man had been throttled to death. The
next man was curled at the bottom of Olagnos's stone legs and
feet. He too had been strangled. Making his way around the
other side of the bed, Polydektos saw that the metic porter had
died the same way as the slaves.

Only Olagnos, lying like a statue between them all, had
been turned to stone.

Polydektos reached over the dead bodies and with a tentative hand grasped the nearest arm of the petrified critic. Even
though the room was humid, Olagnos's body was cool and
solid to the touch. He pulled his hand back quickly.

Polydektos stepped back to the window and stared at the
unnatural death scene on the double bed. The bodies of the
dead servants had been placed around Olagnos, probably after
their deaths, he surmised. Not even Medousa could sneak
up on four sleeping forms, strangle three of them, and turn
another to stone without one of them waking or putting up
a fight. No, they had probably been killed around the small
house, stripped, and then placed around their master to make
the discovery of Olagnos even more shocking.

He wondered who had found the bodies.

"Why not turn everyone to stone?" Polydektos muttered,
looking around the room. Had the Gorgon a flair for drama,
or did servants and slaves not matter to her at all? In all three
cases, only one person had been petrified, while the rest of the
household had either been scared off or, in this case, murdered
by hand. Why not turn everyone to stone, unless she had help?
Maybe a cult, much like the Maenads he had encountered earlier in the year. He had never heard of anyone worshipping
the Gorgon Sisters before, though; they were monsters to be
feared.

Polydektos felt like he was missing something obvious,
something in plain sight that his old eyes could not grasp.
The room looked swept and tidy enough; nothing had been

knocked over or seemed out of place. No struggle had gone on in this bedroom, it appeared.

Blowing out his cheeks, he turned around to face the window. The shutter hung down by one fixture, the other broken. A crack in the plaster below the window ran down before dividing into two prongs resembling forks of lightning. There were scrapes and scoring on the wooden windowsill, and the edge of the sill was slightly splintered. Polydektos tied open the half-broken shutter and knelt to examine the floor. Two feet's length from the window was another scrape on the floorboards. He peered under the bed, but saw only dust and a piece of straw, probably from the mattress.

He stood up quickly. Of course, all this damage could have been there before the grisly murders, but it didn't seem likely. Polydektos peered over the windowsill and down into the weedy and rubbish-strewn alley between this house and the next one. *You could get a horse and waggon down it at a push,* he thought. The former general hung as far out of the window as he dared. There were two grey marks just under the sill, a foot or so apart, like something had been leant or rubbed against the mud, brick, and plaster. Something…like a ladder.

Polydektos felt a sudden rush to his head and pulled himself back inside the bedroom of death. His mind cleared as the balance of the blood in his body returned. Images and theories on how the murders happened flashed through his mind's eye, like oracular visions. Yet that was all they were so far, thoughts and theories. He had no real evidence to prove this idea nor even a main culprit beyond a hideous creature from the past. He could do nothing for the dead, only hope to help the living and catch who or what was doing this. The only real key so far was the black stallions pulling a black waggon. If he could find that, it would lead him to the answers that he sought.

There must be hundreds of black horses in Athens and many black waggons also. Where would he start looking?

"Have you found anything useful?" Perikles called from outside in a testy tone.

Polydektos looked around the room once more and then left to rejoin his friends and the guard captain.

Pheidias wept openly. "How could this happen to poor sweet Olagnos?"

"More to the truth of the matter is why this happened to him," Polydektos stated, looking from the artist to the First Citizen.

"Why indeed, when we have Athens's finest looking into these Medousa Murders?" Perikles said, his words bitter to Polydektos's ears.

"It is Skaios in league with foul creatures of the night—his spirit wants revenge on us all," Pheidias wailed.

"Why would he want revenge on you, Pheidias? Or Olagnos? His wife? Or Hyllos?" Polydektos pressed.

"Enough of this!" Perikles shouted. "Find out who or what is behind these murders and put an end to them, or..."

"Or what, my friend?"

"Or our long friendship ends. I have tolerated you long enough, Polydektos. I defended your drunken behaviour, I kept you on the list of strategoi, even though my enemies see it as a weakness, for you will never lead a company of men again while I rule Athens. I wept when your son was killed by a friendly spear and consoled you when your whore murdered your remaining family. What use are you to me, living off former glories? Find the Medousa and slay it. Then bring back its head, or die in trying, Polydektos." Perikles raged and went downstairs with the Athenian captain of the guard following his chiton tails.

"It is terrible to see such rage and loss in him," Pheidias muttered, as the shouting had dried up his grief-stricken tears.

"He knows nothing of loss," Polydektos muttered gravely. He went back into the murder room to wait for Perikles and his entourage to leave. It took a while and then ages more for the crowds to die down enough to let him slip out the front door and around the side of the house. The Athenian guard had left, but a section of Rod Bearers had remained to guard the house.

The side of the house was hard-baked soil rutted with rocks, stones, and old mud bricks. Tall yellow grass, weeds, and prickly bushes were everywhere. Polydektos drew his short sword from beneath his tunic and stabbed at the hard ground. His blade hardly made any headway into the earth. Even if a wag-gon were backed into the alley, it would not leave an impression in the rocklike soil.

He moved under the window and looked up to make sure he positioned himself roughly where a ladder would have been placed. Sure enough, over a foot apart were two dark indents in the soil. Something very heavy must have gone up the ladder to make such marks in the rocky ground.

Polydektos rubbed at his beard and looked at a pile of rub-ble that led to a mound at the end of the alley. It had once been a low building of some sort, now covered with dirt, weeds, and rocks. He scrambled up it, pulling at the tall grass to help his body reach the summit. At its zenith, it stood as tall as he. He blew out his lips, pondering theories and then tossing them from his mind as they proved unlikely.

"As unlikely as the Medousa, back from the dead to terror-ise the polis," he muttered to himself.

The other side of the mound led down to an L-shaped side passage between a baker's and a house. He used this to slip away from the remains of the crowd around the front of Olagnos's townhouse. Despite the heat, he pulled his himation over his head like a hood and left the polis as fast as he could manage. He'd had enough of the city and its citizens for one day. He con-sidered leaving them all to their plots and vices and just heading off to buy a modest villa on some small island allied to Athens, there to see out the remainder of his days. What was he doing getting involved in political life and strange murders again? It only brought him grief of one type or the other. Polydektos had reached his limit for grief earlier in the year and could stand no more.

By the time he had walked back to Darios's house, he had convinced himself that he was leaving Perikles, Athens, and all his problems behind and taking the next ship out of Pireás on the morning tide. He heard voices as he dipped under the porch, glad to be out of the sizzling heat. He pushed open the front door to find Darios had company. Much welcome com-pany. Polydektos smiled broadly as the man sharing a jug of watered wine with Darios turned around.

"Aristaeos! It's been too long, my young friend." Polydektos embraced the student of the philosopher Sokrates as he turned and stood. They embraced like brothers, and both were joyful at their reunion. Aristaeos had been one of his companions when they had come up against the Maenad cultists nearly half a year ago. He had changed in the five months since Polydektos had seen him. The edge of youth had gone from his face to be replaced by stubble, and his eyes showed that they had seen much in that time. He and his younger brother, just out of the Ephebeia, had sailed north with Sokrates to fight with Archestratos's expedition to stop the revolt in the Chalcidice peninsula. He and his brother had both been injured in the Battle of Potidaea, though it had been a great victory for Athens and its empire. Sokrates had elected to stay behind to lay siege to the city. Aristaeos and his younger brother Philokrates had then headed south to Delphi to recuperate and study.

"I have missed you too, my friends, and Athens so very much." Aristaeos sat down again as Polydektos made his way around the table to sit in the empty chair nearest his visiting friend.

"How was Delphi?" Polydektos sat down and poured himself some wine, mixed with half a measure of water.

"Hot and full of unwise pilgrims, General Polydektos." Aristaeos drank deeply of his cup, hiding his smirk behind it.

"Just Polydektos to my friends and companions in battle, remember that," Polydektos said. "And how is your younger brother Philokrates?"

"He was stricken by the oldest illness of all, and remains behind in Delphi," Aristaeos replied, keeping his cup at his lips.

"What ails the lad? Leprosy, diabetes, or worse?" Polydektos was concerned for the young man.

"No, worse still than that. He fell in love, the poor fool. Never have I seen a youth suffer so keenly from it," Aristaeos replied with a deadpan delivery.

"Surely it is an affliction all young men should both endure and revel in," Darios said, cracking a walnut between his two palms.

"Yet my poor brother suffers from the worst kind of love: the unrequited kind."

"Ah," Darios and Polydektos said in unison as they nodded.

"Yes, he fell hard for a young beauty. A prophétis at the Temple of Apollon. She is sadly most chaste and devoted to the gods, and her young supple body is a temple that only Zeus himself, in one of his guises, might penetrate. Poor Philokrates." Aristaeos raised his cup and so did the other two men around the table. The toasted their companion, lost like so many good men to the wiles and fortunes of Eros.

Darios toasted their absent companion loudly. "To Philokrates, may his senses be returned from the blindness that Aphrodite causes and the wounds to the heart that the arrows of Eros inflict."

"To Philokrates," Polydektos and Aristaeos cried, and all drained their wine cups.

"What of your own wounds—have they healed?" Darios asked, scratching at his knee.

Aristaeos rolled up his himation to reveal a healed pink scar on his upper thigh where he had been pierced by an enemy arrow.

"How was Sokrates when you saw him last?" Polydektos wished his friend was also here this night, for he could use his wise head at the moment.

"In fine spirits. He wears no armour on the battlefield and the arrows seem to avoid him, unlike my brother and me. I've seen a completely different side to him. He is a ferocious man when riled. It is like the gods themselves put an invisible shield before him as walks into battle."

"Sokrates," Polydektos sighed. "Even when we fought at the Battle of Salamis all those years ago, when he was younger than you and I was a young captain, he would never run anywhere." Polydektos smiled at the thought of that battle twenty-two years ago.

Once they had poured a new round of drinks, Aristaeos raised his eyebrows and stared darkly at Polydektos. "Darios has told me a little of what has been happening since I've been away. So, what murderous troubles have you been sucked into like a whirlpool?"

"I do feel like I am a drowning man, Aristaeos. Not only

Athens, but Sparta has pushed me into the depths of Poseidon's deep domain, and Perikles has come after and burnt the ship as I sink by myself." Polydektos frowned and drank more wine.

"Not by himself, though," Darios added, crushing another walnut shell loudly. "Polydektos kindly pulled Alkmaion and I into the water with him, so he does not drown alone."

Polydektos glanced at the man he was the guest of and opened his mouth to speak, but closed his lips tight again. He could only apologise for bringing his friends into danger with him again. At least Talaemenes was at the Ephebeia and out of immediate peril.

"Word travels fast," Aristaeos said, picking a fig from the decorative blue fruit bowl in the middle of the table. "Even on the way home I heard tales that Medousa has found her head again and is haunting the city at night, turning good people to stone. And that Perikles himself has tasked his old friend Polydektos to slay the creature, as he is a descendant of Perseus.

"Last of the descendants of Perseus through the Belid line I may be, so my grandfather told me. What ruin is my family in now? Thin is the blood of Perseus in my veins; no Gorgon-slayer am I." Polydektos shook his head, recalling the fantastic tales his father had told him as a boy. His family could trace their lineage back to Perseus the slayer of Medousa himself. It was a tale he had told Sokos when he sat on his knee as a wide-eyed boy. Polydektos did not truly believe it himself, but it was a good tale to tell and always gave him strength on the battlefield.

"Then when strength of arms and armies fall, we must use the best weapon in our armament," Aristaeos said, tapping his temple. "Our minds."

Polydektos poured his third cup of wine. Each had a lesser measure of water to wine than the cup before. "And what does Aristaeos's keen mind tell to do next? For all my thinking and pondering, people are still being murdered and turned to stone. What can I, a mere mortal man, do to stop such a creature?" He could not believe how the youth had changed in half a year. He seemed so calm now, so mature and self-assured. War could quickly turn a youth into a man.

"We use thought as our method of attack," Aristaeos said in

earnest. "We must stop trailing in the wake of this murderous creature and try and put ourselves in its sandals. If she wears sandals. No matter. The point is we must try to think ahead of the game—work out the reasoning for the attacks and what they have in common, and guess where next the Medousa may strike."

"I've tried to link the three, but have failed to come up with anything solid. Skaios goes missing, no body is found, but the Medousa is spotted nearby. General Hyllos is turned to stone, then Skaios's wife Anthousa, and now this very day Olagnos the critic is found petrified. Three have a slight connection, but Hyllos...I can't fit him into his murder puzzle yet."

"That is because we have yet to find the connection, for there will surely be one. Tell me everything. Like Kerberos, three heads are better than one, eh?" Aristaeos laughed so heartily that even Polydektos had to smile.

Polydektos told Aristaeos everything they knew and had found out so far in relation to the Medousa Murders. Darios contributed to the tale with the odd fact. It was after dark when they had done. Darios set about clearing the table and preparing a cooked hot meal of rabbit stew and vegetables as the night grew chill outside.

The three friends ate in silence and drank water with their meal. All of them were feeling the effects of the wine they had imbibed. The night brought a cold wind from the northeast and they moved their chairs nearer the cooking fire for warmth.

Aristaeos had been quiet for a while, and when Polydektos return from urinating, the younger man, tired from his travel, was dozing by the fire. Darios looked up as he fed and poked the fire.

"Do you think Aristaeos can help?" Darios leant back, pulling his woollen himation over his bare arms to keep them warm.

The rising wind rattled the front door. Polydektos went over to place a rolled-up old blanket at the gap at the bottom of the door to stop the draft circling around their feet. Only then did he sit down and answer his friend. "If he stops sleeping, perhaps."

"I am not sleeping, I am thinking with my eyes closed,"

Aristaeos said in a loud voice, not bothering to open his eyes or uncross his arms.

Polydektos couldn't help but grin. "Then what are you thinking, wise young man?"

"Sokrates used to tell me, 'From the deepest desires often come the deadliest hates,'" Aristaeos replied, opening his eyes.

Darios and Polydektos looked at each other and frowned. Their friend Sokrates always had a more intelligent reply up his sleeve for every occasion, it seemed.

"And that helps us how?" Darios asked, rubbing his cold hands together closer to the flames.

"It doesn't, to commence with. Yet all crimes come from the baser instincts of men and women and even children. What I learnt from Sokrates and my time at Delphi is that hate, love, envy, greed, revenge, lust, and grief are all the lessons we learn from the gods at an early age. They are the foundations of our very existence, and from them, pillars are formed to varying heights according to the men we become and the wishes of the gods. One man may have pillars of equal heights and be content; others may have love and lust as their great pillars, much like our friend Darios here." Aristaeos chuckled and grabbed at his host's knee quickly.

Darios smirked. "I have had no complaints about my lusty pillar, I can assure you of that." Both his friends laughed at his bawdy reply.

But Aristaeos's tone turned grave. "Yet in other men or women, the pillars of love are stunted and dwarfed by the ones of greed, envy, hate, and revenge. These foul murders have happened for some reason we do not yet know. Gods, Gorgons, Titans, and mortal men are all governed in some way by the pillars of their own making. Whether it be Medousa reborn or a mortal man or woman committing them, they must have some core reasoning for the deaths they are inflicting. For a Gorgon Sister to turn these people to stone, her reasons would be hard to fathom. Yet if a mortal man were complicit, I would choose hate, envy, love, or revenge as his motivation. And out of those, revenge seems the likeliest and tallest pillar in this person's temple. Does anyone fit my revenge theory?"

Aristaeos fixed Polydektos with his keenest gaze.

"Skaios," Polydektos replied.

"Yet Skaios is missing, presumed dead by Medousa herself," Darios interjected.

"A perfect cover. Who would suspect a dead man?" Aristaeos gave a shiver as the cold tickled his spine. "If Skaios is behind the murders, would it fit the facts we have of these crimes?"

Polydektos rubbed at his cold arms, deep in thought. "Skaios's work was slighted by Olagnos on many occasions, and he is one of the prime suspects in tampering with the peace sculpture at the Spartan reception. His wife Anthousa was in love with the Spartan ambassador's wife, Eione. Yet I see no connection with General Hyllos at all."

"Skaios would have the skills to carve lifelike stone statues of his victims," Darios added. "And it would explain why his body has never been discovered, not even with that bitch Blue Shrimp and her Pitch Tunics looking into every seedy corner of the city for us."

"You have your high pillars right there. Revenge, lust, envy, love turned sour as week-old goat's milk." Aristaeos leant back in his chair, drew his himation about him, and closed his eyes again.

"We need to find out if Skaios ever served under Hyllos, but who do we ask?" Darios yawned; the wine and the chill around the house were making him sleepy.

"I can visit the Strategoi headquarters in the morning and check the records there. Or someone might know who to talk to about Skaios's military service." Polydektos leant forwards to put more wood on the fire. The winds were howling outside, shaking the shutters and rattling the doors in their frames. He didn't know how Aristaeos could have fallen asleep through the din.

"Good luck with that." Darios yawned and stood to stretch out his arms.

"Why is that?"

"It is the seventh day of Pyanepsion tomorrow; the polis and Agora will be packed for the parade," Darios explained.

"What parade?" Polydektos shrugged and struggled to get up off his chair.

"The Oskophoria festival and procession, remember?"

Polydektos grimaced. All he needed was another festival for Dionysos to remind him of his late family. His wife had always helped him keep track of such festivals, what to wear, what to do or say. "Then I must be up with the sun to get in early before it all begins. If this blasted wind ever dies down and lets me sleep."

"Aristaeos doesn't seem too bothered by the noise." Darios pointed to the snoring figure slumping in his chair by the fire.

"Aristaeos is a young soldier. We have obviously lost the knack of being able to sleep anywhere," Polydektos joked and made for the guest room. "I'm off to my bed; I wish you good-night, my friend."

"And I to mine," Darios replied, heading for the main bed-room, leaving behind the snoring Aristaeos and the howling gales to play out who was the loudest. Polydektos looked at the man sitting asleep by their fire and could not believe the change in him. He fetched Aristaeos a warm blanket and put it over him before he went to bed. The younger man had learnt much from his teacher, Sokrates. Tasting battle and being wounded could also bring out maturity. Many young men thought they were immortal; a brush with death made them realise what they had to lose and made men of them. With his recuperation and study at the Oracle in Delphi, Aristaeos had become a fine, free-thinking citizen that Athens and he could be proud of.

Even though his body was weary, Boreas, the North Wind, and his thoughts would not let him sleep. Even when the wind died down and sleep did come, his dreams were filled with hor-rible monsters and death.

CHAPTER TWELVE

Even with his lack of a decent night's sleep, Polydektos was up just after dawn. He was surprised to find Aristaeos already up, washed, and readying a very early breakfast.

"I didn't expect you to be awake yet," Polydektos said, then yawned as he entered the living area.

Aristaeos smiled at him. "A soldier's habits die hard. I thought I might as well walk with you back to the city. I will head off to my father's house and then go to the procession with my mother and younger sister."

"I will be glad of the company," Polydektos couldn't stop another yawn.

They ate a quick warm breakfast and were on their way early, without waking the sleeping Darios. The wind had turned direction and was blowing warmer from the south, but there was still an early morning nip in the air. A good quarter of the remaining lemons had been shaken from the trees in the grove as they passed by. They talked about Sokrates and the Battle at Potidaea as they walked side-by-side towards the imposing city defences.

"How did you cope with it afterwards?" Aristaeos asked after a brief pause in their conversation.

"With what exactly?" Polydektos replied. He had learnt to cope with many things in his life.

"With taking another man's life. Not some evil Persian invader either. Another Greek's life, who may have a wife and a young family." Aristaeos's face suddenly lost a few years, and he seemed more like the youth Polydektos has first met earlier in this long year of many sorrows.

"Well, you learn not to do that. Humanising the enemy leads only to self-doubt and melancholy. It is hard; I used to do the same. Most men have families, wives, lovers, children, siblings, and parents that love them. Not all enemies are evil men—they are just soldiers like you or me. I used to drink and grasp onto the banner of Athens for help. Killing for the good of the city-state and empire! But that pride doesn't last. The only two things you can hold onto to keep the demons from your soul are these: If you had not killed this man, he would have killed you and others in your phalanx after you. You do not want that burden on your soul in the afterlife. Secondly, if this man lives, he might sack Athens one day and rape your sister and murder your loved ones."

"So, we kill for personal self-protection and to save our families. What about the glory of battle and the might of Athens?"

"Glory and national pride are why we go into battle. Saving our own skins and those we care for is how we soldiers live on after the blood has dried on our swords' blades and spear tips."

The clouds then parted and the warming morning sun shone down on the gates into the city. They spoke no more of battle and parted near the Agora, going their separate ways. They embraced as battle-hardened men of Athens. Polydektos beamed with pride as he made for the strategoi's headquarters, for Aristaeos was a great asset to the empire and a solid citizen of Athens. Sokrates had taught the younger man well.

Polydektos cut across the Agora, where citizens, metics, and slaves were up early decorating the procession route and readying their stalls for a full day's business. The newly constructed Strategeion building had only been open since the summer, cut into the hillside to the southwest of the government buildings. It stood near the round Tholos, making its unusual trapezoidal design stand out more than the other, more traditional buildings nearby. He walked past the guards in their ceremonial uniforms, probably brightly buffed for the festival later. They nodded him through, knowing the general on sight, as most people did in the city these days. Not just for his old skills as a soldier and leader of men, sadly.

He passed into an empty courtyard with an elliptical cistern at one end, with waters pouring gently into it from two nymph-shaped spouts. He passed it and entered the room of records, where on the walls were fixed stone and wooden boards with the names of all the generals who had served Athens gallantly in the past. He found his names, Perikles's, and then Hyllos's with ease. The archivists would have the day off because of the Oskophoria, so Polydektos had to try to find the relevant information on his own.

After half an hour of fruitless searching, he wished that Aristaeos, Darios, or better yet Talaemenes was here to lend a younger pair of eyes. He wasn't much of a reader or scholar, and it took him ages to find out that the records of military personnel were listed by battles and campaigns in date order rather than by the generals who led them.

Hyllos had served as general in more battles and campaigns than he, but Polydektos had more victories than losses than the late strategos. It took another hour and three-quarters of searching for Polydektos to find Skaios in the list of men serving Athens in its time of need. A dozen years ago, Hyllos had led a fleet of twenty ships full of hoplites to harry the Persians who had taken a small, nameless island as their own. It was no more than a rock northwest of Cyprus, a place where no one lived, but it belonged to Greece. The Persians, who were no more than pirates, were turfed off and executed to the last man. Hyllos had not lost a single man in battle, but he had reported three ships lost to storms, although the whispers were that the Persian pirates had captured the ships when they got separated from the main fleet. There had been an enquiry, of course, but no one had had the balls to stand up to Hyllos, lest they find them removed on the end of the late general's blade.

"Here we are at last," he muttered to himself. "Skaios, son of Seleukos, served as one of the Nautical Astoi on that campaign. He served upon the ship *Poseidon's Triton* and returned home to continue his life. He would have been a youth straight out of his two years' service at that time." Then Polydektos spotted Seleukos's name again further down the wooden board listing all the men who served under Hyllos. "Now, this is interesting."

Polydektos moved closer to the doorway of the records room

to allow some natural light to shine on the wooden military records board. "Cineas, son of Seleukos, was a hoplite on board the *Medousa's Gaze*, lost at sea with all hands during a storm."

Polydektos tapped the names on the wooden board and laughed quickly out loud. He went back inside the cool records room, sat down on a wooden bench, and looked at the names again. "Oh, Skaios—you blamed Hyllos's incompetence for the loss of your brother."

Polydektos memorised the names of Skaios's brother and father, returned the record to its rightful place, and left the Strategeion. The Agora was busier now in preparation for the Oskophoria procession at noon. In fact, most of the streets around the Agora were very busy, and it was a struggle to get through the crowds until he left the hub of the city. The minor streets and roads were still full of gaily dressed people in chitons of bright colours. Some of the young men had painted lips and cheeks and wore wigs to celebrate the dual sexuality of the god Dionysos.

He finally made it to Skaios's studio and found Olos inside, alone and half drunk. Two near-empty jugs of wine stood on the workbench to which his stool was pulled up, and his head was leaning down on his arms as he stared blankly at the floor.

"No, we are not open today. It's bloody Oskophoria, remember," Olos cried out without looking up from the dusty grey floor.

"I know, and the city is packed full of happy Dionysos-loving people. I hate it," Polydektos replied, entering the studio anyway. He looked around the place; it didn't look like much, if any, work had been done here since his first visit.

"Polydektos, my apologies." Olos sat up straight, though his eyes were not fully focusing on his unannounced visitor. "Festivals are when everyone is supposed to be happy, but what do I have to be happy about?"

"I know the feeling," Polydektos replied, pulling up a work stool so he could sit next to the sculptor.

"Here's to us, then." Olos grabbed his wine cup and toasted.

"I need to ask you something about Skaios."

"Ask away," Olos burbled drunkenly, draining what was left in his cup

"Did he ever mention his brother Cineas at all?"

"Not often; they weren't very close, even though they were twin brothers," was all that Olos offered.

"Did you ever meet him?"

"No, he died about four years before Skaios and I met. He didn't like to talk about his late parents and brother at all, really." Olos poured himself the dregs of the wine straight from the jug without watering it.

"Did he say anything else about his brother that you can recall?" Polydektos pressed.

"No, like I said before, he never spoke about him at all, not even to Anthousa as far as I know. Not that you can ask her, can you?" Anger flashed in Olos's eyes for a second and then softened as he began to weep.

Polydektos touched the sobbing sculptor's shoulder and stood up. Then another thought hit him. "Did Skaios have another studio elsewhere in or outside the city at all?"

"No." Olos shook his head and wiped his eyes on his tunic sleeve. "If we went to Sparta or Corinth to work, we would set up temporary studios in the cities we were operating in."

Polydektos nodded and rubbed at his beard. "Would you know anyone that knew Skaios and Cineas as younger men or boys?"

Olos just shook his head.

Polydektos went to leave, then stopped and half-turned back. "Who taught Skaios to sculpt?"

"He learnt from a young age from Kallimachos, the perfectionist," Olos said in a sleepy voice.

"Perikles knows him; he did some work on the frieze of the Temple of Athene Nike on the Akropolis. I think I met him a couple of times during the opening of the temple. Where does he live and work?"

Olos didn't answer. Polydektos turned fully around to see that the sculptor was asleep, in a drunken stupor. His head lay on the workbench, his eyes closed. Polydektos took a step closer and then stopped himself. Kallimachos was a well-known sculptor and architect; it wouldn't take him long to find him on his own. He left Olos to sleep off his drinking and headed back into the busy streets of Athens. He couldn't have picked a worse day to try and get around the polis. But he had a good idea who would know where Kallimachos lived or worked, so headed for a tavern he knew a few streets to the southwest of the Agora. It was a well-known place for artists, sculptors, and architects to hang out, drink, and loudly discuss their latest works-in-progress.

Unluckily for Polydektos, the Oskophoria procession was just crossing the Agora as he arrived at the back of a crowd five or six rows deep. He could do little but wait impatiently as the two noble young men, dressed, made-up, and walking like women, led the parade through the city, carrying branches laden with grapes. The procession started at the temple of Dionysos and would head through the city on a winding route out to the stadium, where a goat would be sacrificed and then relay races run for the crowds to join in and enjoy. It reminded Polydektos of family days out at the festivals when his children were young and his wife had still been the only woman for him.

It took half an hour for the parade to pass through the Agora and another twenty minutes for the crowds to dissipate enough for him to work his way across to Sculptor's Tavern. Feeling a simmering frustration rising in him, he entered the tavern. To his relief, the person he wanted to talk to was indeed inside. As he weaved his way over to a table at the rear where two men were sitting, Polydektos was glad to be away from the noise, music, and crowded streets.

He knew the neat, well-dressed person he had come to see, but in contrast, the other man was a rough looking metic, wearing boiled leather chest armour and carrying a short sword for everyone to see.

"Polydektos, my old friend, I didn't expect to see you again so soon. Do you bring me news of Olagnos's murder?" asked the smartly attired, but slightly tipsy, man at the table as the former general approached.

"I am off the beaten track. Yes, I do, Pheidias. May I sit with you a while?"

"Plenty of room for another old soldier at the table." Pheidias the sculptor offered an empty stool between him and his drinking companion.

Polydektos didn't like sitting with his back to the tavern, but had little choice but to sit down. He noticed Pheidias's stern-faced companion was drinking water, as opposed to Pheidias's hardly watered wine. Oskophoria apparently brought out the drinker in most people he had met this festival day.

Pheidias offered his palm across the table to his silent companion and said, "This is Bias of Boeotia." The stubbled, dirty-faced man pushed out his bottom lip and nodded slightly at Polydektos.

"A new friend?"

Pheidias leant closer to Polydektos and whispered, "A bodyguard."

"You think you are in danger, then?"

"Have a drink with me, Polydektos," Pheidias cried out so most of the tavern could hear. Then he leant in again to whisper. "One cannot be too careful after what has happened to poor Olagnos. I might be next on the Medousa's list of death."

"Then I hope Bias has polished his shield for the encounter," Polydektos said, trying to make his casual friend stay uneasy for the time being. He was parched so took some wine, diluted with three-quarters water, just to be civil.

Pheidias waved his hand over to his bodyguard. "See to that." His voice sounded like a rattled mother bird squawking at foxes circling around its tree.

"What help can you bring me, Polydektos?" he went on. "Just your presence here makes me feel safer."

Safer? Polydektos thought doubtfully. Three people had been turned to stone in the city, and he had little clue how to stop it. No one was safe from the Medousa.

"You know all the prominent sculptors in the city."

"I make sure I do, best to keep a wary eye on my rivals."

"Kallimachos did some work on the Akropolis. Is he still residing in the city, and if so, where does he live or work?"

Pheidias's wine paused halfway from the table to his lips. "*Old Katatexitechnos?* Yes, he is still here. He has a rented-out studio near mine. I saw him two days ago. He was working on a piece for one of the ten families, I think. Then he is off to Corinth for the winter, I think he said. Why?"

"I wish to talk to him, that is all." Polydektos didn't want to give too much away, as anything he said would be immediately reported back to Perikles.

"Is he under suspicion?" Pheidias lowered his voice again to ask.

"No. Can you take me to him?"

"What, now?"

"Yes, now," Polydektos nodded.

"But...but the crowds outside. Will I be safe?"

"You have me and Bias here at your side, which makes you safer than most people in Athens, my friend. Half the day is gone already," Polydektos urged as he stood up from his stool and drained the remainder of his drink.

"Oh...well, if you insist." Pheidias stood and Bias rose with him. Looking around like everyone else in the tavern was out to murder him, he left with Polydektos. Bias brought up the rear.

The crowds now congregated around the food and drink sellers or entertainers. Most had joined the end of the procession out of the city. Once past the Agora, the going got easier. Pheidias's nervousness mellowed as the street grew less busy and as he neared the street where he and Kallimachos had their studios.

"There it is," Pheidias said as he reached his large studio and pointed down the street to the smaller building where Kallimachos had set up shop. Four men were loading a heavy piece of marble onto the back of a two-horse-drawn waggon. "Do you wish for me to come with you?"

Polydektos smiled at the tentative offer of help from Pheidias. He knew he wanted to know what business the ex-general had with the older sculptor but was still worried for his life. "No need, my friend—have Bias here take you home and protect you. This could get a bit nasty," Polydektos lied, putting a comforting hand on the sculptor's shoulder.

"Yes, well, stay safe and let me know if you find anything out," Pheidias said in parting and went inside his own studio, which had another stern metic guard at the door. Bias followed him in, keeping a wary eye about the street before the door was shut and barred after. Smiling, Polydektos walked down the street and approached the men about to lift the man-sized block of marble off a temporary, waist-high reinforced wooden support and onto the waiting waggon.

"Is Kallimachos inside?" he enquired to the nearest of the four men.

The man just shrugged his shoulders and returned to the task at hand. These were probably just hired metics or slaves moving an unused piece of marble and no more. Frowning, Polydektos hurried inside the studio to find several more men inside moving and packing vases, busts, and sculptures into straw-lined boxes for transport. One man held a wooden board and seemed to be directing the others. Polydektos swerved around a short man carrying a large bust of a woman to reach the man in charge.

"Sorry, we are closed for now. Apollophane's shop down the street will have a few items on sale in the coming days." The busy man gave Polydektos a brief, cordial smile and returned to order about the slaves and metics.

Polydektos grabbed the man's nearest arm, shifting his attention from his wooden list to his visitor once more. "I am General Polydektos of Athens, friend to the First Citizen. I urgently need to know where Kallimachos is. This is state business."

Polydektos's grip and tone left no ambiguity in their measured strength.

"I'm sorry, General," the man replied quickly, looking down at his arm. "Kallimachos left this morning for the docks."

Polydektos let go of the man's arm. He had his full attention now. "To Pireás? When does his ship sail and where is he going?"

"I'm not privy to that information, I'm just a simple man he has hired to have his tools and certain items sent on a cargo ship to Corinth. His work on the Akropolis is finished, so he's returning to Corinth for the winter, I've heard."

Polydektos looked around the studio with his hands in his hair, taking in everything that the slaves and metics were packing away for transport. "I heard that also," Polydektos said, then rushed from the rented studio.

"Was he there?" Pheidias called from behind Bias in the

comparative safety of his studio doorway.

"No," Polydektos shouted as he ran past. He was puffed out by the time he made it to the Piraean Gate. Luckily, there was a stable nearby where he could hire a horse for the day, saving the need for the long walk down to the port. The horse was worth a couple of obols and would cut the time to get to the docks by more than half. He wasn't much of a sailor, but he knew the ships usually left on the early morning or early evening tides.

He rode the horse hard down the road between the Long Walls, probably its best run out in years. Polydektos was still short of breath, but at least his feet were getting a rest as he spurred on the horse. He zig-zagged between slow moving carts and pedestrians. He was quite enjoying himself by the time he reined the horse in as they reached the outskirts of the port. The horse seemed to have enjoyed the run also and brayed and snorted at having to slow to a trot. Another stable, owned by the same man as the one at Piraean Gate, took the horse from Polydektos. The metic in charge gave Polydektos a token with a horse's head on it so he could claim the hired horse back for the return journey up to the city.

He thought to ask among the local water rats for information about ships heading for Corinth, but their information always came at a price and Polydektos has used his last two coins on hiring the horse. The port was huge, and he counted a hundred or more ships and triremes of various sizes. He needed the correct ship and quickly. He had no choice but to head for the Blue Shrimp Tavern and ask for the lady that bore the same name.

Asking at the bar, he was directed towards two ruffians at a table close to the back of the tavern. One scarred-face man gestured for him to sit down next to him, while the other muscular ruffian went through the rear doorway. The first Pitch Tunic eyed him suspiciously, and Polydektos could do nothing but drum his fingers on the table and wait; the ship Kallimachos was on could be leaving port at any moment.

The rear door opened and the first Pitch Tunic gang member pointed at him and then past him into the room beyond. With a nod to the man at the table, Polydektos stood up and followed the first ruffian down a narrow passage, up some stairs to the next floor, and around an enclosed landing to the left. Ahead was a sky-blue painted door. The ruffian pointed towards it and left Polydektos to it.

"I give you thanks for the help and the excellent conversation," Polydektos called after him before trying the handle. The door opened into a bedroom separated into mini-rooms by sheets of different hues of blue and purple. An incense burner on the table by a shuttered window gave off heavy exotic fruit smells to mask the stench of the fish and the sea. In the centre of the room was a large, opulent oblong bed, not in keeping with the décor of the rest of the shady tavern by the docks.

Out of the bed stepped the Blue Shrimp in all her naked glory, proud and unabashed that Polydektos was in her inner chamber, a place few men or women got to experience. Part of the old Polydektos could not help but look at her tight curves and sinewy arms. The scars on her face, arms, body, and legs showed she'd had to fight for every drachma and every comfort, like this bedroom, probably all her life. To Polydektos, the scars made her look more attractive, not less. Yet he was not the man he was six months ago. Beautiful women, even unadorned ones, had many weapons they could use to bring down a strong man. First the Spartan woman, and now this thief was tempting his eyes. Polydektos was no longer swayed by base emotions like lust; they had led to his loss of the two women he had loved most in the world.

"Do you like what you see?" she asked, moving between the sheer sheets so he could see more of her beautiful form.

"I need your help in finding a ship. It is most urgent I find someone on board if they haven't already left port." Polydektos ignored her question and the sway of her hips as she approached. He could see how she held the command of the Pitch Tunics: by twisting their lusts and emotions to her will. He was sure that she had stabbed a few hearts and taken a few beatings along the way to this lofty position.

"It's always business with you, isn't it? You don't look at me like other men do." The Blue Shrimp stepped on tip-toes until only one sheer blue sheet separated them, her body pressed close to it. Her hard, dark nipples touched the thin material. She held her hands behind her back.

"I can't comment on what other men see. I see your beauty, yes, and your strong determination to be an equal of men in this cesspit of a port. I see beyond your naked allure and note the scars you bear, outside and probably also inside. I see your hands behind your back, where you probably hold a dagger or weapon of some kind. What I notice the most, having been there myself, is how very lonely you are at the top of your tree, even if you are surrounded by fruit," Polydektos concluded in earnest.

The Blue Shrimp smiled coyly out the side of one lip, accentuating a small scar there. Then she pulled not one, but two thin-bladed daggers from behind her back and placed them on the table next to the incense burner. She grabbed a pale blue peplos tunic from where it was draped over an ornate chair and slipped it over her head. She fixed the shoulder with two dull bronze brooches and tied it around the waist with a leather belt.

"You are not as shallow or as straightforward as the rumours and information tell me." She smiled with her lips, but frowned at him with her eyes, looking him up and down. "Now what do you need, and what has it to do with the Medousa Murders?"

"I need to find a ship heading for Corinth that has a man called Kallimachos on it."

"You bring me such easy tasks. He sails on the *Midnight Aphrodite* this very evening." The Blue Shrimp picked up a pair of sandals from under the chair and began to lace them on.

"Can you get me onto that ship to talk to him?"

"With ease, my new friend. The captain of that ship owes me several favours, and we have already procured one of Kallimachos's busts to help ensure a smooth passage to Corinth." The Blue Shrimp put the two daggers in the back of her belt and pulled her peplos over them.

"Are we friends now? Don't I get a say in this matter?" Polydektos asked as she ducked under the last sheet separating them.

"You have seen me as naked as the gods bore me into this world. Not just the flesh; you see a lot for a drunken old general of Athens from a famous family of heroes. You entered, and will exit, my bedroom without paying in blood or drachmas;

this makes you unique in my eyes. You look at me without lust, even though I have heard stories of your sexual appetites from the girls at the House of Javelins. We are friends for the moment at least, but that doesn't mean I won't stab you in the eye for an obol at a future date." The Blue Shrimp smiled back at him as she opened her bedroom door and led the way out of the tavern.

Walking beside the Blue Shrimp was an interesting experience for Polydektos. From leading an army, he was used to a certain reverence of command, but with her beside him, it was something slightly different, like he was carrying an invisible shield of the gods inside the slender frame of the woman beside him. Men and woman parted in mid-conversation to make way for her to pass. Men glowered at her, looking on with lust but also fear. She had built up something no sword or fearsome man could match; she had created a legendary reputation with the Pitch Tunics and her name.

"So, what is your real name, then? As we are friends," he ventured as they headed down one creaky plank towards the dock at which the *Midnight Aphrodite* was anchored.

"I had a name once, but that girl died a hundred humiliations and a thousand beatings ago. Only the gods know her now, and I will keep it that way until I meet them at Olympos and demand my rewards for the suffering I've endured in life. We are as close to friends as I will allow, so you can call me Blue if you wish, but never Shrimp. Shrimps get eaten."

Polydektos nodded and smiled to himself. What would his father Praxilios have thought of that idea? From Perikles the First Citizen to the Blue Shrimp of the Pitch Tunics; Polydektos had friends now in the lowest and loftiest places. Yet, at this moment he was not sure who posed the more danger to him.

They marched together to the gangplank of the ship bound soon for Corinth. A swift whispered conversation with the captain had them onto the gangplank in seconds. The captain of the *Midnight Aphrodite* escorted them past his sailors and belowdecks via a ladder, into a dingy, salty, wood-smelling world. He pointed to a cabin door, his own quarters given over to the famous sculptor and architect for the duration of the first leg of the voyage.

The captain nodded solemnly to them and headed back up on deck to give his final orders before they sailed that early evening. Polydektos looked at his companion, who shrugged her shoulders before he knocked on the cabin door.

"Captain?" a voice called from inside.

"Not quite," Polydektos answered, pushing the door open to find the ageing Kallimachos lying on a hammock reading a scroll by the light coming through a small open porthole in the side of the ship. The cabin was cramped and loaded with some of the sculptor's and the captain's belongings.

"Who in Hades's name are you?" Kallimachos asked, sitting up so sharply he bumped his head on the beams of the deck close above where he lay. He rubbed his forehead hard. "Don't I know you from somewhere?"

Polydektos thought about closing the cabin door, but the Blue Shrimp would only listen at it if he did. She stayed outside, silent and out of sight from the ship's only passenger.

"I am Polydektos, friend to Perikles and general of Athens," he announced, knowing that at one time both of these statements had been true, although he wasn't quite sure of their current validity.

"Oh yes, wasn't there a trial for murder or something?" Kallimachos dabbed with his fingertips at the place he had hit his head.

"Of which I was found not guilty, and the real culprits later found justice on the edge of my blade," Polydektos replied, trying not to lose his temper with the sculptor.

"Good for you, but why are you disturbing me in my cabin? Is there an issue with one of my works? Has Perikles sent you to bring me back to fix something? I'm about to set sail for Corinth, you know. I always winter there, better for my health."

Polydektos cut the older man off before he could burble on some more. "No, everything is fine. I wish to ask you about a former pupil of yours, Skaios."

"Oh, I see. Well has this something to do with him going missing? I've seen him twice since I've been back to Athens, but not to talk. We had an artistic falling out many years ago and have not talked since, you see."

"Did you know his brother Cineas?"

"Oh, of course I knew him. I was a friend of their father, Seleukos, and I taught them both to sculpt." The older man nodded and stopped rubbing his head.

"They were both talented sculptors, then?"

"Yes, I taught them both in my Katatexitechnos style. You could not tell them apart through their looks, but their skills in sculpting—there was a vast difference. Skaios was brilliant, precise, and dedicated to his work. Cineas had talent also, but his skills were slow and laboured, and he was always under his brother's shadow. Even though they were twins, like Hypnos and Thanatos, Skaios always bested his brother in athletic ability, and also with the girls, I remember. Skaios had just been betrothed to Anthousa before they left this very port to go on some military expedition. I can't remember where. They were both madly in love with her, you see, but only one brother returned alive, and Skaios seemed a changed man by the loss of his brother. We had an argument that he was wasting his life and talents, and we never spoke since. I heard he married sweet Anthousa and did quite well for himself in the end." Kallimachos looked down at the scroll in his hand with a sorrowful look of recollection.

"Did you ever try and reconcile your differences?" Polydektos casually put his hand on the cabin door frame. The gentle lapping motion of the sea against the cargo ship brought back memories of more arduous journeys of the past. The mind might forget, but the body didn't, it seemed.

"I sent messages over the years, but he never replied to any of them, you see. In the end, I gave up."

Polydektos rubbed his stomach as a cold queasiness spread out from his core. He would have to hurry this up. "Your style is to make your statues as lifelike as possible. Was Skaios also a perfectionist like yourself?"

"Oh yes, as a young man he was; that is all I can comment on first hand. I've seen some of his later works around Athens and other cities; his style seems grittier and leans more to warriors and creatures from history than it did in his youth. Men change and grow, and the way they perceive the world changes also. It is natural that change is reflected in their work." Kallimachos nodded.

"So, could Skaios make such a lifelike statue of a person in stone as to fool people into thinking a Gorgon had petrified the victim?"

"He could, but so could many sculptors, including myself. I thought Skaios was missing, presumed dead."

"No body or stone corpse has been found."

"Then you think Skaios might behind these awful Medousa Murders? He was one of the most talented students I ever had, and gentle and caring with it. I can't see him killing anyone, let alone his beloved Anthousa." Kallimachos frowned as he shook his head of wispy white hair.

"As you say, time changes men, not always for the good." Polydektos rubbed at his stomach. The gentle bobbing of the ship at port was increasing now. "I give you thanks for your time and answers, Kallimachos. I hope Poseidon speeds you to Corinth with calm seas."

"May Zeus shrine his celestial light upon these ghastly murders and show you the way to stop them, Polydektos."

Polydektos exited the cabin and closed the door behind him. He hurried up the ladder to the deck and off the *Midnight Aphrodite* as quickly as his shaking legs would allow.

"Polydektos, are you well?" The Blue Shrimp chased after the sea-sick former general.

Bending over a barrel, Polydektos breathed hard and closed his eyes. Being back on the dock helped a lot, and soon the cold feeling of nausea left him. He waved an angry hand in her direction. The last thing he wanted was to appear weak in front of the leader of the Pitch Tunics. After a while, he turned and sat on the barrel, thanking Asklepios the god of healing that he did not vomit in front of the Blue Shrimp.

Blue patted her hips with her palms. "So—did that aid our quest at all?"

"*Our* quest?" Polydektos raised his eyebrows at her inference that they were in any way partners in this investigation.

"I've always loved the tales of Perseus. To help you defeat Medousa would set me up amongst the Heroes too, wouldn't it?" The Blue Shrimp cocked her head to one side and gave a crooked smile.

Polydektos could not help himself; he slapped his knee and laughed heartily. Not at her, but with her. "If you really knew me, Blue, you would know that you are putting a wager on the wrong sprinter. I do this because I promised two women on my honour to find or stop the murderer. One of them is already dead, a victim of the Medousa. There is little glory and no drachmas in this, only the distinct possibility of failure, exile, or a swift hemlock death."

"You do yourself a disservice, General Polydektos, great strategos and vanquisher of the Maenad cult of Dionysos." The leader of the Pitch Tunics moved closer and held out her arm to him. "I find betting on long odds, though risky, brings all the more rewards."

Polydektos took her arm in his and grasped it at the elbow, letting her help him off the barrel. "I could do with some food and a little well-watered wine to ease my stomach."

"Then I know just the place, General." She smiled and led the way back to the tavern that bore her assumed name. Polydektos, in spite of his trust issues with women, was warming to this leader of thieves, smugglers, and dock rats. She could not be more than four years older than his late Kyra, but she had lived such a brutal life that the two couldn't be further apart.

"So, what did your little trip to see the sculptor on the ship do in helping us find the Medousa Murderer?" the Blue Shrimp asked as they finished their meal in her private rooms, next to her bedroom.

Polydektos wiped his mouth and set down his knife on the metal plate. He studied her face in the light of the two oil lamps on the table. He weighed in his mind whether sharing information with her would help or hinder his cause. She wanted the murders to cease because it impacted her gang's profits. Scared citizens would group together in their homes and employ guards for their property. Male citizens would avoid the dark docks at night, reducing the money made from cutpurses, wine and food sales in the taverns, and prostitution. Even with her claims of wanting to be a hero, which were false, he trusted her to some extent. Notoriety and infamy were good in her line of business; fame, though, would bring the authorities down on her. At this point, he had little to lose, and her eyes and ears in low places around the city would be helpful.

"Skaios had a twin brother who died serving under General Hyllos a decade or more ago. So, if we rule out the possibility of a Gorgon Sister stalking around Athens at night and turning people to stone, all the roads lead to Skaios being involved. I... we have learnt today that he had motives for killing all three of the people that have been petrified so far." Polydektos chose, for good or ill, to trust her with most of the information he had gathered.

"Then you are saying Skaios faked his own disappearance. He has been dressing up as Medousa, sculpting exact replicas of these people, and replacing them," the Blue Shrimp stated before drinking from her cup of wine.

"Or he was kidnapped and forced to sculpt these life-like statues for someone else with a grudge. If our thinking is true, it could even mean that these victims may still be alive and held captive somewhere," Polydektos mused, drinking some of his own much-watered wine.

"It explains the black horses and waggon that have been spotted around the houses of the victims," Blue continued, putting down her cup. "The statues would have to be transported to the houses and then put inside to appear the victim had been turned to stone."

"And they could use the waggon to transport the victims somewhere to be held captive or bury them outside of the city." Polydektos clicked his fingers as the image of men loading and offloading stone statues and bodies formed in his mind. "Apart from Hyllos, the first victim, the other two were on the first floor. It would take blocks and tackles and many men to lift a boxed statue through Olagnos's bedroom window. The stairs in his rooms were too tight and low to accommodate the stone replica of a man. I found straw in his bedroom and evidence that someone had been through the window, probably by ladder. Wouldn't people have noticed such an effort? The first two victims had their servants scared off by the Medousa, but Olagnos's servants were throttled to death and then placed around his stone body afterwards."

"Why not take the bodies and leave stone replicas?" the Pitch Tunic leader asked.

"Because Skaios did not know them well enough or have time to produce a reasonable likeness in stone," Polydektos replied.

"And there might not be room to safely hide four bodies in the waggon," the Blue Shrimp pointed out.

"Skaios could have been sculpting his victims months in advance. It would take a while to carve new victims chosen since his disappearance."

"We need to find where he is hiding out and taking his victims, then."

"We need to find that waggon and horses. It might lead us to Skaios—or worse, the Medousa," Polydektos added grimly.

"I will have my people scour Athens for it," she replied.

"Good." Polydektos stood. "I think it is time I got back to Darios; he does worry so."

"Can't keep the faithful hound waiting. Then I will accompany you to the edge of my domain, the stables at the edge of the port."

"I have a horse waiting there for me."

"I know," she replied with a wink and led him out of the room.

CHAPTER THIRTEEN

It was dark by the time Polydektos made it back to the city. He dropped the hired horse back to the stable, where the owner gave him back his money.

"I don't know what I've done to get a refund," he told the stable owner.

"The Blue Shrimp sends her regards." The owner gave him a gap-toothed smile and led the hired horse back into the stable for the night.

The mood of the Oskophoria festival had changed from fun and games to a child-free drunken revelry. It had been a long day, and Polydektos was feeling weary of mind and body. A few men were dressed and painted as women, and a few bolder unmarried women were dressed up as soldiers. The noise and the sound of laughter were not music to his ears, and he made his way through the crowds of the Kollytos District towards the Itonian Gate, which led out of the city again towards Darios's home.

It was night, so he had to wait for the guards to open the gates. At least he was away from the festival crowds. He would brief Darios on what he had learnt today and then seek his bed swiftly after. Polydektos yawned and waved at one of the guards he knew by sight from using the gate so much since lodging with Darios. The gates opened wide. Polydektos went to exit but was halted by a waggon trundling into the city. He waited on the side of the road as the waggon made its way through the gate. The hooded, long-bearded Greek man driving the waggon was dwarfed by his bulkier companion next to him. The latter man seemed Egyptian to Polydektos's eye and looked as wide as two men and two heads taller than most. He has not seen such a bulk of a man for many a year.

He let the dark waggon pass and then looked to see what it was carrying, but the rear was empty. The waggon continued up the road and into the city. Polydektos watched it trundle on its way.

"We are about to close the gates again. Are you coming or going, General?" The guard asked him. Polydektos looked at the guard and saw that he was standing in the way of the gates. For some reason only the gods knew, he stepped back into the city.

He looked down at his weary, sandaled feet and then up the straight road that led to the part of the city called Limnai. He wondered why his legs had seemingly moved without him ordering them to. He started slowly and then increased his pace, following the dark waggon from a safe distance. He felt like Athene was leading him, somehow. Was this the waggon that transported the stone likenesses of the supposed Medousa victims around the city? There were hundreds of waggons in the polis; why was he suddenly drawn to this one?

He pulled his himation up to cover his head, gripped his hidden sword, and followed the slowly rumbling waggon as it rolled down the roads of Athens. He kept to the shadows at the roadsides, or followed behind other people if they were going in the same direction for any amount of time. The waggon turned right before the Odeon, then north again into the Diomea Quarter of the city. The buildings were sparser here, and fewer and fewer people were on the road.

Even though his feet, shins, and ankles were aching now and the night growing chill, Polydektos continued to track the black waggon north through the city.

The driver stopped his horses halfway around the corner of a house at a crossroads. Polydektos could only see the rear end of the halted waggon, so he crept up the side of the house to get a look at what the two men at the front were doing. The hairs on the back of his neck bristled and, on instinct, he drew his short sword from under his outer himation. He peeked round the corner, only to see something moving towards his head at high speed. He jerked his head back as a huge fist crashed into the side of the house, cracking a hole in the bricks. His army-trained reflexes saved him, but also caused him to fall backwards on the hard road surface. The giant of a man loomed over him like the moon eclipsing the sun. The night was gone from view. Only the Titan-sized Egyptian could be seen.

Polydektos raised his sword to stab at the man, but the hulking shadow caught the blade and easily wrenched the weapon from his grasp. He watched on, wide-eyed in the dark, as the giant snapped the blade in half with his bare hands and threw a piece away to either side of him. Polydektos tried to scramble backwards on his behind, but the Egyptian giant grabbed his left ankle and dragged him back.

Polydektos ignored the cuts on his back from the stones in the road and kicked at his attacker's forearm with his free foot. It was like kicking a boulder and did nothing to dislodge the giant's grip on his ankle. A bloody hand gripped his tunic and pulled him to his feet, then up off the ground entirely. Polydektos glimpsed the shadow of the other man near the waggon as he punched the giant with all his might. The Egyptian's head cracked back a little, but so did at least two of the former general's fingers.

He couldn't help but cry out in a furious rage at the pain.

"This is your last warning. I have no bone to pick with you, Polydektos," the man in the shadows said in strangely accented Greek.

"Who are you? Why are you doing this?" Polydektos cried as he tried to pry open the tall man's grip with his undamaged hand. "Skaios?"

"You should have left it alone, Polydektos. Give up now before you lose everything. I am sorry for your loss," the bearded man in the shadows stated.

"What?" Polydektos exclaimed, a moment before a massive fist slammed into the side of his head, knocking all sense from him.

Polydektos awoke to a world of pain. His eyes fluttered into slits as harsh morning sunlight glared into his eyes, causing more pain to his already throbbing head. The creak of wood and the judders of the road screamed to his mind one fact: he was in the back of a waggon.

The pain in his hand, his puffed and swollen face, and his light-blinded eyes were all ignored as he sat up in the back of the waggon, fully expecting to be knocked down again into darkness any second. His left eye wouldn't open more than a tiny slit, and he felt arms grab him gently. He struggled for a second, fearing the giant of a man was going to finish him off, but he saw only a woman on the back of a donkey-drawn cart. This wasn't the black waggon from last night, and his companion was the Blue Shrimp.

"Easy now, General, you have taken a bit of a beating," she said in as near an approximation of a caring voice as she could mimic.

"Where am I? What happened?" Polydektos asked, but his voice sounded strange to him. He touched the side of his face with his good hand to find it bruised and swollen, making it hard to talk properly. He had a splitting headache.

"On the road, back to your dog's house."

Polydektos blinked tears from his eyes and could see they were not far from his friend's home.

"Ow," he said, touching various tender parts of the left-hand side of his face. "How did I get here?"

"One of my eyes and ears found you beaten unconscious near the temple of Hera. I came and got you and am bringing you home. It looks like you found someone who didn't like you, but not enough to kill you." The Blue Shrimp gave him one of her lopsided grins as she pointed to his hand. "I set your broken fingers and bound them. I'm amazed that did not wake you up."

"It was them...I found them," Polydektos said quietly. His lips, jaw, and ear hurt when he spoke.

"Found who? What are you talking about, man? Found a few fists, more like." The Blue Shrimp offered him some wine. Polydektos drank some, then used more to rinse out his mouth and spit over the side of the cart. It left a red stain on the dry sandy rocks by the roadside.

"The black horses drawing the black waggon. There were

two men on board. A Greek man with a long bushy beard and a huge Egyptian-looking one. He hit me once and that was enough to knock me senseless. He was as tall as a Titan and as strong as Herakles."

"Where did this one-sided fight happen?" Blue asked, intently staring at him with her vivid green eyes.

"In the Diomea District, by the second crossroads there."

"I will get my eyes and ears onto this. They seem an odd pair and should have been noticed by one of my many friends around the city. We will find these men or the waggon and put an end to all of this mischief-making." She looked up over the driver of the cart. "We are here."

Polydektos blinked his watering eyes and saw they had indeed passed the lemon grove and had entered Darios's small-holding outside the city walls. The Blue Shrimp patted the cart driver on the shoulder. "Help me get him inside."

The man nodded and got down from the cart and went to the rear to help Polydektos down. The two Pitch Tunics pulled him out and onto his feet. Polydektos could just about stand, but the thumping dizziness in his head made it hard to walk straight, so they helped him inside.

"Dog! Your master is here," the Blue Shrimp called out as she kicked open the front door.

"Darios," Polydektos called, before turning to the leader of the Pitch Tunics. "He has a name, you see."

"I'm a bitch, he's a dog. You are the only lofty general with Heroes' blood I know," she said with a chuckle. "Check the bedrooms."

The cart driver did as he was ordered as his leader helped Polydektos into the centre of the room. "No one here," the man said as he returned from his quick search of the small house.

"He may be outside, throwing pots," Polydektos suggested.

The cart driver opened the rear door, and with her arm around his shoulder, the Blue Shrimp helped Polydektos outside into the morning sunshine again. The low morning sun was in their eyes, but they could see Darios sitting at his potter's wheel, looking in their direction.

"Darios," Polydektos called out, blinking his moist eyes

rapidly against the blinding sunshine. It didn't help that his left eye was nearly swollen shut. They moved closer, but his friend did not seem to hear him.

"Up, you dog, your friend Polydektos needs your aid, man," the Blue Shrimp called out as they crossed the yard to the potter's hut.

Even though it was a warm morning, Polydektos suddenly felt like an icy blade had been plunged down the back of his spine.

The words of the bearded Greek man last night came to mind. *You should have left it alone, Polydektos. Give up now before you lose everything. I am sorry for your loss.*

"Darios!" he cried and pushed the Pitch Tunic woman aside to stagger towards the open door of the potter's shed. As soon as the shade of its roof covered his eyes, he could see what his heart had feared.

His friend, companion, and fellow soldier looked back at him with unseeing stone eyes.

"By the gods!" The Blue Shrimp, following Polydektos, saw what had happened to his friend.

"The Medousa has been here," the cart driver called out in panic.

"Stand your ground," his leader snarled at him and then went to Polydektos's side.

Polydektos half-slumped to the ground, resting his elbow on the potter's wheel to steady himself. His left hand touched the face of his friend. How stupid had he been? He had seen the black waggon enter the city, but he never thought its previous deadly destination had been here. His fingers touched the cold stone face as tears flowed down his swollen cheek. A rage so fierce boiled up inside of him as his mind screamed to Olympos; *not again, not again!*

"Polydektos, this is an evil act beyond anything I have ever done or seen. He was a good man; I liked him a lot." Blue tried to touch his shoulder, but he shrugged her off and punched the potter's wheel with his bandaged hand. He heard either bone or the wheel break before a tidal wave of pain engulfed his fatigued body and he fainted away again into the welcoming numbing darkness.

Polydektos awoke in his own cot in the guest bedroom of Darios's house. He turned his numb head to see the Blue Shrimp looking down at him, mopping his brow with a wet cloth. Her face was lighter and more compassionate than her usual severe look. She could almost be his daughter, such was the blurring of his vision.

"Kyra?" He reached up and touched her face with his good hand.

Compassion turned to concern as she moved back from his touch. "Who is Kyra—your daughter?"

"She was," he gulped; his throat was hoarse and dry. He blinked, the gentleness of Kyra's face replaced with the beautiful but scarred and worn face of the Blue Shrimp.

She helped lift his head so he could drink a cup of water. Half of the liquid spilt down his chin and neck, but it refreshed him. "I've sent my man for a doctor. I think that Egyptian may have cracked your skull. He will then take word to your friend, Alkmaion. Do you wish me to contact the boy you stood trial with...what was his name?"

"Talaemenes. No, I would keep him as far from this as possible for the moment, lest he suffer the same fate as everyone I love."

"As you have no love for me, I will take my chances, old man, and stay to keep you safe." She gently let his head fall back onto the pillow.

"I am a broken man, cursed by the gods to live on as everyone around me dies. Why do you stay?" Polydektos was nauseous, and his spirit felt like it was floating just above his body at the moment.

"I too am cursed by the gods, Polydektos. Even though we are worlds apart, I see you as a kindred spirit. I love no one and can't fully understand the loss you have borne this year, yet I know pain and suffering. I have no high friends like Perikles or Sokrates, only lowlife scum like myself, but I will not see the city I was born in suffer these terrors and deaths. I hate my life and I hate Athens, but it is the only home I have ever known."

"Then together, unloved and cursed, we will hunt these

murderers to the edges of the known world and not rest until
they are ended. I have had my fill of being on the back foot; we
will take the fight to them." Polydektos grasped her hand in his
tightly, even though it jarred his head and made the room spin.

"First, you must get better. Wait! I hear a horse approaching.
Stay here and remain silent." The Blue Shrimp drew her daggers
and left the bedroom. Polydektos tried to turn his body over,
to rise from his bed, but the movement caused black spots to
appear before his eyes. He had no choice but to lie down again.

Blue returned with a white-bearded and sparse-haired doctor, one she often used to patch up the bare-knuckle boxers she
owned.

Alkmaion arrived just after the doctor left. The Egyptian's punch
had indeed mildly fractured Polydektos's skull. He would need
at least three days' bed rest, and the injury would slowly heal
itself. He hadn't bled from his nose or ears, which was a good
sign, and the doctor said he should make a full recovery in time.

Alkmaion knelt by Polydektos's sick bed, clasping his hands
over his friend's uninjured one. "I shall make arrangements
for Darios within the week, my old friend." He was weeping
openly; the three of them had been close comrades for over
twenty years. Alkmaion was the eldest of the three. "You shall
come and stay at my farm until you are better."

"No, I cannot risk your and your wife's lives also. It is too
dangerous to be my friend at the moment."

"You can't stay here on your own, Polydektos; it's plainly not
safe," Alkmaion pleaded with his former military commander.

"I will look after him, somewhere safe, away from here and
the city," the Blue Shrimp offered from the doorway where she
leant, her arms crossed.

"Surely you do not trust her with your life?" Alkmaion spat.

"I trust you, Alkmaion, to follow my wishes to the letter.
No word of this gets out, and do not tell Talaemenes. We keep
the fate of Darios a secret, like it never happened. We will bury
the stone body by the lemon grove; until we find his flesh and
blood body, he is not dead to the world. I will go with Blue—best
you do not know where. Then we will make our plans against

these men masquerading as Gorgons and end the terror they have brought to Athens. Perhaps their hubris will get the better of them if no word of Darios's demise gets out. It might put them off their step. Blue's people will scour the city shadows for them and any that have seen them. When I am better, we will wreak the bloody vengeance of Theseus upon them, my friends," Polydektos swore gravely.

"You called me Blue." The Pitch Tunic leader turned away and left the bedroom.

Alkmaion dug a grave and buried the stone body of their friend by himself. He wasn't completely sure that this wasn't their old war comrade, turned to stone by a creature from the Time of Heroes. He did his best to give a fitting send-off to a friend he had fought alongside for twenty years. He mourned for his brother-in-arms; there would be no laying out or day of mourning for Darios.

He said his final farewells and returned inside, out of the warm sunshine, to wash his face, hands, and armpits. Polydektos lay inside on his bed, talking in whispers to the Pitch Tunic girl who had suddenly become a trusted ally. He had a long draught of wine before heading into the bedroom to see how his general was.

"Is it done?" Polydektos turned his eyes to look in Alkmaion's direction, as turning his head made it ring as though a huge bell were right next to each ear.

"Yes, my general," Alkmaion replied, glancing with unease at the Blue Shrimp, who sat on a stool on the other side of the bed.

"My men should be here soon," she said, picking at her nails.

Silence fell among the awkward trio, and Polydektos drifted off into an uneasy sleep.

The jarring travel back into the city and then out between the Long Walls was maddening to Polydektos's injured head. He threw up into a wooden bucket at least three times on the journey down to the port. Alkmaion had left them at the Piraean Gate to return to his farm, though he was loath to leave Polydektos in the Pitch Tunics' care.

"Your friend does not like me." Polydektos opened his eyes and looked keenly at the woman to whom he had he entrusted his life. After Gala's betrayal, he had vowed never to trust another woman fully again. Not that he trusted Blue completely, but they had the same goals for the time being: to stop the Medousa Murders. The stink of fetid salt water and fish told him they were deep inside the port now.

"He doesn't trust you."

"And do you trust me?" Blue cocked her head to one side to get closer to Polydektos's line of vision.

"I have little choice."

She pouted, feigning sadness. "That wounds me, Polydektos. I thought we were fast friends, like you and Perikles perhaps."

Polydektos laughed grimly and then groaned as the crack in his skull flared with pain. "It is true, Perikles and I are old friends, but I don't trust him either."

"Politicians, lovers, and thieves, eh?" she said, repeating part of an old Athenian saying.

"Where are you taking me?" he asked as the covered waggon lurched to a painful stop.

"Where every man would count you lucky to be…my bed," she replied, blowing him a kiss as the rear flaps of the waggon were thrown open from outside.

Polydektos, unlike any other man in the port who would have gladly swapped places, hated his time in the Blue Shrimp's bed. The inactivity was terrible, gnawing at his mind like he had maggots inside his brain. He could not do anything to help catch the murderers of Darios, making him a terrible patient. He just went over and over in his mind all the mistakes he had made since starting this quest to stop the murders.

The Blue Shrimp spent her nights naked next to him; after all, it was her large bed. Apart from the late hour when she would undress and clamber in beside him, her visits were maddeningly infrequent. As a general, he relied on reports to form any future strategies. He had spent the first day throwing up every time he tried to do anything, even reach over for a cup of water.

The second day, he could at least drink without being sick, and on the third he managed to pull his legs out and sit on the edge of the bed. The purple and blue-veiled, perfumed bedroom swam around him like he was looking through a large crystal, but he kept down his stomach contents. His bruises had come out livid purple and yellow, but the swelling around his eye had gone.

"Progress," Blue said as she came through the door and saw him sitting on her bed pulling on his tunic, which has been washed since he had been there.

"Yes, I can now dress myself like any two year old. But unlike them, I cannot stand without the world spinning and sending me crashing to the floor. Any news?" he asked through gritted teeth.

"We have checked all the stonemasons, carvers, and quarrymen we know. They have not seen or heard of the pair that attacked you," she replied, working her way lightly between the sheer hanging sheets.

"Someone must know them!" Polydektos cried angrily. He put his palm to his head as a wave of pain ripped through half of his skull.

"You would think they would stand out like your broken fingers, but they seemed to be a mystery to even my eyes and ears around the city. Unless they do not work with stone, or use some middle metic we have yet to find. I will not go to my grave with this mystery hanging over us, I swear." She finally made it under and around the hanging sheets to sit gently next to him on her bed.

"Graves," Polydektos muttered.

"What did you say?" she asked, putting a gentle hand on his leg. "I did not quite catch your words."

"Gravestones, markers. They have a black waggon and horses. We have been looking at sculptors when we should be looking at death itself. They are carriers of the dead, gravestone masons. You see such horse-drawn carriages in the city every day. There is not a day goes by without one funeral or another happening. They hide in plain sight as carriers of the dead."

"I will get every man, woman, and child onto this," she said, getting up from the bed.

"I will come too. I can't lay in your bed forever," he said, reaching up his hand to her.

"I don't know, I've gotten used to you being there, Polydektos. A naked, handsome man in my bed that wants nothing from my body is a rarity in my life. I hope I am not that unattractive." She cocked her head again and eyed him from head to toe.

"The old me would not have wasted the opportunity of lying naked next to such a beauty, but I am not that man anymore. I'm not sure what kind of man I am, or what use I am to Athens now, but take it as no slight. You have strength like Herakles, beauty like Aphrodite, and the cunning of Dolos. I need your help, Blue," he said reaching up to her again.

"Elektra," she whispered, looking down at her feet for a moment. Then she grasped his arm and pulled him to his feet. "My real name is Elektra."

He smiled grimly at her. "Let us catch these killers together, then, Elektra."

"I trust you like the father I never knew or wanted. You have a truth and honour about you, Polydektos. Something we rarely see around this port. But do not *ever* say my name aloud again," she warned.

"I understand," he nodded. "I swear on my daughter's grave to take your name to my own." The movement of his head made the room pitch and roll for a moment, like he was on the deck of a ship on stormy seas. The Blue Shrimp steadied him and then handed him his washed and dried clothes to wear. His head and face felt tender, but once he walked down to the rear exit of the dockside tavern he was feeling more like himself. The air outside the small, rubbish-strewn courtyard was less than fresh, but it woke his mind from the bed lethargy.

"Wine?" she offered from the back doorway.

"Water or apple juice," he replied, taking in a deep breath of the salty port air.

"I will find us a table to sit down at."

Polydektos went to nod, then stopped himself, raising a hand instead. He took many breaths of the cool sea air through his mouth. He wondered how he had ended up here, in Pireás among thieves and killers, when he had started the year in his own villa with his wife and daughter around him. He looked down at his bare hands. He may be bruised and slightly broken, but he still had breath in his body. If you can breathe, you can think and fight, he believed. He had hit the bottom of a deep well, and there was nothing but water below his feet. The only way now was up, and he loved a fight against all the odds.

CHAPTER FOURTEEN

Polydektos found walking much gentler on his cracked skull than taking the Blue Shrimp's cart or one of the horses from the stables near the port. He had put his trust in Elektra once more as she shaved off his greying beard and gave him old clothes and a dirty stained cloak to wear to conceal himself. He had rubbed his face, neck, hands, and forearms with blackberries to give himself a swarthier complexion. He carried his short sword hidden beneath his disguise as he took the long walk back up to the city. He chewed mint leaves to aid his painful headache as he walked in a bent manner, holding a staff he had purchased back in the docks. He looked and smelled like a rather fruity old beggar, or that was his hope.

The Blue Shrimp had other matters to attend to in her realm of thieves and cutthroats. Polydektos didn't want to know what these matters were, and she didn't offer. He knew her contacts were scouring the city for the men who attacked him, but he couldn't and wouldn't lie idle in her bed, comfortable as it was, doing nothing.

He reached the city and bought a waterskin and more mint leaves at a stall by the roadside. He wondered as he walked the streets of Athens: with Talaemenes busy with his military training, and only Alkmaion in the know, if he died on these streets in his beggar's disguise, would anyone really miss him? Trekhos, Aristaeos, and a few old army comrades might, in time. Perikles would mourn him outwardly in public, but probably would be glad to get shot of him.

Polydektos needed to feel like he had a purpose to his life once more. He had drifted along since his ex-lover had murdered his family. Even with the Medousa Murders, he had been half-hearted in his pursuit of the culprits. Perikles thought him a failure, and he hadn't wanted to disappoint the First Citizen. Now that Darios was gone, it was suddenly more personal. He would catch these men and stop the deaths and fear that hung over the city. Perikles might have a better opinion of his old friend then, but that wasn't what drove him now; he wanted to prove to himself that he was a useful citizen of Athens once more. He also wanted to make amends to his dead family and undertake heroic deeds before he joined them in death.

He made his way through the city, unnoticed and unac-costed, through the Street of Tombs and then out through the Dipylon Gate. He wanted to visit the graves of his family, but there were too many people around, and he did not want to blow his disguise so quickly this morning.

A funeral procession soon arrived, and Polydektos kept out of the way, pretending to mourn at an old, worn gravestone. The waggon was black, but the horse was chestnut-coloured and its driver, a bald man with a large gut, was not the one he was after. He waited until the body of a young woman was taken to her funeral pyre before moving. The waggon and its driver moved out of the way and waited as a mark of respect until the funeral was over. While the mourning family and friends gathered closer to the pyre, Polydektos approached the driver of the waggon.

The driver tried to shoo him away. "Get away from here—show some respect to the dead, you Thracian scum."

"Thracian? You aren't much of a traveller, are you?" Polydektos replied with annoyance; he had been going for the Egyptian look. "I want to ask you something."

"Ask yourself the last time you had a bath. Now hop it, before I get down and kick your dirty arse out of the cemetery," the driver said, jerking his thumb back towards the Dipylon Gate.

Polydektos turned his back on the funeral so only the wag-gon driver could see him open his beggar's cloak. He showed the man an obol in his left hand and his short sword in his right. "I have some questions for you, driver, and I don't care which hand of mine gets the answers, but you might."

The driver heard the strength and menace in the beggar's voice and realised the man before him was not as old and feeble as he thought. He pointed to the beggar's left hand. Polydektos flicked the coin up to the driver.

"Do you attend to many of these funerals?"

"Nearly every day of the year. What is it to you?" the driver answered, resentful of being harried at a funeral when he was working.

"Have you seen a couple of men in the same line of work as you? One a Greek with a long beard, the other a towering, Egyptian-looking bruiser?"

"I can't say I have," the driver replied haughtily.

"Do you have anyone else that works with you, or for you, to ask?"

"I work alone, and I have not seen these men you have described. Now leave me be—I have a job to do."

Polydektos pointed his sword at the man and then hid it away under his cloak again. With a grunt, he wandered off into the cemetery without another word.

He waited in Kerameikos for the rest of the day. Haranguing, bribing, or threatening the funeral waggon drivers for information got him nowhere until nearly the last funeral of the afternoon. He wearily approached a younger waggon driver with a kindly demeanour. The youth answered without the need for threats or coin.

"I've not seen such men, but my cousin Nisos sometimes does funerals after dark, and he has seen many a strange sight in Kerameikos after the sun has set."

"They have funerals at night?" Polydektos hadn't heard of such a thing.

The young man nodded. "Very popular with some of the older families, and some oddballs that follow the ways of Hades and Kore."

"Could I talk to your cousin?"

"I'm heading back to the yard now. I'd be glad of the company," the happy-go-lucky young man said, patting the seat beside him.

"You are a tribute to your parents and Athens for doing such a kindness to an old beggar like me," Polydektos said, climbing up to sit next to the young man.

"Anything for a hero of Athens like you, Polydektos," the young man said, and cracked the reins, directing the horse to turn the funeral waggon around to face the road back to the gate.

"You recognise me like this?" Polydektos could hardly contain the disappointment in his voice.

"You are one of my heroes, General. The populace loves you," the young man said.

"And you saw through my disguise. What is your name, son?" Polydektos said, rubbing at his blackberry-stained chin.

"Erebos." The boy nodded and drove the waggon back towards the city walls. "I just thought you had some sort of allergic reaction to something you ate."

Polydektos couldn't help but smile and then laugh at the cheery way the young Athenian lad spoke.

"You have keen eyes, Erebos." Polydektos patted the boy's back. "So, you are named after the god of darkness?"

"Yes, my mother and father had a bet on whether I'd be born during the day or night. My mother said night and won. My father thought he knew everything, you see, so to spite my mother he named me after the darkness deity," Erebos said cheerily as they passed through the Dipylon Gate.

"With that name, were you teased as a boy?" Polydektos asked to make conversation as they rode through the city. It also took his mind off the pain the jarring ride was causing to his head. Also, he liked the sound of the boy's voice; it was ever so uplifting.

"A little, but I always warned other children I'd curse them to live in eternal darkness. That used to shut them up. Could be worse—my parents had another bet when my younger sister was born."

"And what is she called?"

"Well, my father lost the bet again, so he named her after the goddess of luck, Tyche," the lad laughed.

Despite the pain in his head from his wounds, and in his heart from the loss of Darios, Polydektos could not help but laugh with his new friend.

The woman with the red cloak left the shadows from where she watched Polydektos pass, smiling at his laughter. He had been through many trials that would have broken lesser men, and he still had more dark roads ahead of him, she descried. She moved unseen back into a dark alleyway and was lost unto the night.

Erebos, along with his older cousin Nisos, had a small yard near the Diochares Gate. They had two horses, but only the one waggon. Erebos, in spite of his godly namesake, worked during the day five days a week, and Nisos worked the other two days and some nights when required. It worked out to an average of three funerals after dark each week.

They had four rooms above their shop and yard, which was also where Tyche lived with her parents until a suitable husband could be found for her. It was cramped living, but the cooking fire was warm after the chill night fell and it felt good to be in the company of a family again. Polydektos would live in a cave on a remote mountainside in abject poverty if it meant he could have his family around him once more.

The father and mother welcomed him into their home as a friend and treated him like a living demigod, giving the finest food and wine they could spare. Tydeos, the father of Erebos and Tyche, had served with him on an old campaign under Perikles's command. The father liked his wine, tales, and wagers. Polydektos had to talk of old wars and better times before he could politely get Nisos alone when he went to feed the horses. The sun was fully set, and only a torch lit the dim stable from outside.

"So, are you working tonight, Nisos?" Polydektos leant against a wooden support post as the cousin of Erebos gave the two horses some hay.

"Sadly not, but I have two funerals for tomorrow night." Nisos, unlike his cousin, had a more sombre tone to his voice. He looked in his mid-twenties.

Polydektos cleared his throat and pushed himself off the post. "You like the work, then?"

"Yes, it gives me time to think, and be away from here at night," Nisos replied in a quieter voice.

Polydektos caught a grim look on the man's face in the torchlight.

"Your uncle likes his drink?" Polydektos ventured.

"So do a lot of men, but not all fritter away the family's hard-earned money on frivolous wagers that rarely come off. I am glad he and my aunt took me in after I was orphaned, but if we held onto the money Erebos and I earn, we could expand the business and buy another waggon." Polydektos could hear the bitterness in the young man's words.

"It will not always be like this, Nisos; you will get your day in the sun." Polydektos walked over and patted the lad on the back. "I am looking for some other nocturnal funeral drivers Erebos told me you might have seen. One is a long-bearded Greek, and the other a huge Egyptian fellow."

"I have seen those men. Twice in Kerameikos, after dark, and once in the city heading up Arcarnai towards the Gate."

"Have you spoken to them at all? Do you know where they reside?"

"They keep to themselves, taking in a foreign language I've not heard nor can understand."

"Was it Persian, perhaps?" Polydektos pressed.

"No, my uncle knows a few words of Persian from his time in the army. He did not recognise them. If you say this hulk of a man is Egyptian, then maybe that is what they speak," Nisos said with a shrug.

"So they always speak in this foreign tongue, never in Greek?"

"When they are alone, yes. If they talk to mourners, only the bearded man speaks, in Greek. He has a strange accent to him, but the way he talks sounds like he is from Athens originally. I did hear two words I recognised when they spoke together, Greek words mixed in with the other tongue they converse in," Nisos said to give Polydektos hope.

"What words?"

"Mine and Tartaros." Nisos shrugged again. "I'm not sure how that helps you, or what the words mean."

"I do, boy," came a new voice at the entrance to the stables, followed by a loud burp. Polydektos turned to see the father of the house pissing against the side of the stable wall. He cleared his throat, smiled at Nisos, and waited for Tydeos to finish his business—which seemed to go on forever, to the embarrassment of the ex-general and Nisos.

Tydeos coughed, shook himself dry, and looked up at Polydektos with the bloodshot eyes of a man who knew the dregs of a wine vessel all too well. "What did you want again?"

"You said you knew what the words *mine* and *Tartaros* have in common, apart from the place evil kings are sent after they die."

"When I was Nisos's age I worked in a mine north of the city. It was dubbed the Mine of Tartaros, as we found a deep abyss below the place where many men worked. They dug down in search of silver and good masonry stone but found only a sinkhole to the darkest place in the world. The silver had run out, and the mine was deemed too dangerous for even captured enemy slaves to work. They called it the Mine of Tartaros after the floor collapsed. It has been abandoned for over two decades now, haunted by the ghosts of the men who died. If you go inside, near the lip of the abyss, they say you can hear the souls of the men below crying out to be rescued." Tydeos sniffed and staggered forward and then back for no apparent reason. "May Hermes take their poor souls to the fields of everlasting sunshine."

"Whereabouts is this mine, exactly?" Polydektos moved closer to steady the drunken father.

"Less than half an hour by waggon, an hour by foot. Down, or should I say up, the north road to Acharnai. There is an eastern dirt road that leads off once you get past the second sacred burial site. If you hit the river crossing, you have gone too far. It is in the hills to the east. I'm sure the road will still be visible, if a little overgrown. The eastern dirt road leads right to its entrance; it was built for no other purpose than to bring stone and silver back to Athens." Tydeos seemed to hitch and throw up in his mouth, before swallowing the bile back down with an acid look on his drunken face.

"I give your family many thanks for your hospitality and information." Polydektos pulled his coin purse from his sword belt and then threw it at Nisos. "Here should be enough to buy a second waggon for your business, Nisos."

Nisos caught the coin sack with a look of wonderment on his face. "Your meeting with my cousin was a true gift from the gods, Polydektos."

Polydektos smiled and turned to the father, who was eyeing the coins Nisos was tumbling into his palm from the purse. "I will be back to check on Erebos and the new waggon. Tell Erebos farewell, but I will see him again soon."

"Oh yes, yes, my patron, Polydektos." Tydeos nodded in shock.

Polydektos leant into the father's ear and whispered. "If there is no new waggon when I return, Tydeos, I wager you will live to regret it."

With a wave, Polydektos wandered out of the yard. He covered himself with his beggar's cloak and made the long journey back to Pireás.

The Blue Shrimp tavern was at its height of evening business, rowdy and crowded to the hilt. An Armenian girl was dancing on one of the centre tables. She was oiled and bare apart from thin golden chains around her wrists, neck, and ankles. Two long, feathered pink fans both protected her modesty and gave glimpses of her exotic delights as she writhed, gyrated, and danced on the table. Polydektos made his way to the rear of the tavern, though it took a while and nearly started two fights with men who were straining their necks to see the flashes of bare flesh from the dancing girl. One of the Blue Shrimp's bodyguards saw him and let him up the stairs to her bedroom.

Polydektos cast off the beggar's cloak on the stair bannister and rubbed at his face. He felt drained after his first day out of bed, and his head was pounding like a team of miniature horses was running over and back across the top of his skull. He was thirsty, his left jaw ached and clicked, and he wanted the Blue Shrimp's soft bed more than anything.

"And what time do you call this?" Blue said sternly with her arms crossed as he opened the door to her bedroom. She was dressed in a simple blue peplos, tied at the waist with a golden belt but split at the side to reveal her skin from ankles to armpit.

"I found some vital information during my day as a beggar. Grab that wine jug and bring it over to the bed, as I am parched and tired," he said, standing up straight and looking her in the eyes.

"Generals and beggars. I have taken both to my bed for coin in my ragged youth, but never have they been one and the same person. Grab the wine yourself if you want it, and wash that blackberry off your face or you'll not get within a diaulos of my clean bedsheets," she warned with her scar-twisted smile. As she made her way to the bed under the sheer sheets draped across the bedroom, her belt and then her peplos fell to the floor. Polydektos caught a glimpse of her well-rounded bottom and the lovely curve of her spine before she disappeared under the warm covers.

Polydektos took a drink of wine from the jug and then rid himself of his sweaty clothes and sandals. He washed his face, hands, armpits and groin before bringing the wine jug over to the bed. He set it down on the bedside table and then slid inside the clean sheets next to the Blue Shrimp.

"So, from your time looking up, rather than down on the populace of Athens, what did you find out?" she asked, turning towards him and leaning her elbow on the mattress, revealing her right breast from under the covers.

Polydektos failed badly to keep his eyes looking into hers, so he turned his head to face the sheer blue sheets hung over the bed. "I met a lad called Erebos, in the Kerameikos outer cemetery, who showed me the light—contrary to what his name suggests."

"I see. Is that why you won't look at me, Polydektos? Because you met a lad who took your fancy?" she teased, a mock look of hurt on her scarred but attractive face.

He frowned and glanced her way briefly. More of her alluring body was now on show. "Now who is looking up from the gutter? You are as strong as you are beautiful, Blue, and must have a line of suitors from here to the Piraean Gate and back, all more young and handsome than I."

"The Dipylon Gate at least," she stated. He could almost hear the curved smirk that was surely on her face. He didn't look to check; he loved their sparring, but sleep was creeping up on him.

"At least. As...I was saying. This lad helps run the family funeral waggon business, taking the corpses to the cemetery to be burnt or buried. His cousin, Nisos, sometimes works the funeral waggons at night and has seen the men that assaulted me. He said they come into the city from outside via the Acharnian Gate." Polydektos paused to yawn and rub at his tired eyelids.

"So, we are nearer to finding them? You do well down here amongst us thieves, whores, and murderers. Maybe you belong here...now," she said with a low tone to her voice, her free hand moving to rest on Polydektos's hairy chest.

Polydektos glanced down at her hand as her forefinger traced the circumference of his left nipple. He glanced over at her face. Her eyes were cast to his chest as her fingers played with his chest hairs. She had everything, this woman: strength, youth, beauty, and power, even though her domain was one of cutpurses, violence, and both male and female prostitution. He was naked in her bed, and they had an alliance of a sort, but he couldn't risk trusting her. Not after what had happened with Gala, where his wife and daughter had paid the price. He put his right hand on hers to hold it in a bond of friendship and to stop it moving down under the covers.

He moved her hand up and kissed the back of it, right across an old white scar. "You haven't heard the best of it yet. Nisos heard them speak in a foreign language, probably Egyptian, but two words he heard in Greek: the Mine of Tartaros."

The Blue Shrimp frowned and edged closer to press half of her body across his. She lay her head on his chest and wrapped her leg over both of his, drawing him closer. He could smell the delicate lemon-scented perfume she wore and felt the warmth and comfort her body heat gave to his own fatigued frame. "I have not heard of this place."

Polydektos wrapped an arm around her, holding her close, but also at bay. "It lies north of the Acharnian Gate, before you hit the river. To the east, down a track, is an abandoned quarry and mine. This could be where the villains are based. It would be a perfect place to get the stone for the Medousa statues without going through a middleman. There is an abyss inside that opened up, killing many miners and forcing the mine to close years ago. A perfect place to dispose of any bodies." Polydektos closed his eyes and sighed. He felt so tired and was struggling to stay awake. His head, deep in the middle of the soft feathered pillow, had stopped hurting now.

"Then tomorrow I shall gather together some of my most trusted scouts and fighting men and we shall go to this place as allies and put a stop to these Medousa Murders, for the good of all the people of Athens. General Polydektos, hero of Athens, and the Blue Shrimp, waif of Pireás and Queen of the Pitch Tunics, united as one. Perhaps...united in other ways?" she purred...then looked up to see that Polydektos was asleep on his back, breathing gently while she was entwined about him.

She smiled and laid her head back on his chest, listening to the beating of his heart through his ribcage. The rumours and tales that she had heard from the House of Javelins about this man were of a fat drunkard who would fornicate with anything with a pulse, living off old tales of his younger military exploits. Some of that she deemed true, but that seemed to be the old Polydektos, before his hetaira lover and secret Maenad cult leader murdered his wife and daughter to get him all to herself. The death of his family and the betrayal of his slave-girl lover had changed him. He was as athletic as his age would allow, noble and almost a demigod to be around. And handsome, she thought. He seemed at least to see her as an equal in their brief partnership, giving but not wholly trusting of her. She felt the same way back, even more so. He could have made his move on her any time in the last few days, but he hadn't. Men had taken from her all her life. Her virginity at eleven, the drachmas she earned while she slept with one vile rough-handed man after the other, her share of the cut when she thieved and murdered. It had made her hard, made her ruthless to the core; she had assassinated her older lover and former leader of the Pitch Tunics to take his place. To prove her worth, she had to care less and kill more ruthlessly than any man. Now, in the port and around the docks of Pireás, she was both respected and feared.

Yet deep in her core, something was missing. There, in a locked cage of her own making, was the eleven-year-old orphaned girl of Athens; frozen in a moment before the rape and the beating and the scars were formed. Little Elektra crying out for more, for love, for a father figure.

Maybe in Polydektos, she had found that figure, at least for a time. Until he ultimately let her down, as all men did. But for now, in the warmth of her bed, holding onto to his sleeping body, she could in the darkness pretend for a while.

Polydektos woke in the darkest hours of the night with a dead arm, and with the leader of the most feared dock gang clinging to his torso, her legs entwined with his. He smiled and kissed her forehead before gently rolling her off his numb arm. "Sorry, Elektra," he whispered and rubbed life back into the arm.

He considered whether to take Alkmaion, Talaemenes, and perhaps Aristaeos with him tomorrow, so he had at least some men around him he trusted implicitly. But he dismissed the idea. He'd had enough of putting his loved ones and friends in danger, and he could not bear to lose anyone else close to him. He would trust in the gods and the Blue Shrimp's Pitch Tunics alone. He turned away from the sleeping woman next to him and waited for the pins and needles in his arm to pass before going back to sleep.

The Blue Shrimp was gone when he woke up a second time. He had only just sat up in bed when the door opened and she came in carrying a silver oval tray of hot breakfast foods for them both. She weaved through the hanging sheets with dexterous ease.

"A hearty meal to start this most glorious of days, my general," she said with an enthused grin.

"Am I your general?" he asked, rubbing the sleep from the corners of his eyes.

"What do you mean?" Blue carefully put the silver tray onto the centre of the bed between them, before climbing in herself.

"Today, and probably this day only, I will lead you and your men into whatever dangers that mine holds. Are we in agreement?" Polydektos stared deep into her eyes.

She nodded. "For today and today only I will let a man command me again."

He took her hand and placed in on his bare left breast. "Then you do me a great honour in putting your trust in such an old failure."

"It also means you go first into the fray," she winked.

Polydektos raised her hand and kissed it. "I wouldn't have it any other way."

They dressed after breakfast. Polydektos donned a short fighting tunic and a blue cloak clasped around his neck to hide his short sword and a dagger his host provided. The Blue Shrimp wore long blue trousers in the Scythian style and a pitch-black tunic, and had many daggers hidden among the folds of her clothes.

They met her assembled thieves, scouts, and fighting men in the rear yard of the tavern: eight of them, making their party ten strong. They were led by a balding man with a thick black beard, going by the name of Theas. They were all dressed in different garb, some with boiled leather tunics, some bare-chested to the waist, others covered head to foot. The predominant colour they wore was black, showing their allegiance. Polydektos and the Blue Shrimp stood out amongst them. Polydektos deemed them suitably fierce killers for the task ahead.

The Blue Shrimp addressed her followers. "From this place to the entrance of the mine, I am your goddess, and you will obey my every command. Inside the mine, you will take your lead from Polydektos and follow his orders as if they were my own. Is this understood, my Pitch Brothers and Sister?"

The assembled men nodded, grunted, and said yea to her.

"Then let us depart—we have a long way to go this morning." The Blue Shrimp led the way out of the rear yard through two fixed wooden fence planks on hinges, unseen by any eyes. They made their way through the dirty alleys and streets of the port as the low morning sun made them shield their eyes every third corner turn. They reached the stables at the perimeter of the port, where two waggons, each with a pair of horses hitched to the front, were waiting for them. Plus, two outriders on fast steeds, to scout the roads ahead. The stable master nodded to the Blue Shrimp and Polydektos as they took one waggon. Polydektos climbed up onto the driver's seat next to her and took the reins.

"You forget yourself, my general—I lead here. You get in the back under cover and out of sight." She thumbed behind her with her lopsided smile on full show.

Polydektos deferred to her and handed over the reins. "As you command," he said, clambering into the back to settle beside a fighting man near his age and the only other woman in the group apart from the leader. She wore a red scarf over her nose and mouth, and apart from her first glance at him, she took no notice of Polydektos for the entire journey. Her name was Red Scarf, and she was one of the Pitch Tunics' best thieves and scouts. She wore the scarf to cover up the pox she had picked up as a prostitute, a scarring that had eaten away half of her nose and top lip.

The fighter, who introduced himself as Straton, was far more sociable, even too much of a chatty companion as they made their way towards and through the city. Straton claimed he had once served under Polydektos many years ago, in a winning battle. Polydektos nodded and smiled at the man's tales of arms. He had met many men like Straton who boasted of their exploits, strengths, and victories. He didn't fully trust them in battle. Most men who faced the horrors of war were usually reticent in telling of the blood and gore that they had witnessed on the battlefield.

It was a great relief when they passed through the Acharnian Gate and left the city behind. Coin crossed the hands of the gate guards to ensure that neither of the Pitch Tunics' waggons were searched. Not that they had anything to hide, apart from the presence of one of Athens's most famous sons inside one of them. After the farms and outer homesteads had gone by, the Blue Shrimp patted the seat next to her on the driver's board. Polydektos was slightly irked to be at a woman's beck and call, but it got him away from the overly chatty and slightly malodorous Straton.

It was good to be in fresh air untainted by the city and to

feel the sunshine on his face. They looked like a travelling band of merchants with a fondness for black clothing, apart from the joint leaders of their quest.

"When we reach the road to the mine, we will leave the waggons and horses behind with one man to guard them and proceed on foot, with the scouts going first," she informed him.

"I concur," he nodded. This was his quest, but they were her men.

She grinned at him. "See, a man can follow the orders of a woman and still be a man at the same time."

He gave her a quick glance. "And I thought we were equal partners in this quest."

"Partners, perhaps—equal, we shall see when the fighting begins, eh?" She dug him in the ribs with her elbow.

Polydektos resisted the urge to rub his hurt side. He kept a ghost of a smile on his lips and his eyes on the road ahead of them.

Two of the Pitch Tunic horsemen rode back to the main column.

"What news, Arion?" the Blue Shrimp called to the lead bareback-riding man.

"We eventually found the eastern dirt road to the mine. It was covered and disguised with large bushes, potted in large urns sunk in the road. A casual passerby could easily miss the road entirely. The urns can just about be lifted by two men, but are heavy with earth. We scouted a little way ahead and saw track marks in the dirt road," Arion reported, trying hard to control his snorting and winded horse.

"And you saw no one?"

"No," Arion said, patting and stroking the neck of his horse to calm him down.

"You have done well, Arion." The Blue Shrimp praised her scout and whipped the reins to start her horses and waggon moving again.

"Let us hope that our murderers do not want to leave the nest before we reach them," Polydektos warned.

"Or have already flown the coop," Blue replied.

CHAPTER FIFTEEN

The man-made barrier across the eastern dirt road was still intact when they reached it. They left the waggons and horses in a wood-rimmed dell down from the hidden dirt track. One of the men from the other waggon was left behind to guard them as the rest of the group set off on foot.

They moved around the potted obstructions in the dirt track and kept to the right side of the road, following a line of olive trees. The trees gave way to undulating, rocky dry hills, where the only cover was provided by boulders and the contours of the hillside. They took the long way around to keep off the skyline and out of sight behind the hills. Getting low and then crawling on their bellies, Polydektos, the Blue Shrimp, Theas, and Red Scarf scrambled up a loose bank of small rocks and pebbles, to find themselves overlooking a rough circular quarry dug into the hillside.

A set of metal gates barred the large entrance to the mine, which headed into the depths of the rising hills beyond. It was wide and high enough for two horses to ride abreast without their riders having to duck to leave the mine. There were no guards on duty, no signs of life outside, and nothing to see past the gated entrance but darkness.

Red Scarf kept watch while Polydektos, Blue, and Theas scrambled back down to talk tactics.

"I suggest one, perhaps two scouts approach the mine entrance first," the Blue Shrimp said. "Red Scarf and Arion would be my suggestion."

"I would send one scout, the girl." Theas pointed up the slope to where Red Scarf was keeping watch.

"What do you think, my general?" the Blue Shrimp asked the brooding Polydektos.

"That we should move round to a place above the mine entrance and lower someone down by rope. Someone who is silent as a mouse and has the ability to pick any lock that gate may or may not have."

"Let us get on with that plan of action then," the Blue Shrimp agreed.

Taking Straton, Red Scarf, and the Blue Shrimp, Polydektos carried a coil of rope around the lip of the quarry until they were over the entrance to the mine. The rest of the men stayed with Theas to keep a watch for any movement in the entrance. At the summit, the edge of the sheer quarry wall was dotted with bushes and coarse yellowed grasses. There was a slight overhang, so as Straton and Polydektos lowered Red Scarf down, she did not have to touch the side of the quarry for very long, making her descent almost silent. The female Pitch Tunic didn't weigh much at all.

Then she did something that amazed the watching Polydektos. As her feet neared the top of the mine entrance, she grabbed the rope and agilely flipped her body upside down. Her feet and legs entwined around the rope, leaving her arms free to help her manoeuvre down. She waved for them to stop as she listened, then flicked her hand twice, so they lowered her half a foot's length. Polydektos watched as she peeked into the entrance of the mine.

The Blue Shrimp and Polydektos exchanged a tense look, then returned their gaze down the side of the quarry. After a nervous wait, Red Scarf flicked her fingers six times. Polydektos judged the length she needed to be let down and then mouthed the command to Straton behind him to stop her descent.

Red Scarf produced a dagger from the folds of her black tunic and cut away at the knotted leather thongs securing the gate. The weak protection showed that they liked to keep the entrance shut, but weren't particularly expecting any visitors. With the thongs cut, Red Scarf righted herself and waved for them to pull her back up.

"The gate was only secured with tied leather thongs," Red

Scarf reported once they had done so. "The entrance is wide and goes into the hillside on a gentle slope. I saw torches flickering deeper down, but nothing close to the entrance. There are two ruts where a waggon or cart has been taken in and out of the mine on many occasions. I smelled horse dung and pitch, and I'm pretty sure I heard a horse whine from deeper inside."

"It is your quest now, my general," the Blue Shrimp said to Polydektos. The former general nodded back, and they headed back round to rejoin the rest of the group.

Polydektos addressed the Pitch Tunics gathered in a semi-circle in front of him. "We go now, with weapons drawn and no scabbards or bow quivers. All unnecessary and noisy clothes, coin purses, and items will be left outside to maximise a stealthy approach. We will enter as two columns, led by Red Scarf and Arion, with the Blue Shrimp and myself next. Then two archers behind us, and the rest in single file. We will hug the walls of the mine and keep in shadows. We will take torches, but light none of them unless it gets too dark to see. Look out for trip-ropes, traps—and somewhere in the mine is a black abyss that goes down to the deeps of Tartaros. And does anyone have an apple on them?"

"Feeling hungry, General?" said one of the men, known only as Scar. He hefted a spiked club with a sarcastic grin.

"For vengeance, yes," Polydektos replied grimly as Arion passed him an apple.

"I think I know what it is for," the Blue Shrimp stated, taking off her sandals.

"Then we will see if you are right." Polydektos winked at her as he discarded his cloak. He pulled his sword arm free of his tunic, exposing the right side of his hairy chest, so he was free to fight unhampered. "The Egyptian Titan will have to die, but I want the bearded Greek man alive at all costs."

"Is that understood, my ugly bunch of murderers?" The Blue Shrimp backed Polydektos up, eyeing them all one after the other.

"Yes," they all replied in turn.

"Then, without words or noise, we go into battle," Polydektos concluded.

He led the way down the southern side of the ring, around the outer quarry, with the others behind him in single file. Once they were at ground level they skirted the side of the ring cut out of the rock hillside, to avoid being seen from the mine entrance. He approached the entrance at a low crouch, and as he neared the closed metal gates, he crawled like a whipped dog. From his lowly position, he peered through the gates into the darkness beyond. The mine was as Red Scarf had described, tall and wide and dark. It was hard for his eyes, squinting against the harsh outside daylight, to make anything out. He waited, making sure none of the shadows moved, and then, taking the biggest risk, stood up and moved silently across the double gates. Glancing at the Blue Shrimp quickly, he exposed his manhood and began to piss on the lower and middle hinges of both sets of gates. The higher ones he just could not reach. Wiping his hands on his war tunic, he swapped his sword to his left hand and tried the iron gate nearest to him. He held his breath and lifted the gate and pushed it inwards at the same time. The hinges at the top grated, metal on metal, but the noise was negligible. He let out his breath, and then took another deep lungful of air and pushed the gate inwards another two feet. Deeming that the gap was wide enough for even the biggest of the Pitch Tunics to enter, he turned to face the Blue Shrimp. She had her eyebrows raised and a slightly shocked smile on her face. He ignored her and waved her and her men on, into the mine.

Polydektos returned his sword to his right hand and went inside. Instantly the temperature dropped as he made his way over to the right-hand side of the main entrance tunnel. He edged a few feet forwards to give the others room to enter and form up. The Blue Shrimp made for the left-hand side of the main shaft, carrying a lethal-looking dagger in each hand. Red Scarf moved in front of Polydektos, and Arion took his place before the Blue Shrimp. Behind Polydektos, a Pitch Tunic with a bow, and then Straton, brought up the rear of the right-hand column. Another Pitch Tunic archer came up behind the Blue Shrimp, followed by Theas, with Scar at the rear. They could still see fairly well as the sun streamed through the entrance. Polydektos waited for the Blue Shrimp to look at him, then waved the two separate columns forwards into the darkness of the mine.

The comfort of the sunlight at the entrance soon faded behind them, cooling the sweat on their bodies and raising the tension in their necks, arms, and legs. The smell of horse dung and pitch grew in strength as they moved down the wide tunnel. There was still some ambient light from the entrance as their eyes adjusted to the darkness. To the left, Red Scarf made a clicking sound with her tongue, and both columns froze on their haunches.

Polydektos squinted across the tunnel to see Red Scarf moving her left arm into a small opening beside her. Polydektos nodded, clicked his tongue twice to the roof of his mouth, pointed two fingers at the female scout and Theas in the column behind her, and then turned his hand sidewards and pointed for them to scout out the side tunnel. Both of them, along with the Blue Shrimp, nodded at him as they left the column to explore the tunnel, which was only wide enough to accommodate one person. Ten feet ahead of Polydektos, on his side, a torch was flickering in a sconce fitted to one of the wooden beams that braced the side of the mine shaft in intermittent spacing.

A horse moved and snorted, the sound echoing down the shaft. Beyond the torch there must be a cave or made-made room where the horse was stabled. Polydektos was considering whether to move forwards when Red Scarf and Theas returned from the side tunnel. Red Scarf pressed her fist against an open palm: a dead end. Polydektos nodded to her. Now they could proceed.

As they neared the torch, they could see that the right-hand side of the tunnel opened up into a large chamber carved into the hillside. The sound of a nervous whine from the horse forced Polydektos to stop. He hand-signalled for the rest of the group to stay where they were, went past Red Scarf, and crept up around the corner.

A large, squarish stable area had been carved out from the main entrance tunnel. It was divided into two sections by a chest-high wooden fence. Nearest to the corner was an empty, black-painted waggon, the one the murderers used in their nocturnal body-moving activities, both official and unofficial. In the next stall were two large black workhorses, eyeing his movement with unease. Polydektos pulled out the apple and cut it in half with his sword blade. Keeping his eyes at their hooves, he approached the horses. He leant his short sword against the upright of the stall and offered a half of apple to each nervous, snorting horse. The two dark steeds took the apple halves from his hands with relish.

Polydektos moved into the hay-covered stall between them to nuzzle and stroke their necks, making calming noises. He retreated from the horses and picked up his sword. He clicked his tongue and waved the others forward quickly, while the horses were finishing off their apple halves. Four horse lengths ahead, two torches were in sconces, one either side of a solid tunnel support. Beyond that, the sides of the tunnel vanished, and some sort of chamber of indeterminate size lay beyond.

Arion and Red Scarf moved slightly ahead of the slow-moving columns to scout out the chamber ahead. The torches cast only a small circle of light, but both had the feeling that this was a large cavern.

As they pressed on around the rough natural rock edges of the chamber, something grabbed Arion around the neck, lifting him off the cavern floor. He just had time to croak out a frightened cry and soil himself before his head was dashed against the rock wall.

Red Scarf wailed a warning to the others as she watched Arion drop to the cavern floor, dead, with half his skull caved in. Spotting the Titan-sized attacker, she jumped at him, intended to stab his neck deep with her dagger. Yet the giant caught her in mid-attack, his large hand nearly encircling her neck. Holding the struggling woman in midair, he moved to the left and shouted out a warning in Egyptian. Red Scarf stabbed him in the arm, but the giant of a man hardly flinched, and he certainly did not relax his crushing grip. Then she was flying through the air, before darkness enveloped her vision.

She didn't hit the cavern floor, but continued to fall into Stygian darkness. Her namesake red scarf came loose as she fell. She had time to wonder what Tartaros had in store for her, before the bottom of the abyss shattered nearly every bone in her body.

The rest of the group formed a defensive semi-circle as they entered the vast cavern. Polydektos heard Straton quail at the very sight of the huge Egyptian. They saw Arion in the torchlight, on the chamber floor with his brains dashed out, but Red Scarf was lost to the vast dark places.

"Arrows," Polydektos shouted to get the stunned group to focus. The giant man charged as Polydektos dashed sideways to grab a torch from the right-hand sconce. Fear had taken half of the Pitch Tunics already, yet two arrows did fly before the Egyptian Titan crashed into the group like a battering ram, scattering and knocking them sidewards. One missile went wild and hit the high cavern roof unseen, while one found its mark in the brute's side. The giant of a man grabbed the two Pitch Tunic archers and smashed their heads together with a sickening sound.

Polydektos saw a dark figure run from a half-lit side passage to the left and around the cavern walls until the permanent night cloaked him from view. He wanted to chase after him, but could not let the Pitch Tunics face the colossus unaided. As he rushed to aid them, he saw the Blue Shrimp leap from the shadows onto the Egyptian's back trying to plunge her two daggers into the sides of his thick neck. The giant reached back, grabbed her tunic, and threw her screaming into the darkness of the cavern. Theas attacked next, his kopis sword heading for the giant's face. The Egyptian caught the blade in his left hand, stopping the attack, but losing two fingers to its keen edge. With his free hand, he punched Theas unconscious with one mighty blow.

Polydektos ran in from the Egyptian's blind side, ducking low to hack at the back of his exposed right leg, slicing it deep. The Egyptian roared in pain and swung round to grab at Polydektos. The former general ducked at the last moment but kept the torch high, where his head had just been. The giant grabbed the torch instead, crushing it before the flames caused him to roar like a wounded mountain lion. Polydektos used the painful distraction to his advantage and hacked at the Egyptian's wrist, slicing it deep.

The Egyptian grabbed at his hand, now fixed onto his wrist by only skin and gristle, and kicked out at Polydektos. It was only a glancing kick to the general's midriff, but it sent him sprawling and winded to the rough cavern floor. The Egyptian lurched angrily towards the fallen Polydektos, who could do little but raise his sword in a weak defence as he gasped for air.

Luckily for him, some of the Pitch Tunics were still up for the fight. Scar leapt up and bashed his spiked club into the back of the giant's skull. The mighty Egyptian staggered forward two steps, wrenching the still-embedded club from Scar's grip. Even Straton ran forward and speared the Egyptian under his left armpit. The giant brought his arm down, breaking the spear in two, and Straton retreated back into the shadows. Yet it had distracted the colossal Egyptian and given enough time for Polydektos to catch his breath. He leapt up and shoved his short sword hilt-deep through the man's throat, slicing his tongue in two before thrusting into his brain.

The giant sank immediately to his knees, all fight suddenly gone from his body. He reached out one bloody hand towards Polydektos and then collapsed sidewards onto the cavern floor, finally vanquished.

"Straton, Scar, light the torches," Polydektos barked as he moved forwards to place his foot on the Egyptian's chest so he could draw his sword from the man's throat. He stared down into the beaten face of the giant. "You fought like twenty men, my enemy. May the gods you pray to welcome you over to the other side with honour."

Stratton and Scar lit two torches each. Polydektos took one off Straton and surveyed the cost of their victory. It had been a hard one. The two archers and Arion were dead. Theas was groggily coming to, and Polydektos knew all too well the power of the Egyptian's punches. The two women of the group were missing in the darkness.

"Elektra?" Polydektos bellowed, his voice echoing around the vast dark cavern.

"Over here, help me!" he heard her cry in reply.

He and Scar hurried over to where her voice had come from. Their torches illuminated a vast hole in the cavern floor not far from where they had been battling the Egyptian giant. The Blue Shrimp was down the side of the abyss, holding onto a thin raised lip with bleeding fingers. The two men dropped their torches and reached down to pull her from her precarious position.

She let Polydektos help her to her feet. "I give you thanks for the rescue, and for the help in slaying the Egyptian Titan. But you said my real name aloud in front of my men." Her voice went from warmth to chilling cold in a few words.

"Fine, kill me later, but I saw the other murderer slip off into the darkness. We must find him with the haste of Hermes. He cannot escape without confessing the true reasons for his crimes."

They picked up a torch each and returned to where Theas was getting to one knee, shaking his bruised and bloodied chin.

"Is this all that is left? Where is Red Scarf?" the Blue Shrimp asked, looking around the dead men on the floor.

"I fear she was thrown into the very abyss we rescued you from," Scar replied.

"We have to find the other man," Polydektos urged the remainder of their band.

The Blue Shrimp came over and helped her second to his feet. "Theas, are you well enough to cover the exit so the other murderer does not slip round us in the dark and escape on one of the horses?"

"That Egyptian hits harder than a demigod, but I am able to keep watch," Theas replied, probing at his bloodied mouth for loose teeth.

"I suggest we split up and skirt this abyss, Blue," Polydektos suggested, already making for the left-hand side of the cavern where he had glimpsed the other man before. "Straton, with me."

Straton picked up one of the fallen archers' short swords and glanced at his gang leader. She nodded to him and led Scar the other way, keeping to the edges of the vast cavern. Straton rose and hurried after Polydektos, who was already a horse length away from him. The Pitch Tunic caught up with his former general just as the older man found a natural tunnel in the left-hand wall. It had been excavated to let a man walk through it unhindered, and Polydektos was sure this was the place he had seen the bearded Greek run from.

"Straton, I think this is where our other murderer was when we arrived. I need you to scout it out while I press on."

"On my own?" Straton held his torch out into the narrow tunnel, apprehensive to explore it by himself.

"Do you see a phalanx in reserve that we forgot about? Get about it, man, and then catch me up," Polydektos barked. He did not wait for any further conversation. To his mind, his orders had been given and needed to be followed.

Straton watched the back of his former general move off into the darkness, then glanced across the large cavern to see two torches bobbing and moving around the right-hand wall. Straton hoped Polydektos was correct in his assertions that there was only one surviving murderer on the loose and that the Medousa would not suddenly pop up and turn him to stone. He took a deep breath and pressed on into the tunnel, holding the torch before him, keeping one eye closed just in case that might help save him from the Gorgon's petrifying stare.

Polydektos followed the wall of the cavern, which ran surprisingly straight for a natural formation. He glanced back across the dark subterranean world and saw that the Blue Shrimp's and Scar's torches were a long distance away; they seemed to have stopped to examine something unseen from where he was. Ahead of him, another opening appeared in the dark grey rock. It started at one man's width and widened out as it went in.

He thought about waiting for reinforcements to arrive, but what if this tunnel led to an exit far across the hillside? Instead, he hurried inside, worried that the long-bearded Greek might escape his clutches one more time. The way widened even further as he moved along, so he kept to the right-hand wall and held the torch out towards the centre of the tunnel. Ahead, it seemed to open up even further, and Polydektos could see a table with food bowls upon it and one stool nearby.

A sudden heavy clang of metal against metal caused him to freeze to the spot, and he heard a muffled voice and footsteps approaching. Polydektos tensed his right arm and tightened his grip on his short sword.

He was about to press on when a female figure shuffled around the corner of the cave towards him. She wore a black ragged and worn tunic, but it was her face that made him gasp. Out of the dark shadows of the cave and into his torchlight came the hideous visage of the Medousa.

CHAPTER SIXTEEN

Polydektos raised his blade over his eyes and looked down at the creature's feet. The image of her malformed cheeks and tusk-like upthrusting teeth made him shudder and recoil. Maybe he had been wrong all along and these men were purely servants of the Gorgon. Then he saw her feet, bare and crusted with dirt and grime. Small delicate feet nonetheless, with toenails that had once been carefully manicured. He raised his gaze; these were no feet and ankles of a monster. He thought one last time of his wife and children and then lowered his sword. The creature was still shuffling towards him, but her arms were behind her back and her eyes were full of fear, not petrifying hatred.

"Who are you behind that mask?" He was shocked at the loudness and echo of his voice in the tunnel.

The female stumbled on the rocky floor and fell forwards and to the right. The mask fell off her as she landed heavily on the tunnel floor. He could see her hands were tied together behind her back.

"Anthousa?" He cried out in shock to see Skaios's wife still in the land of the living. But he had no time for answers from her gagged mouth. Over her sprawled body leapt the bearded Greek, slashing at Polydektos with a short sword. The ex-general managed to parry the first blow, as luckily his sword was up anyway; but it made him stagger back two steps.

On his back foot, all Polydektos could do was defend himself from the bearded man's wild and ferocious attacks. "You killed Ipunakht," the man grunted, as he continued to slash and stab wildly.

Polydektos thrust the torch at the wild man's midriff, sacrificing it to gain some momentum in the melee. The man knocked the torch aside, but it gave Polydektos time to counterattack and force his foe backwards. Anthousa kicked out the back of her captor's right knee with her free legs. The shock of the rear assault drove him to one knee. Polydektos pressed the advantage and sliced his short sword sidewards into his attacker's grip. It sliced off his thumb and sent his sword skittering across the tunnel floor. Polydektos kicked the bearded man in the chest, sending him sprawling onto his back, and then thrust down until the tip of his blade was pointing only a little finger's length away from the other man's nose.

"Yield!" Polydektos roared at him, his blood pumping and breath coming hard and fast like the beat of his heart.

"I give in, but my vengeance has already been sated," the prone, bleeding man replied, holding his maimed sword hand.

Hurried footfalls behind Polydektos signalled the arrival of the Blue Shrimp, Scar, and Straton at the rear.

"It seems you have caught the Medousa and the malefactor behind it." Blue seemed almost impressed at this feat he had managed alone.

"She is no Medousa; she is Anthousa, Skaios's wife. Set her free," Polydektos ordered. Straton saw about freeing her arms and mouth from their restraints.

"She is no wife to Skaios, only a whore who will bed any man or woman who takes her eye," the bearded Greek shouted at her in his tainted Athenian accent. To Polydektos, it seemed he spoke like someone who had spent too many years living in some far-flung colony of the empire.

"And who are you to speak of Skaios? Is he still alive? Is Darios?" Anger suddenly turned to hope in Polydektos's heart. "Guard him."

Blue and Scar moved forwards to pull the bleeding prisoner to his feet as Polydektos rushed around the corner to find two wrought iron cells fixed into the right side of the cave beyond. One was open and empty, presumably the one Anthousa had been held in. The other had a straw mattress with a bound and gagged man lying on one elbow upon it.

"Darios, by all the gods, you are alive, my great friend!" Polydektos cried with joy to find his close companion alive and well. He spotted an iron key on the nearby table and quickly unlocked the cell as the rest of the gang and the new and former prisoners were brought round into the cave.

Polydektos rushed inside to cut the leather thongs tied around Darios's arms and ankles and then removed his gag. They embraced like long lost brothers. "I thought you killed. Never in my life have I been so grateful to see a man come back from the dead."

"I am far too handsome to die so young," Darios laughed as Polydektos helped him to his feet. "have faith in the gods, my friend." His ankles and arms were a bit numb, but the blood would soon be running back into them. "What took you so long?"

"There's gratitude for you," Polydektos laughed, causing the Blue Shrimp to smile at the joy in the old general's face.

"I see you have found your lost dog," Blue said as she opened the cell door wider to let them out.

"I see you still have the rabid bitch around to guard your hind-end, my friend," Darios joked, his eyes not leaving those of the Blue Shrimp.

"Enough—we have mysteries to unravel before this day is done," Polydektos warned them both with a severe look. He led them back to where Scar was restraining the surviving Medousa Murderer, while Straton was holding up the hideous mask to his torch.

"You caught our captor, thank the gods," Darios muttered bitterly, his eyes like daggers towards the bleeding man.

"Polydektos turned to the bruised and shaken woman. "Anthousa, are Skaios, Hyllos, and Olagnos held captive here also?"

But it was her captor who answered. "Hyllos and Olagnos took the long fall to Tartaros."

"Did Skaios share the same fate?" Polydectus raised his voice and moved threateningly closer to the bearded murderer.

"No," the bleeding man laughed back at Polydektos. "You just don't see it, do you, General?"

Polydektos stepped up into the prisoner's face and pulled Scar's torch closer to get a better look at the bearded murderer. Polydektos felt the heat of the spitting flames on his cold cheek as he gazed at the man's face. The eyes and the brow seemed familiar, but the nose had been broken at least once. The man had scars enough to show that he had suffered greatly until recently. Polydektos stepped back and tried to imagine the man without the long wild beard.

"You set sail under General Hyllos, but your ship was lost in battle, and you were feared drowned in Poseidon's graveyard. You are him—without the beard, you are Skaios's twin, Cineas." Polydektos pointed his finger from his nose towards his prisoner's nose. "Why did you capture Skaios? To let him take the blame for your Medousa Murders? But why take Skaios's wife and Olagnos? What had they ever done to you?"

The twin just laughed even harder in Polydektos's face.

"He never touched Skaios," Anthousa said in a soft, shaky voice.

"Then what happened to him?" Polydektos raised his arms in despair. He had killed the giant Egyptian, he had rescued some of the victims and captured the man behind the Medousa mystery, but something remained elusive. He turned on his prisoner again. "Did you kill Skaios?"

"No, but you might, if you don't let me bandage my hand," the twin replied, raising his bound hands.

"What?" The Blue Shrimp articulated what everyone was thinking.

"He *is* Skaios!" Anthousa almost screamed the words out.

The cave was stunned. It was Polydektos who broke the silence. "Straton, find something to bandage his wounded hand so he does not bleed to death before we can bring him back to Athens to meet the justice of the law courts for his crimes."

"If he is Skaios, then who was the other man pretending to be Skaios all these years?" Darios asked, confused.

"Cineas," the bearded man said. "The lazy brother who wasted his talent and lost Anthousa to his twin. It was Cineas, not I, who returned with General Hyllos and his ill-fortuned campaign. In the midst of battle both twins ended up in the sea, one saved by Hyllos himself and the other captured and forced to row, shackled to his oar in the bowels of a Persian ship. Whipped, tortured, and praying to the gods for the release of death, every single day of his captive life. For eleven years I endured pain and torment, wishing only to see my beloved betrothed Anthousa again, and Athens, the city of my birth. Ipunakht, my faithful companion for five years, kept me sane and alive. With his help, we killed our guards and jumped ship. Luckily, a Greek merchant ship spotted us and picked us up.

"I came home full of hope and love, to be back in the city only to find betrayal around every corner. My parents were dead, and Hyllos lauded as a great general when he should have been tried for not returning to pluck so many dead Athenian men from their watery graves. Worst still, Cineas had claimed my name, married my Anthousa, and stolen my career. I had nothing left but hatred and revenge."

Polydektos looked at the man who had spoken and felt a pang of sympathy for him. Betrayal by the people who claimed to have loved you the most could drive any man to despair, as he well knew. "You could have reported this. Gone to the courts."

"The law courts, hah! I wanted blood and justice. My twin had the ear of Perikles and friends in high places—who would believe me? Anyway, I wanted blood, suffering, and fear throughout the whole of Athens for the years taken from me at the oars of our enemy. They might be cruel, but not as cruel as my family and fellow countrymen," the real Skaios bellowed.

"Did you know any of this?" Polydektos asked Anthousa.

"Not until I was drugged and brought to this mine. I always felt something was wrong since Skaios returned from war to marry me. I thought at first that battle had changed him. We drifted apart; he had other lovers, and I had mine. We kept up the pretence of a happy marriage. In Sparta, I fell in love and so did he—I with another woman and he with the fame his sculptures and building works were giving him. I should have known he wasn't the real Skaios, deep down, but I chose to ignore it and lead my comfortable, dutiful life," Anthousa finished truthfully.

Polydektos turned to face the man behind the murders and

kidnaps. "So, what happened to Skaios—I mean Cineas?"

"We had a brief family reunion, and then I threw him down the abyss," Skaios replied without any remorse in his voice. Polydektos didn't really blame him; he would have probably done the same thing in Skaios's position.

"Why the mask?" Polydektos pointed to the cruel-looking Medousa head which Straton held.

"Happy accident. When I vandalised the Spartan peace sculpture, I knew my brother might drink himself silly. I followed him out of the tavern and confronted him. A fog had enveloped the city, like the gods of vengeance were on my side. Coupled with the fact that it was the night of the festival of Nemesia, I got lucky. I faced my brother, we had a fight, and I knocked him to the road, where he hit his head. When he was out cold, I stripped him and took him back to my waggon. I had dressed Ipunakht in a Medousa mask to hide his identity and scare off passersby. I had no thought of using the Medousa to cover my kidnaps and murders until the day after I kidnapped my brother. Rumours were awash over the whole city that Medousa had returned from the dead during Nemesia and would turn to stone all men who were not pure in heart and worshipped the gods. So, I became what everyone suddenly feared. I had sculpted doubles of all of my nemeses since I returned, out of the very stone I cut from this mine. At first, I beat their statues and cursed them until my plans for revenge formed in my darkest hours." Skaios smiled under his beard, his mouth had many chipped or missing teeth.

"In the excitement, I forgot to tell you, Polydektos—we found more stone statues in another cave off the main cavern," the Blue Shrimp informed him.

"We will need to bring them as evidence. Who are they of?" Polydektos asked the gang leader.

"Straton, put down that mask and go tell Theas to ready the waggon and horses in this mine," Blue ordered. "Once you have completed that task, head to where our horses and carts are hiding and, with Timonax, bring them to the mine entrance."

Straton looked at the Medousa mask and shuddered. He went to cast it on the floor, but Polydektos stopped him and took it from him before he left the cave.

"Who were these new stone statues of?" Polydektos looked from Skaios to the Blue Shrimp. Skaios just stared back at him and smiled, while the Blue Shrimp shrugged her shoulders.

"It's easier if you come and look," she said, and started down the passageway to the vast cavern. "Oh, and we found a basket full of snakes too."

Polydektos let the others go first. Darios and Scar dragged Skaios each by an arm and Anthousa hurried after the Blue Shrimp, trying to keep her distance from the man who had imprisoned her. They headed left, skirting the cavern wall until they came to another wide, short tunnel leading to a cave filled with polished copper shields and trays on the walls and many lit and unlit torches and lamps to provide as much light underground as possible. This was Skaios's workshop. Wooden rollers had been set on iron spindles and set in the floor to form a track out to the main cavern, an easy way to transport the large blocks of stone the sculptor had used to carve his doubles of Anthousa, Hyllos, and the others.

Inside, two new sculptures had been completed, while another had been started from a fresh oblong block of mined stone. The two sculptures were plain and it was easy to spot who they were intended to replace: Perikles and Polydektos.

"I look pretty good for my age," Polydektos had to appreciate the skill and the likeness to his features. "Would I have ended up down the abyss too, Skaios?"

"I had no problem with you, Polydektos, until you confronted us the other night," the murdering sculptor replied. "Now I wish only a long slow death for you, for killing Ipunakht."

Polydektos did not rise to the bait. He kept his back to the man and approached the life-like statue of Perikles. "The features aren't bad, but the back of the head is far too normal. My friend the First Citizen looks more like a sea-onion than this."

Skaios said nothing in reply.

"You sound more and more like a common Pitch Tunic every day I know you," the Blue Shrimp complemented him.

"It's the company I keep," Polydektos replied. "We need to take these to Perikles as well. How are they getting on with that waggon?"

Polydektos walked past where Scar was holding onto the wounded Skaios and into the great cavern again. He could see torches moving in the far distance, near the entrance tunnel to the mine, and heard the echoed sounds of the horse and waggon being readied. He took two unlit torches from a pile stacked on some jars of supplies and lit them from the Blue Shrimp's torch. He held it down near his ankles and slowly approached the dark abyss in the centre of the vast natural cavern.

"What are you doing?" Blue asked from a safe distance behind him. She had already got close enough to the edge of the abyss and felt fear for the first time in a long time.

"Seeing how deep this hole really is." He crept closer, finding the rounded rough lip of the abyss. His torch did little to dispel the blackness below.

"Do you really think it leads all the way down to Tartaros?"

Polydektos got as close to the edge as he dared and threw one of the torches into the abyss. It fell for an age, it seemed, and then was lost from his sight by the lip of the hole. "How am I, a mere mortal, to know? But if you had fallen into it, you would have been as dead as anyone in Tartaros."

A roar, and the sound of running, caused him to turn around. Skaios was rushing out of the darkness, head down and charging at him. The Blue Shrimp slashed at him with her dagger but missed. Polydektos could do little but drop his remaining torch into the abyss behind him and dive to the left, hoping he found solid ground underneath him. His leg came up as he fell, connecting with Skaios's ankles, and the Medousa Murderer went over the dark edge and fell screaming down into the vast sinkhole to his black end.

"My general!" The Blue Shrimp hurried forwards with her torch, grateful to see him still in the land of the living.

"Curse that fool to die and be reborn a thousand times, and to suffer a brutal early death every time," Polydektos spat as the Pitch Tunic's leader helped him back to his feet.

"We still have the corpse of the Egyptian giant and the words of Anthousa and Darios to tell all they know," she soothed him.

"Death was the easy way out. He should have stood trial." Polydektos moved away from the edge of the abyss. "I'm going outside. I've had enough of darkness and death for many men's lifetimes."

He shrugged her off and headed around the edge of the cavern towards the exit, where Theas was leading the black funeral waggon inside, lit by four torches.

The sun nearly blinded Polydektos as he left the mine, causing his slit eyes to weep in protest. Was this his life now? No family, no lovers, just chasing death in the darkest corners of Greece. A father, husband, and general no more; seeker of truth in the darkness that lay in the hearts of many men and women of Athens. Was this the life the gods intended for him? Bathed in blood, choked with the funk of corpses, and always weary from the chase?

He sat down on a broken and discarded block of stone that had been dumped outside the mine. He looked up at the sun and the thin white clouds in the dazzling blue sky and wondered what Athene and Zeus had in store for him next.

CHAPTER SEVENTEEN

It took an hour to load the sculptures, the corpse of the Egyptian, the Medousa mask, and all other evidence of the murders they could find onto the funeral waggon. This proved too heavy for one horse, so both were bridled up.

The Pitch Tunics found little money or anything of value in the mine. Polydektos said the waggon, horses, and tools could be theirs to sell, once Perikles had seen them with his own eyes. The corpses of their fellows had been thrown into the abyss under the Blue Shrimp's callous orders. It was a crime not to bury a corpse in Athens, but what did they care about another wrongdoing put against them?

"They are under the ground," Blue Shrimp simply replied as they rode together back to the city. They were her men, and Polydektos was too fatigued to argue with her. He had Darios back from the dead and had saved Anthousa also. The Medousa Murders of Athens were at an end.

The Pitch Tunics and their two waggons parted company with Polydektos, Darios, and Anthousa before they got to the city walls. Polydektos was taking the evidence straight to Perikles, a place where criminals would rather not be.

"We make a good pair, you and I. I hope this isn't the last I will see of you, my general," the Blue Shrimp said and pulled him into a close embrace, kissing him by his left ear before she whispered, "In my bed also."

Polydektos kissed her cheek and whispered back. "Why would you want an old fool like me in your bed?"

"Because I said if you called me Elektra aloud in front of

anyone I would kill you. Killing you with my endless unbound carnal desires seems the most pleasant way of doing so for the only man in this whole rotten empire that I respect."

"Then when I tire of life, I will seek out your bed once more, Elektra," he said in a hushed tone.

She kissed him long and full on the lips. "Now I will have to kill you twice over." She skipped back to her carts and men, laughing.

Smiling broadly, Polydektos climbed back onto the funeral waggon next to Anthousa and Darios. He whipped the reins of the horse and led them down the road to the Acharnian Gates.

"What was that all about?" Darios asked him.

"I could tell you, my friend, but then she would have to kill you." Polydektos thumbed back at where he had left the Blue Shrimp and her men.

"I've died once already—that is enough for my idle curiosity for the time being," Darios smiled back at him.

It wasn't until they passed through the gates that they sensed something was amiss in the polis. There seemed more guards and Rod Bearers in the streets, and people pointed at him and looked away muttering as he rode past on the funeral waggon.

"Why do these things keep happening, oh great General Polydektos?" a woman wailed at him as they passed.

"What things?" he shouted back at her, but she was lost in the crowds behind him.

"What have we missed while being held captive?" Anthousa asked.

"I have no idea," Polydektos replied. A few streets closer to Perikles's official residence, he saw the Rod Bearer captain he knew well from sight, but not by name. "What is going on in the city today? Why are the people so agitated?"

"There has been a lot of unrest after the latest murder, but surely you know more about it than I, General," the Scythian shouted back to him over the din of the crowd his men were holding back.

"Know about what?" Polydektos asked, bemused.

"About the latest attack by the Medousa in the early hours of this morning—the son of the Spartan ambassador was found in his room at the residency of the proxenos, turned to stone like the rest."

"How can this be?" Darios looked at his old general and friend.

"It can't be possible. Blue had men watching every gate and the northern road all night for the black waggon. Skaios could not have got into the city unseen."

Darios sat shaking his head. "I saw the murderers Skaios and Ipunakht several times last night. One of them would check on us every hour. There was no way, unless they had the help of Hermes himself, for them to get to the city and back, let alone have time to capture the ambassador's son."

"And if they had, where is the lad?" Polydektos wondered aloud as he urged the waggon through the busy streets. "Isandros, I think he is named. Skaios had no other prisoners and made no mention of him."

"I, too, saw them several times during my fitful sleep last night. It would take half the night for them to do such a deed, surely," Anthousa ventured in a tired voice.

"We must head back to Palamon's house and find out what is going on here. I have a terrible feeling about this, and I hope I am wrong."

The funeral waggon only got a further street nearer the proxenos's residency when two lines of twelve guards marched around the corner and stopped them in the rutted tracks of the side street.

"General Polydektos, the First Citizen has been looking for you for two days now," the young captain of the guard called up to him.

"Then the gods are smiling on you today, Captain, for my greatest desire is to meet with him also." Polydektos smiled broadly down at the young soldier, putting the captain off his stride.

"I have orders to bring you to the house of Palamon, the proxenos, with all haste," the captain said, finishing the speech he had worked over and over in his head, in preparation for catching up with the famed general.

"Then why are we standing around here orating like we were at the bouleuterion? I urgently need to see our exulted leader also." Polydektos cracked the reins and urged the two horses on down the street. The funeral waggon was wide, so the guard had to hurry and scurry out of the way, to avoid being run over.

The red-faced captain quickly reorganised his men to walk a brisk pace after the waggon.

"We are leading a parade now, General," Darios joked, finding his humour again for the first time since he was captured.

"And so we should be. After what I tell Perikles, they should be bathing and kissing our old behinds," Polydektos snarled and urged the horses on.

Anthousa raised her eyebrows in shock but said nothing.

A further phalanx of soldiers was waiting for them. They pointed their spears at first as they ringed the entire residency, but the sight of Polydektos and the guard jogging behind to keep up made them swiftly stand down.

They were let through the tradesmen's entrance around the rear of the wall property, as it was the only gate wide enough for the funeral waggon to pass through. There were sounds of shouting and a heated argument coming from inside the villa.

"Wait here. Darios, guard the waggon. Let no one see what we have covered up in the back." Polydektos pulled his sword and handed it to his companion before he jumped down from the waggon. "Come with me, Anthousa."

"What are you going to do, Polydektos?" Darios called after his friend, who with Skaios's wife walked purposefully past the guards to the rear entrance of the Spartan rooms of the residency.

"Hopefully prevent all-out war," he called before entering the cool buildings. The residency was much cooler than the outside, but the words inside were as heated as Hephaistos's forge. He ushered Anthousa to conceal herself behind an outer column as he walked unnoticed towards the confrontation ahead.

Lydos was dressed for war. He and his retainers, as well as his wife Eione, had their swords drawn and were wearing shields, ready for a battle that they could not win. Perikles, Pheidias, and more Athenian soldiers were on the other side of the large inner courtyard, also armed for battle. Palamon and three of his armed men were caught in the middle of the two warring factions, trying to keep the peace.

"I will avenge my lost son. Perikles, you will pay for his death with your head!" Lydos roared and raised his sword upon high.

"The Medousa kills at will, it seems, my Spartan friend. It is not I that you should be angry with, but the gods themselves for allowing this atrocity to happen in my fair city," Perikles replied in a loud, but calmer voice. Yet, he too gripped his sword tightly in his hand.

"My life means little to me now. If I die here on enemy soil or return home to Sparta, the outcome will be the same: war!" Lydos edged forward two steps, and so did his armed wife and a small band of hopelessly outnumbered retainers.

"Men of Athens, men of Sparta, lay down your arms. Only together as Greeks can we hope to defeat this monster of the night." Palamon almost squeaked the words out, so fearful was he of being caught in the middle of the two sparring sides.

"I would listen to what the Proxenos is saying," Polydektos shouted over the din as he moved closer to the armed and angry groups. "There is no need for battle, bloodshed, or war; I have ended the Medousa Murders once and for all."

Perikles looked as surprised as anyone present to see his old friend. "Polydektos, where have you been these last few days? I've had men looking for you. Even wily old Alkmaion did not know your whereabouts, but he did tell me that Darios had fallen victim to the curse of the Medousa also."

"Darios had fallen foul of this insidious plot to bring mighty Athens to its knees with fear, and it is true his stone corpse was found by me not more than four days hence. Yet let it be known that Polydektos, son of Praxilios, went into Tartaros and brought him back from the dead."

"What addled nonsense does your general speak, Perikles? Is he drunk?" Lydos shouted angrily across the courtyard at the Athenian leader.

Polydektos smiled, he was distracting them from blood and death at least.

"Why do you smile, Polydektos," Eione demanded, "when my only son lies in an enemy bed, his eyes unseeing rock in their sockets? Are you so cruel? I always thought of you as the best man in Athens, but now do you come to prove my heart wrong?" She dropped her shield to the floor and beat at her left breast.

"I come not to mock or bring tinder to fuel this fire of hate I see before me. The Medousa Murders were a vengeful ruse of a desperate man. I slew his companion, and the true malefactor I saw die with my own eyes. Masks, false death statues, and darkness were their ploys as they spread fear throughout the city. Yet I, Polydektos, saw these tricks and stone cadavers. I stared into the eyes of the Medousa and was not found wanting. I faced the fear and slew it. I bring you this news to stop this mistake occurring again. To stop bloodshed and war happening in this very residency, where peace and honour should come before any objectives of a single man, whoever that man may be."

"You speak in riddles, my old friend," Perikles said in a quieter voice.

Eione pointed her sword directly at Polydektos, anguish all over her face. "Our son is stone cold dead in an Athenian bed—we have a right to vengeance, a right to spill blood because of this. What could you possibly say to stop this Spartan woman from stabbing any traitorous Athenian in his weak heart?"

"I can say nothing to ease your loss, but I can give some you something that might mend your cleaved heart. A token of peace that will lead at least to a temporary ceasefire in this courtyard and give me time to sort out this mess." Polydektos turned and clicked his fingers. "Come forward."

With timid steps of her dirty bare feet, Anthousa emerged from her hiding place. She came to stand next to Polydektos, her weeping eyes only for Eione. Forgetting her place, her husband, and the situation, Eione threw down her sword and rushed over to take her lover into her arms and kiss her dirt-covered cheeks.

"I saw you buried," Eione cried and pulled Anthousa closer

into her tight embrace. "Is it true, then, Polydektos? Have you, like the Heroes of old, ventured into the Underworld and brought my Anthousa back to life?"

"In a manner of speaking," Polydektos nodded. "Darios too is alive and well after his encounters with the false Medousa. I beg thee, Ambassador Lydos and First Citizen Perikles, give me an hour's grace, and I will end this evil plot here and now and let no war begin today between Athens and Sparta. What say you?"

Eione looked at her husband. Lydos looked across at Perikles and lowered his sword.

"For my wife's sake, I will give you your hour, General Polydektos. It seems Athens has one man of honour left within its spineless walls."

Perikles looked with anger from Polydektos to Lydos. He would look foolish not to give in to his friend's demands for just an hour. "I agree. But Polydektos, I do not see how this one metic widow of Skaios proves anything."

"Then let you, and you alone, come to the waggon I have outside and prove the faith you bestowed on me when no one else believed in these old bones. You tasked me to find and stop the Medousa, this the quest you set me upon and the quest that I have completed this very day. Let us walk and talk together, my old friend, and I will explain everything to you." Polydektos showed his arm towards the exit to the rear gardens and outside courtyard beyond.

Perikles handed his sword over to Pheidias and walked out to save face in front of the Spartans. They headed through the rear gardens in silence until they came to the funeral waggon, with Darios sitting upon it.

"What does this funeral waggon prove?" Perikles asked as they stood over to it.

"Well on its own, nothing. But Darios and Anthousa returning from being stone cold dead statues, and other things I have to tell, will convince you by the end that the Medousa threat is now over." Polydektos smiled and waved at Darios as he led the First Citizen around the back of the black waggon. The horses were panting loudly from the heat, but apart from a few birds in the trees of the gardens, the residency was quiet for a time.

"We shall see," was all that Perikles could give his old friend.

Polydektos knelt at the rear of the waggon and unhinged the secret compartment that transported the stone statues and kidnapped victims around the city unseen. "Where the lifelike replica statues of the victims were carried, and the victims themselves after they had been drugged or knocked unconscious."

"Or used to smuggle stolen goods," Perikles haughtily gave another use for the hidden space under the waggon.

"Stolen people, at least. Then let me show you the foreign Titan I killed." Polydektos clambered up onto the rear of the waggon and uncovered the dead Egyptian giant of a man.

"I see a corpse," Perikles shrugged. "He is a brute of man, I must admit, but just another dead body, my friend."

"Then this might have you singing my praises to Athene." Polydektos whipped off the rest of the sheets and sacks to reveal the stone likenesses of himself and Perikles. "One of us was next, my old friend."

Perikles's face blanched, and he had no words this time.

"I told the sculptor that he should have made the back of the head longer and pointier, but you know how artists hate to be criticised." Polydektos could not help but pour scorn on his friend and his abnormally sized cranium.

"I was the next victim?"

"Or I; I never did find out before he died."

"Before who died? Who is responsible for this and where is he?" Perikles's anger quickly returned.

"He is dead by his own hand."

"Who is, and why did he do this?"

"Skaios, but not the man you knew, Perikles. Come sit up here a while, my friend, and I will tell you everything," Polydektos reached down his hand to the First Citizen.

Perikles took it, and once pulled up into the rear of the waggon, he bent low to examine his stone double.

"So it was Skaios all along, but why?"

"It was, and then by Zeus, it wasn't. Sit down Perikles, and hear my tale of betrayal, death and vengeance."

It took half the allotted ceasefire time for Polydektos to tell the whole story of the Medousa Murders and of the twin brothers that caused it all. Darios added what he knew, at Perikles's behest, until the full tale was told.

"I can hardly believe it all," Perikles muttered to himself.

"You don't want to believe, though, do you, because it leaves you in a tight spot?" Polydektos said as he clambered over the First Citizen to get down from the rear of the waggon.

"Where are you going with this? What do you mean?"

"You are going to take me to see Isandros," Polydektos replied.

"His stone cadaver, you mean?" Perikles jumped down off the waggon after his old friend.

"You can take me to see that first, if you like," Polydektos led the way through the garden to the rooms of the Spartans. Perikles had to hurry to catch up.

"Wait, my friend, we need to talk," Perikles caught Polydektos by the shoulder and spun him around.

"Talk about what, Perikles? How the stone statue of Isandros will look like him, but it won't have been carved by Skaios's hand? Perhaps it will look more like the work of Pheidias. You heard my words: Skaios was in the mine at the time that Isandros was turned to stone. I have two witnesses to that fact. All the gates of Athens were being watched under my orders last night. Skaios did not do this thing, but I have a good idea who ordered it," Polydektos openly berated the leader of Athens.

Polydektos entered the quarters given to the Spartans during their stay. Polydektos pushed aside a young guard blocking Isandros's bedroom. The guard followed him into the room to restrain him, but Perikles waved him from the building so the two old friends could talk alone.

Polydektos was bent down examining the stone figure of Isandros as he lay on his bed.

"You see the evidence before your very eyes." Perikles's words were scornful as he followed his old friend into the bedroom. "Perhaps you did not catch this Medousa in time; perhaps she is real and still on the loose. The populace would see you as the failure that you are, Polydektos."

Polydektos stood up, looked over the stone corpse towards Perikles, and laughed heartily. "I am not you, my old friend. I have no fear of failure. I have no reputation to lose, unlike you. This isn't the petrified body of Isandros, and you know it. I am no critic of art, but this is a shabby shade of the statues that Skaios carved. Are you not concerned that you might have been next?"

Perikles jabbed a finger across the bed. "I have no fear, you know this. Nobody, not even old friends can stand in my way. I have the will of the people and will lead them as I see fit. I do this for the good of Athens and the ultimate victory."

Polydektos's voice rose in anger. "What does Perikles's War do for Athens, apart from taking a generation of young men and blooding Attica with their sacrifices to stroke your ego? It is hubris beyond reason. You see yourself as a demigod, answerable to no one, not even the gods."

"What happened to you, my old friend, that you fear war and battle now?"

"I fear nothing, not even death's cold embrace. I have nothing to lose, so that makes me a dangerous man, First Citizen. Yet there is a way out of this day. Bring back Isandros from where you hold him captive. I will claim I killed Skaios after he switched the live youth with his stone twin. I will claim I saved the boy and brought him home to his parents. Then the Spartans and Anthousa can leave the city, unhindered."

"I see what you hope to achieve this day, Polydektos, so that you are a hero of Athens once more: General Polydektos, slayer of the Medousa. They will put up statues of you for this, my friend, I can see it now. I can make you my first general once the war with Sparta has begun. I will give you the command of an army to vanquish the Spartans and her allies."

"I have seen enough death and suffered more loss than any man should witness. I want peace, not the war that you are bent on having with Sparta. A war which will do little but to stoke your inflated ego and see thousands of good Greek men die. You are a clever man and you will find some other way to have the war you so desperately need, but not this day. The guilt will not rest on my shoulders."

Perikles lowered his voice. "What if I don't bring Isandros back—what then?"

"Then I will tell the Assembly, the Boule, the Strategoi, the Prytaneis, and I will cross the floor and enter politics on your enemy's side. Would you rather have Polydektos, Slayer of the Medousa and the Maenads, as your friend or foe? Let the boy go," Polydektos warned his old friend.

"Now you threaten me," Perikles scoffed, with a dry laugh.

"I only do what the gods and my own conscience tells me to do as a good citizen of Athens. You are better than this, Perikles."

"You would destroy our friendship to save one Spartan and stop a war that is inevitable?"

"War delayed today means there is a chance for peace tomorrow."

"You sound like Sokrates. At least he knows his duty towards Athens."

"If war comes, I will stand shoulder to shoulder with any man. But the quest that I am entwined with will not be the cause of it, I swear by Athene and Zeus," Polydektos said with rising passion to his voice.

"I was wrong," Perikles chuckled. "You sound more like a politician than a philosopher."

"You will give Isandros unharmed into my care?"

"If the gods will it, and the Spartan find his way into the back of that waggon, be warned any friendship and protection in my city I have given you over the years dies this day," Perikles said darkly.

"I think our friendship started dying the day you became First Citizen and lost your way," Polydektos replied gravely.

"Wait by your waggon, citizen," were Perikles's final words as he left the room.

Polydektos waited a few moments and did as his First Citizen commanded.

Isandros was returned, alive but unconscious, and placed in the rear of the funeral waggon just before the hour mark was up.

As Lydos and Eione rushed over to their son, Polydektos caught Anthousa's arm as she followed them. He pulled her to one side behind a late-flowering garden scrub.

"I need you to do something for me, for the good of Athens, Sparta, and the rest of Greece," Polydektos said in a serious voice.

"You saved my life, Polydektos, and brought me back to Eione. I would do any favour you ask."

"Then I will need you to lie for me."

The Spartan delegation left that night under cover of darkness and with no formal fanfare to match their arrival. Polydektos, Darios, and Alkmaion were there to see them off and escort them a part of the way west. Polydektos still feared for their safety, but knew because of his new fame and adulation around the city that Perikles would do nothing if he was with them.

Polydektos got off his horse at dawn to say his final parting to the Spartan delegation and Anthousa, who was going with them.

Lydos and the now-conscious Isandros gripped his arm and thanked him as fellow Greek warriors. Their words were brief and simple, and Polydektos found that fitting. Anthousa's thank you was a tight embrace and kisses to his lips and cheeks.

"Thank you with all of my heart, Polydektos. No man could have done more for me than you," she said as they parted.

"It was my duty and also my pleasure," he replied as Eione approached him.

"You saved my son and my lover from the Medousa. If you were a Spartan, I would reward you beyond all dreams of mortal men, Polydektos." She kissed his lips softly.

"Sadly, I am but a humble citizen of Athens," he replied.

"That does not have to be so. You have sacrificed much and have only a parade your friend Perikles has arranged for tomorrow to show for it."

"I fear that after this, the First Citizen and I are friends no longer."

"Then come with us to Sparta and be exalted amongst the gods as a great hero of the age. I see little left for you in Athens.

Forge a new life in Sparta with us." Her words were softer than he could ever recall, and tempting.

"I am no traitor to my ancestors or my family. Their graves are in Athenian soil, and one day I shall join them there. I was born and will die an Athenian. I am glad you have Anthousa and your family. Treat them well, Eione. I will bid you farewell," he said, and then leant forward to kiss her cheek.

"Farewell, for now, Polydektos, but the gods and the fates have told me, this is not our last day together. I will see you again." She turned without another word and helped Anthousa into her chariot.

Polydektos got back onto his horse, and he and his friends watched them until a bend in the road took them from sight behind a hill. Then they turned their horse and rode back into the city, just in time for Polydektos's victory parade.

BIBLIOGRAPHY

The Athenian Navy: An investigation into the operations, politics and ideology of the Athenian fleet between 480 and 322 BC by Samuel Potts.

The Ancient Greek by Nicholas Sekunda & Angus McBride

Greek Hoplite 480-323 BC by Nicholas Sekunda & Adam Hook

Women in Ancient Greece and Rome by Michael Massey

The Penguin Historical Atlas of Ancient Greece by Robert Morkot

Athenian Society by Jennifer Gibbon

The Rise and Fall of Athens by Plutarch

History of the Peloponnesian Way by Thucydides

Note: I have given the Greek gods their original Greek names and not the more popular Latin versions i.e.: Herakles instead of Hercules and Athene instead of Athena, Apollon instead of Apollo..

ABOUT THE AUTHOR

Alexander Arrowsmith has had a lifelong fascination with Ancient Greece; its myths and its culture. It is a country he loves and has visited on many occasions. He has had eight books published in other genres, but this the first in his series of historical crime novels set in those times.

He lives in Surrey, with his family and two cats.

Curious about other Crossroad Press books?
Stop by our site:
http://www.crossroadpress.com
We offer quality writing
in digital, audio, and print formats.

Made in the USA
Lexington, KY
15 November 2019

57104055R00136